New

silverboy

Also by N. M. Browne

Warriors of Alavna
Warriors of Camlann
Hunted
Basilisk
The Story of Stone

silverboy

N. M. BROWNE

BLOOMSBURY

First published in Great Britain by Bloomsbury Publishing Plc
Published in the United States by Bloomsbury U.S.A. Children's Books
175 Fifth Avenue, New York, NY 10010
Distributed to the trade by Holtzbrinck Publishers

Library of Congress Cataloging-in-Publication Data
Browne, N. M.
Silverboy / by N. M. Browne. — 1st U.S. ed.
p.   cm.
Summary: When Tommo, aged about fifteen years, runs away
from an apprenticeship as a spellgrinder, he begs for sanctuary and
is forced to attempt an impossible journey to leave his country,
but help arrives in very unexpected forms.
ISBN-13: 978-1-58234-780-6 • ISBN-10: 1-58234-780-8
[1. Magic—Fiction. 2. Birds—Fiction. 3. Fantasy.] I. Title.
PZ7.B82215Sil 2007   [Fic]—dc22   2006014900

First U.S. Edition 2007
Typeset by Hewer Text U.K. Ltd, Edinburgh
Printed in the U.S.A. by Quebecor World Fairfield
2   4   6   8   10   9   7   5   3   1

All papers used by Bloomsbury U.S.A. are natural, recyclable products
made from wood grown in well-managed forests. The manufacturing processes
conform to the environmental regulations of the country of origin.

For Ed, Luke, Lani and her imaginary friend, Akenna

CHAPTER ONE

Tommo had just eight days before his sanctuary band was worthless. He twisted its fraying leather with nervous fingers. It was a bad night. The rain soaked through his thin work-wool tunic and made it smell rankly of the cow byre, of pungent dung and sour milk and his own old sweat. His hair was plastered to his face and dripped icy droplets down his back. He was weary and cold, and everyone knew it took ten full days not eight to get to port, to Bentree Harbour. He had not time to rest or sleep, all he could do was walk and then after that maybe crawl. His eyes were gritty and sore, and there was a cold emptiness in his stomach, which was the hunger he was trying to ignore. There had to be a better way to avoid the noose than this desperate sanctuary flight, but he was twice damned because he couldn't think of one, so he walked on, buffeted by the wind, doused by the rain and colder than a cellar jar in winter.

It was obvious that he wouldn't make it and sure enough by the fifth day of his reckoning – which was most likely wrong – he found himself on his back in a ditch and staring exhaustedly at the pewter grey of a rain-filled sky. It was warmer in the ditch and the mud which filled it yielded squishily to the shape of his back. But for the fact that it was cold, it might even have been comfortable. It was hard to say which was worse, death in a ditch or death from a noose – though the ditch was at least more private.

His life did not flash in front of his eyes. Maybe, he thought, that only happens when you're drowning and dying of hunger, and cold is an altogether less interesting type of death. Not that there was much about the fifteen or so years of his life so far that he really wanted to relive.

Childhood had been good until his mother had died bearing his brother, whose own death had followed swiftly a few weeks later. His father had been someone of importance, so they said, married, obviously, in a three-heir dynastic contract – and not to Tommo's mother. His mother had never said whether he had half-siblings somewhere or not and he didn't much care. He'd been alone right enough when the coin for his upkeep had run out after his mother's death. There was no one to take him in and so he'd swapped good linen and velvet for work-wool and sackcloth; gentle lessons with a tutor for an apprenticeship at the spellgrinder's. It was not a job to make a boy rich or to broaden his mind. It tended to kill off apprentices at a remarkable rate. Most died of the quivers, the uncontrollable bouts of trembling that made eating impossible. Of those with strong constitutions who escaped the quivers, more than a few died of their wounds when the turn-knife slipped and sliced them. His only friend, Ahurn, had died that way and so Tommo had reckoned he'd little to lose but his head and he'd run away. The moment the cellar door was open he'd pushed past the startled spellgrinder and run as if Unga's demon hordes pursued him.

Unfortunately, he'd not realised quite what an easy job it was to track a spellgrinder. The grind-dust settled in the folds of your skin and gave it a ghostly silver sheen, oh and – hard to notice in the dark cellar in which he'd lived – it turned your hair white as bleached cambric. There was a reward of course – another thing he'd not known. A couple of havers, a labourer's monthly wage, for returning an apprentice, and so his fate had been sealed the moment he'd climbed, blinking blindly, out of the cellar and into the never forgotten daylight. He couldn't blame the motherly-looking woman whom he'd pestered for directions for handing him in to the Sheriff – she'd looked poor enough and wore no marriage chains round her neck or wrist. The penalty for running away from an apprenticeship in an accredited craft brotherhood was to be hanged by the neck until you were dead. After, when they cut you down, they chopped off your head, just to be sure, if you were a spellgrinder's apprentice anyway, in case the grind-dust interfered with justice. There were stories of apprentices surviving the gallows through the unpredictable and largely unknown effects of grind-dust, but no one, as far as he knew, had ever survived both hanging and beheading – at least not in his lifetime, which the way things were going was unlikely to be very long.

3

In the happy times of his childhood he'd enjoyed his mother telling him the story of how the old High Priest of the Inward Power had been captured and mortally wounded outside the Thaumaturgical Chapel at Tipplehead. It was a dramatic story in which Gildea, all his powers exhausted, had knelt by the hitching post and made a speech on the virtue of the Inward Power, of the gifts of Urtha, which have no need of outward symbols nor of the unnatural help lent by spellstones. His mother had made it seem very brave and noble. Anyway, although the old High Priest was charged down and trampled by horses, as recognition of his courage the Convocation of Thaumaturgists had decreed that any man, woman or child prostrating themselves by the hitching post by White Urtha's shrine could claim sanctuary in Gildea's name. To the best of his knowledge it was a rule which the Protector had not revoked, even though the Convocation had been disbanded, and its members had died of the blue pox or the spite of the Protector.

Tommo knew that hitching post well and, on being taken to the Sheriff's manse nearby, had waited anxiously for the one heartbeat's measure of time when he was not watched. It had come when the old woman went with the Sheriff to collect her dues. As the Sheriff unlocked his brass-banded coffer, Tommo had run for it. He thought his heart might burst with the fear and the unpractised speed, and his side was almost split in two with pain from the unusual exercise. Who knows but maybe the grind-dust helped give his feet desperate fleetness, but no one caught him until he'd fallen to the ground and prostrated himself by the hitching post, screaming with what little breath was left in his lungs: 'Sanctuary, sanctuary, in the name of Gildea, High Priest of the Inward Power, I claim sanctuary!' He'd lain there panting like an over-pressed hound, while a small crowd gathered to watch what might happen next.

The other thing, or at least one of the other many things he did not know, was the exact terms of sanctuary. The Sheriff, when he finally arrived, having been informed by the street runners of the whereabouts of his erstwhile captive, was aggrieved by the apprentice's desperate bid for life. In front of a public gathering of nosy shoppers and wonder-seekers, he issued his decree, which he then had spellstone inscribed indelibly in runes on a pig-leather sanctuary band. The band wearer, one unclaimed and thus fatherless soul, without known patrimony or hope thereof, this apprentice spellgrinder, known commonly as Tommo, had eight days to leave the shores of the borough or face the hangman's noose. This declaration was accompanied by some low-grade pyrotechnics of scarcely recognisable symbols in crude colours to exhaust the remaining power in the rather poorly cut green spellstone. This satisfied the nosy shoppers if not the wonder-seekers, who clearly hoped for better from the spellstone capital of the Protectorate, and it doomed Tommo to an only slightly delayed death.

The moment the declaration was made he heard one of the shoppers mumble within earshot, 'Best start running now, lad. It's a ten-day walk to the coast and the only place to get a ship in this stormy time is Bentree Harbour.' The woman dropped a mince dumpling for him too, only slightly chewed and dusty and within his arm's reach. He took it gratefully and ate it as he began to run. No one stopped him but none helped him either and he realised that he ought to have thanked the woman with the mince dumpling as the only kindly spirit in the Borough of Tippo. She was the only person to offer him Urtha's charity in all the muscle-rending, foot-blistering, wearying days of his running. The thick sanctuary band on his wrist, glowing with magically inscribed runes, his silvery skin and white hair seemed to guarantee that he would be avoided at every turn, that people in his path unexpectedly found some other place to go, and that curious eyes would never meet his own. When he could not run any further, he spent the night in a cow byre until he was discovered in the morning by a pale-eyed girl who screamed up a storm. And pelted him with still-warm dung.

So, in the end, he had come to this ditch and a quiet death. A flock of birds flew overhead making a rather incompetent attempt at flying in formation, though curiously the formation seemed to be the magical rune symbol for 'Note well'. Tommo recognised that his thinking was obviously becoming deranged by his imminent demise, as no birds flew in such a way. Two or three of them landed and perched on the hardened crust of earth that marked the top of the ditch wall and began singing. Their singing, too, sounded like the ancient words for 'Listen and learn', which marked the beginning of the good student's litany he had learnt long ago by his mother's knee. He would have laughed at his own stupidity in fantasising such an unlikely scene, until he looked more closely at the gathered birds. His heart, which must have been slowing, winding down like a grinding wheel without a spellstone, suddenly beat wildly with terror and he cried out. The faces of the birds were human – unusually small but recognisably human.

'Listen and learn,' they chorused. And Tommo sat up.

CHAPTER TWO

Tommo felt distinctly light-headed. His stomach hurt and he was finding it hard to focus, but rubbing his eyes did not make the birds go away. The one closest to him, a bird with the face of a young boy, tilted its head to one side intelligently. Of course, it was possible that the bird was not a product of his hunger and exhaustion, but of a rich man's imagination – a well-cut spellstone, a yellow hue or maybe a pink, could make the most unlikely vision a reality. Perhaps the bird was some kind of joke or a birth-giving gift that had lost its way.

His experience of what people actually did with the spellstones once he had assisted in their grinding was extremely limited. He couldn't think of any reason why someone would want to create a bird with a human face. He squinted at the boy-faced black bird so that the double image he was seeing merged into one slightly blurry creature. How did it feed itself without a beak and with no hands to help it? Surely the bird must be as weak and hungry as he was? He stopped worrying about whether the bird was real or some fever fantasy of his own and started looking round for something to feed it with. He was intrigued. Perhaps he wasn't yet ready to die after all.

He got rather awkwardly to his feet. His legs trembled badly so he stayed on his knees and began scratching in the dirt for worms. The smell of the earth, a heady, loamy smell, brought sudden tears to his eyes. He was lost for a moment in the sunny garden of childhood memory, digging in his mother's smallholding for lettuce and onions. He found a couple of thin worms and let them lie wriggling in his hand, pink and naked-looking. He offered his open palm to the boy-faced bird that did not fly away. The bird picked delicately at the worm, grasping it in teeth as fine as needles. There was something disturbing about watching the tiny face struggling to chew the writhing worm and Tommo found himself looking away, but if the bird could do it so could he. He dug about in the earth and, finding a fatter specimen, shut his eyes and thrust it into his mouth. He had some trouble swallowing it down and the boy-faced bird looked at him reproachfully. He didn't like the texture in his mouth and it didn't make him feel any less hungry either. He would have to find some real food from somewhere if he was to stand any chance of surviving.

'Fish! Fish! Fish coming!' sang the boy-faced bird and his song was echoed by his two companions, a bird with the face of a baby and one with the loose flesh of an old man. They wrinkled their tiny noses and sniffed the air and then Tommo smelled it too – the unmistakable scent of fresh fish, of salt and succulence, making his mouth water and the worm sit even more uncomfortably in his shrunken belly. He felt weak again – too weak to struggle to his feet – and he wished that he could fly like his unlikely companions. They continued to sing 'Fish! Fish! Fish coming!' in three-part harmony from mid-air. From far away Tommo heard the clatter of wooden wheels, the regular sharp tattoo of iron-clad hooves on the metalled road, and he slowly worked out that someone was coming.

A cloud of what must have been gulls or some other scavenging bird flew above the cart squawking shrilly so that he could guess its whereabouts long before he could see it. In the meantime he tried to look a little more respectable. It wasn't easy.

He could see just by looking at his hand that his skin was marred by a patina of glowing, silver dust that would not wipe away however hard he scrubbed at it with the dirty sleeve of his frayed tunic. He had no doubt that his hair was full of twigs and leaves, and probably mud-covered too, so he combed it roughly with his fingers. It was long enough to tie back off his face – and no spellgrinder ever lacked a scrap of leather for that purpose. He tried to stand to wait for the arrival of the cart, but he was swaying dangerously and was afraid that if he fell back into the ditch he would never climb back out, so he sat cross-legged on the floor as if he were working. The scent of the fish was driving him mad.

When the cart came into view, he could see it was a ramshackle, old-fashioned affair with peeling paint and a much-mended waxed cover protecting the fish from the eager beaks of the wheeling gulls. The horse was old and far too thin, and the driver was a skinny boy of no more than ten with a scowling face. When the cart was close enough for these details to be obvious, Tommo shouted 'Hoy!', which was the all-purpose greeting of the country. His voice was so weak and tentative, and the boy took so little notice, that he tried again. 'Hoy there!'

'I heard you the first time,' the driver snapped. 'Hoy yourself!'

From high above he could hear the boy-faced bird and several other similar voices calling, 'Listen and learn! Listen and learn!'

Much to Tommo's surprise the driver halted the cart and glanced upwards at the singing birds as if he heard them too. They were real then.

'What is it you want?' the boy said brusquely, looking at Tommo with narrowed eyes and an expression of acute suspicion.

'I thought maybe you might have something to eat,' Tommo said and struggled to his feet.

The driver looked at Tommo for a long moment without changing his expression, as if weighing him up.

'Why are you that funny colour?' he said eventually.

'I was a spellgrinder's apprentice.'

The boy nodded. 'You ran away?'

Tommo nodded.

'Well, I've got enough trouble of my own,' the driver said bluntly and flicked the reins of the weary horse.

'No, wait! Please! If I don't eat, I don't think I can go on . . .' Tommo hadn't wanted to beg, but he knew he wouldn't last much longer without something besides worms to eat.

The boy's brow furrowed even further and he hesitated.

'How can you pay me?' he asked grudgingly.

'I can grind spellstones. I was the best grinder in my cellar . . .' Tommo began.

'There's not much call for that round us,' the boy answered with an impatient shake of his head. 'Ever gutted fish?' Tommo would have said anything for a piece of fish, but as he opened his mouth his questioner interrupted him.

'Doesn't take much skill anyhow – just a steady enough hand with a bit of speed. Best step in the cart and I warn you if you try to rob me, you won't find nothing but my gutting knife in your gizzard.'

Tommo nodded weakly, and stumbled forward to try and get into the cart. The boy watched him struggle without offering to help. The cart was high and it took Tommo all his remaining strength to clamber up. He all but fell into the hard seat.

'I'm grateful,' he said when he'd got his breath.

'Don't worry. You'll pay me well enough for the ride.'

The boy groped under the waxed cloth that covered the cart and produced a small package wrapped in the same material.

'Yesterday's fish,' he said, flatly. 'Have it. I've had a bellyful. Not much selling since them bird-catchers have been out and about. You can get a brace of birds for under a haveling.'

Tommo couldn't speak for the fish he'd stuffed in his mouth. He tried to nod intelligently, but doubted that he looked convincing.

'When did you eat last?'

Tommo shrugged. 'Four days – could be five. Don't know.'

'There's beer behind,' the boy said a little more softly, indicating the same place under the canopy with his thumb. A couple of the human-faced birds alighted on the horse's back and the boy glanced quickly at Tommo to gauge his reaction. He didn't much care – his world had narrowed to the joy of fish and the beer, sweet and wet, running down his throat.

The boy watched him from the corner of his eye.

'You might as well sleep now. We've a way to go.' He tossed Tommo some coarse cloth, waxed like the canopy over the cart. He didn't take his eyes off the road. 'You'll need your eyes open to gut fish,' he said brusquely.

Tommo didn't have the words to thank his rescuer and was struggling not to cry tears of relief. Something unfamiliar made his eyes tickle, perhaps it was the dust. Somehow he didn't think the skinny boy would be too impressed with that.

'I'll gut fish till my fingers bleed,' he said as robustly as he could manage.

The boy nodded. 'Them that call me anything call me Akenna,' he added.

'But that's a girl's name,' Tommo said unthinkingly – the food, the beer and his exhaustion making him less cautious than he ought to have been.

'So?' Akenna said, opening her tunic to show the gutting knife. The air was suddenly heavy with the tension of a lightning storm.

'I mean, I . . .'

'Forget it,' Akenna said abruptly, as if thinking better of picking a fight. 'It don't worry me none, but don't think that because I'm a girl I can't take you and seven more like you in a fight.'

'No, no, I wouldn't,' Tommo said quickly, only grasping his danger too late.

'They call me Tommo,' he added. 'And I'm pleased to meet you.'

'That's fancy talking for an apprentice,' she said suspiciously. 'Go to sleep – I'm done gossiping. Chatter won't get this cart home.'

She shut her mouth like the Master Spellgrinder shut the trapdoor of the apprentice's cellar.

Tommo fell almost instantly asleep.

CHAPTER THREE

Someone was sobbing. Tommo lay still in the darkness. Back in the cellar the new apprentices often sobbed at night and the old ones sobbed too, for that matter, when the quivers started. It was the hands that got it first – when the head started to tremble you didn't have much time left. But then he remembered. He wasn't in the cellar. He was a sanctuary runaway, a fugitive, alone and temporarily free. Who then was crying? His neck was stiff and painful but he moved it anyway to look around. He had fallen asleep while the cart had been moving, but now it had stopped and he could smell the salt smell that he knew must be the sea. He could taste it on his lips. Bentree Harbour – he had made it to Bentree Harbour. He might yet have a chance at living! His sudden ebullience was quashed at once by the persistence of those sobs. They made his chest ache. He had always been too soft and had found it hard at first among the street boys, the mountain-herd lads and the poor farmers who were his fellow apprentices; they'd had most of the spirit beaten out of them before they got close to the spellgrinder's cellar and most of the kindness too. Tommo had had to learn to harden his heart. Whoever was crying, it was no business of his. But then he never could help his curiosity.

They had stopped by some kind of low, dark building. The horse had gone and he was left alone in the cart. Where was Akenna? Was she the source of the sobbing? He untangled himself from the waxed covering to sit up properly and was dazzled by his own silvery glow. It was as if he were alight with a thousand tiny firefly sparks. He hadn't noticed it so much before; he was sure the ethereal glimmer had grown worse and surely his hand as he wrapped himself in the waxed cloth shook slightly. He didn't want to think about that. It was probably just the relief that made him tremble, nothing more. He could not have been so blessed by White Urtha, only to be cursed by Red Unga. His hand did not shake; he was tired that was all. The sobbing quietened and Tommo sank back into his seat – there was no need for him to act. He would most likely only get the sharp end of Akenna's gutting knife for his trouble. If she had left him here in the dark, outside, perhaps she had wished him to remain hidden. He was exhausted and it did not take much to persuade him that he was better off staying where he was, hiding his skin that was bright as starlight, under a waxed cloth covering. He settled to sleep again and tried to ignore the disturbing truth – that his hand continued to shake for quite a while after his deliberate movement had ceased.

He woke a second time to birdsong and the cawing of

gulls and the strange, inhuman voices of the human-faced birds. There were more of them than there had been the previous day.

'Look and listen, hoy!' They sang high and clear in coldly precise harmony that was at once beautiful and chilling. It was not a sound he could sleep through. He hadn't quite roused himself to full wakefulness when Akenna emerged from the rough door of the tumbledown turf cottage. He could see that she was badly bruised, her right eye almost shut and shaded a livid red.

She put her finger to the thin line of her compressed lips and beckoned for him to follow after her. His skin did not sparkle quite so obviously in the pale sunlight, but he kept the waxed cloth draped round him anyway. The birds unaccountably stopped their singing, almost as if they'd seen her signal, and she led him down a steeply descending rocky path in eerie silence. Even the great cawing sea birds were quiet as Tommo stumbled wearily after Akenna's small, rigid form towards the grey mass which he concluded must be the sea. He had never seen it before and he could not help but stare at it in fascination. There was a mist and it was hard to know where it ended and the sky began. It frightened him for no good reason.

Akenna hissed at him and he gathered himself together. She climbed easily up the outcrops of dark rock that surrounded the small shingle beach to form the ragged arc of a bay. He followed after, clumsily. His soleless canvas slippers were worn through after his days trudging the countryside and the black rocks were spiky and pointed like shards of crystalline spellstone. He knew better than to cry out or to try to stop her. He cut himself once or twice and was relieved to see that his blood still flowed dark and red; he had feared that it too might have turned silver. When Akenna disappeared, he did not panic. He had gone beyond that. He had so nearly died the day before and yet had survived, even the sight of his hand trembling as he held on to a spindle-shaped crag of rock for support could not depress him; nor could the fading gleam of the spellcast runes on his sanctuary band. His time of sanctuary was almost over. He sat down on the flattest expanse of rock he could find and looked out to sea. The mist was lifting and all he could see was the sleek back of the sea, a vast beast, silver-grey and flecked with sunlight, stretching all the way to the cobweb-thin thread of the horizon. He didn't have a word for the exact colour of the sea and it changed as he watched so that he almost lost himself in it. Akenna's sharp whistle startled him back to full awareness. He turned to follow the source of the sound and saw her pale and pained face squinting at him from the heart of the rock. Her face made it clear that he was to follow and was a dolt for failing to do so immediately. He shambled after her and found that she was peering from a cave, the mouth of which was almost as thin and narrow as Akenna's own. Inside, the cave was dark and dank. He unwrapped the waxed cloth, which he was still wearing, and discovered that his own faint personal inner light was more than enough to illumine the space that opened out in front of him.

'Da's got a skinful so won't be fishing for a while yet – you can hide here.'

'You don't want me to gut fish?'

Akenna scowled. 'Not now. I'm not stopping here no more.' She wiped her nose with the back of her hand and Tommo tried not to notice that her eyes were glistening wetly. 'Need you to help me take the boat.'

He thought about this for a moment. 'Take it where?' he asked, trying to keep his sudden flame of hope from showing too much in his voice. It didn't do to let people know what you cared about – it made it too easy for them to hurt you by depriving you of it.

'Anywhere but here,' she said quietly, and looked at him with interest. 'Knew you made enough light to see by.' She fiddled for a moment with a string of dark-coloured beads round her neck and then unwrapped a length of rope from her skinny middle. 'I won't cut you if you don't fight. I've got to leave you here until full dark tonight and I don't want you running off,' she said, and proceeded to try to tie his hands tightly together. He didn't fight; why should he? If she took him from the shores of the borough and better still from the Protectorate itself, he would be free. His imagination could not envisage anything further ahead than that: where he would go and what he would do were problems for another time.

'Keep still!' Akenna did not seem to realise that the shaking in his hands was involuntary and for a moment he thought she might reach for the gutting knife, which he could see still hung prominently from her belt in its rough leather sheath.

'I can't keep still. It's a sickness.' There, he'd acknowledged it. Akenna let go of his hands as if they burnt her, and backed away. No one in the Protectorate was sanguine about sickness. It was not that many years since the Protector came to power by the popular will after the members of the ruling Convocation and most of the country Names had died of the blue pox. They'd not died alone: a good portion of the working priesthood had gone too, choking on fresh air. Neither the old wandering quacks, the merciful wives, nor the educated leechers and physickers had ever worked out why that vile pestilence attacked the powerful and left the poor alone, which was not to say that they didn't all have their different theories. Most suspected Fallon, the Protector, had something to do with it, but as no one knew for sure it was generally held that the pox could return at any time. Akenna covered her nose and mouth with her grimy shawl.

'It's not the blue pox or anything like it, and it's not like the winter sow-croup. I don't think you can get it. Only spellgrinders and their apprentices have it – I think it's to do with the grind-dust. We call it "the quivers". It's very common.'

'Does it kill you?' Her voice was sharp and she was to the point.

'Yes.' It was not so hard to say; he hadn't died in the noose and he hadn't died in the ditch so let the quivers do

20

their worst. 'But it doesn't take you straightaway,' he added quickly, seeing Akenna's expression darken and her hand hover near to her gutting knife.

'Does it take your strength?' she demanded, and Tommo had enough wits left to lie.

'I am fit enough to help you and besides everyone knows the grind-dust gives you thaumaturgical powers.'

It was an old joke in the cellar that, a story spun to encourage the parents of the benighted apprentices to give up their sons to the craft. No apprentice truly believed it, but Akenna would not know that. In the unearthly light of his own skin Tommo saw Akenna's eyes widen.

'You're having me on.'

'You wait and see,' Tommo said, trying for the mysterious but confident tone he'd overheard the spellgrinder use with his customers, agents and intermediaries. He thought he might even have pulled it off. She did not look entirely convinced but she was certainly more wary of him when she tugged at his bindings, though that could have been because she feared to catch the quivers.

'Have you anything to eat?' Tommo asked at last because his stomach was making the kind of noises more usually heard in a kennel.

Akenna shook her head. 'There's fish and turnips back at the cottage. I'll bring you some later.'

'And something to drink?'

'There'll be milk when I've milked Katrina, the goat.' She added, 'My father named her after my mother. He's like that.'

21

'Is your mother dead?'

Akenna shook her head. 'She ran off without bearing the male heir she was contracted for. My father never forgave her. He didn't think a girl was good enough. He's going to regret that one day.' Her small face was hard and fierce. Tommo had the strong feeling that the apprentices would have had trouble taking advantage of Akenna.

'I'll be back later,' she said abruptly. 'If you try to escape, I'll find you and you'll be sorry – and then dead.'

Tommo nodded. 'I'll be here,' he said simply, 'but I would be more use to you if I wasn't so hungry.'

Akenna looked at him as she might inspect a goat. 'I said I'd bring food, didn't I?'

And with that she stalked irritably away.

Tommo was almost relieved to be left alone – Akenna wasn't exactly easy company, but if she got him away from the borough he could forgive her anything. He held on to that thought and, closing his eyes, fell immediately back to sleep.

CHAPTER FOUR

Vevena, the Protector's wife, regularly tried to spy on her husband, but her efforts were usually thwarted. There were several reasons for this, the most obvious being the number of spies in the Fortress of Winter who were in the pay of her husband. Added to this was the difficulty that the most beautiful woman in the Protectorate had in going anywhere unnoticed. The most serious impediment to her many attempts to find out anything useful about his weaknesses was the thaumaturgist's curse that bound her: she could do Fallon no harm by word or deed. As there was nothing she wanted to do more than cause him considerable harm, this made her a deeply unhappy woman, as well as a bad spy and a wholly unsatisfactory wife. The Protector had discovered through bitter experience that not even the Chief Spellstone Wielder of the Protectorate, gifted with the most powerful yellow-hued spellstone that had yet been discovered, one cut by a master spellgrinder when all the portents were good, not even this could cast a spell powerful enough to overcome Vevena's natural revulsion and make her love him.

Vevena did what she could. The curse could not oblige her to smile or even to speak, and so for the greater part of her days she did neither. She avoided Fallon's presence wherever possible, though it was impossible for her to stray too far from his person. She had tried it once riding her palfrey to the edge of the estate, but had become violently ill and passed out as soon as she attempted to cross the boundary. Such events did not make her dislike Fallon any less.

She was very frustrated. Sometimes she could devise innocent questions to ask the servants which might cause some crumb of useful information to fall into her lap, but such triumphs were rare and try as she might to be in the right place at the right time anything important always seemed to be going on somewhere else.

On the second night of the winter month dedicated to White Urtha, the night the peasants called 'All Spirits' Eve', she chanced upon one of the Protector's guards, a senior spy, talking in an undertone to a small and undernourished gafferboy.

'You say you had it from your brothers in Tipplehead?'

'That's right, your honour, by Unga's udders.' He paused and bit his lip so hard that he drew blood, as if aware that wasn't the best language to use before some high-up in the fortress. 'I mean,' he continued, 'by Red Unga and White Urtha both. My runner, Moran, saw it happen.'

'He saw the apprentice?'

'Yes, your honour, and checked his name in the Sheriff's Ledger of Malfeasance. He gave it to me good. He's as honest a legman as you'll find. Moran said there was this lad, known as Tommo, and a fair spellgrinder. He'd been with Master Irons in his cellar on Greeve Street for seven or more years and looked the part – white hair and flashy like those boys go.'

Vevena, who was wearing her riding hood, pulled it further over her eyes. She was sure she had lost a bead from the trim of her cloak – yes, surely it was here somewhere.

The guard barely glanced at her, he was so busy checking the gafferboy's story.

'Tell me again what he did.'

'He claimed sanctuary in the name of Gildea at White Urtha's shrine in Tipplehead.'

'You are quite sure of the name and of the penalty?'

'Never surer, your honour. I double checked on Moran, but he's real reliable.'

The gafferboy fiddled nervously with the cloth cap in his hand.

'You go in there and report what you've told me to Lord Fallon, the Protector, himself. Look lively and don't fancy up your tale or you'll be sorry. If he finds out I've brought him a fabulist, I'll be for the dungeon and you will be dead by the next watch, so tread careful and be honest.' The guard ushered the boy into the council chamber and Vevena swept past him as though nothing she could hear from such a source could be of interest.

Gildea was dead so what did it matter if some apprentice called on his name? Why did the spy think that tiny snippet of information important enough to disturb the Protector?

Gildea had been the High Priest of the Inward Power, the greatest thaumaturgist who had ever lived, the man who had introduced the spellstones into the Island of the Gifted. He was the man who had developed the theories on which all thaumaturgical understanding was based. He had declared publicly not long before he was killed in the marketplace of Tipplehead that spellstones were living beings which must not be ground and used at the whim of man.

Vevena had met him once as a young child and remembered him as a kindly grandfather figure with white hair and beard, a large nose and eyes the colour of a winter sea. He had given her a toffee and declared her 'White Urtha's child' for the unblemished clarity of her skin and her unearthly loveliness. Vevena had always been rather disappointed that even as great a man as Gildea had not seen past her pretty face.

Her brain refused to think about the meaning of this chance encounter with the guard and the gafferboy. Every time she tried to focus on it she would find herself thinking about flower arranging and the colour of her new gown. In truth Vevena was interested in neither and such disruptions to her thinking were the result of her ensorcellment. The thing she mustn't think of . . . the roses and the lilac. No . . . the grey gown with the peridot and pearls. No . . . the old man who'd given her a toffee. Yes! He was still a danger to her husband. She started to sing and to embroider a very complicated piece. What if she could find a way to get her father released? Then he could find out what she could not and . . . lavender and wild thyme improved the scent of any bouquet and the green velvet would look best with her emeralds. She jabbed her embroidery needle hard into her finger. It hurt. She had thought of something dangerous again, she had to hang on to that thought then find a way to act on it . . . lily of the valley was pretty in its way and rubies went well with her pale skin. Her father had bought her rubies. Her father needed to be free! Her blood was red as rubies. Let blood and rubies remind her of her father . . . and roses of course and the colour of her new cloak embroidered with gold. Rubies. Father. Still singing, she took out some fresh white linen, from which she carefully cut a square and laid it on her work table . . . white as snow and old men's beards. She took one ruby earring and a sapphire and laid them both on the linen cloth . . . how pretty they looked, the sapphire, blue as larkspur, so useful in a posy, blue like the summer sky. Let the sky stand for freedom; let the ruby stand for her father and the white for the beard of the old man who was danger. She put them into the small and extravagantly jewelled purse that hung from her girdle and promptly forgot why.

'My lady.' Her handmaid, Dolina, was on her in a moment. Vevena knew that she was a spy – they all were, all the people she was allowed to meet reported on her movements to the Spymaster and sometimes directly to Fallon himself.

27

'I think I will walk a little in the garden,' Vevena said. More wretched flowers again. What was it that she really wanted to think about? She still wore her heavy hunting cloak, the good one that was waxed against the weather, the one that hid her face from view. She did not change but waved Dolina away. 'I require solitude. I wish to consider which jewels to wear for the All Spirits' Feast.' As if she cared. How could she go on when even her thoughts were not her own?

The curse would not even let her die. She blinked back tears of frustration that she would not let fall in front of one of Fallon's people, and walked purposefully to the garden.

Fallon had demanded the spellstone wielders turn the Fortress of Winter into a folly of wild excess. He wanted to flaunt his power she was sure, but even ensorcelled she was not so blind that she could not see he also wanted to impress and amuse her, and she despised him for it. She could not imagine why he thought she would be amused by a life-sized golden statue of her, the Lady Vevena, wearing a dress of rubies. Rubies. Blood. Father. There was something she wanted to do. What could it have been?

The garden distracted her. The spellstone wielders had excelled themselves and with magic had constructed rainbow fountains and cascades of pearls, a pathway of precious stones and trees made from ice, from living flowers and from flowing water. Vevena would have preferred it if the spellstone wielders had merely planted a few trees and shrubs, but they had created a wonder instead, and one which changed every day to Vevena's irritation. All the flowers which had been blue yesterday were now white and at least four times the size of any bloom found in nature.

'Not again,' she said to herself and was surprised when another voice answered.

'You do not like change?' It was the voice of Fallon's right-hand man, the Chief Spellstone Wielder, Kalen.

'I think that Red Unga-under-all created better bodies than those of your spells, Kalen. If it were left to me, this garden would be full of trees and grass and that is all.'

'And I would be in the dungeon, my lady, for failing to please your husband with my ingenuity.'

Dungeon . . . dragon flowers, pink silk damask. Danger.

Vevena didn't say anything, but she fiddled with the clasp of her purse until it opened with a snap. There was something inside. She pulled out a white cloth from which spilled a single ruby earring and a single sapphire. Ah. She remembered something.

'Gildea. Father. Free,' she said.

'What did you say?' Kalen looked at her with sudden interest.

She had been saying something and had dropped some stones on the ground . . . how pretty the ruby looked against the grass. She must wear her green velvet gown with her ruby choker for the feast and perhaps wear the gold tiara in her hair. Kalen was still looking at her strangely.

'I will do what I can, my lady,' he said. 'You are an inspiration to us all.'

His eyes looked quite moist as he turned away. Funny, gawky man – she had no idea what he was talking about.

CHAPTER FIVE

Tommo woke to a dry mouth and a horrible crick in his back. Both reminded him that he still lived so they distressed him less than they might have done. He had no way of knowing how long he had slept, but Akenna had obviously returned at some point as a small package of fish, turnip and a clay bowl of milk had been left by his feet. His hands shook as he tried to bring the milk to his lips. He was terrified of spilling any. Akenna had done a good job of binding his wrists so his task was complicated by the limited movement she had allowed him, but he managed somehow and the rich taste of the milk revived him. He had not drunk unwatered milk for a long time; it reminded him of his childhood and for a moment he could almost smell the new-baked pot-bread and scrubbed wood of his mother's homestead from the good days before his fortunes changed.

When he had eaten as clumsily and awkwardly as he had managed to drink, he began to give serious thought to escaping his bonds. He didn't mind helping Akenna, indeed he probably owed her his help in return for the food she'd given him, but he saw no reason why he should be trussed up like a chicken for her satisfaction. In the eerie light of his glowing skin, he examined the knot she had used. It was some complicated sailors' affair. He thought briefly about untying it with his teeth and the idea made him smile. He had eaten badly for so long he doubted his teeth could munch through a good steak let alone the heavy-duty hemp rope that Akenna had used. Outside the cave the rocks were sharp as razors. He would use them as saws to free himself.

Somehow the fact that he had the quivers liberated him from many of his usual fears. He did not have too long to live whichever way he looked at it and now that he was rested he wasn't going to waste time waiting, bound in the dark, on the whim of some scrawny girl with plenty of problems of her own.

He stumbled around a bit before he made it to the narrow cave opening and the searing daylight brightness that made his eyes water. His legs had grown numb and uncooperative as he slept and when he started moving they needled him with a thousand pin pricks as he forced them to work again.

Outside the wind lifted his hair and whipped it round his face, the fresh salt tang of the sea and the spray from the wild waves breaking on the nearby rocks made him lick his lips to taste the day: it was wonderful. The mist had cleared and the sun shone on a liquid silver sea. It was so beautiful he was transfixed by it: the wide sky and the endless sea and the birds high above, calling. It was as far from the cramped, dim, constricting cellar as it was possible to be, and he felt his spirits soar, against all reason, for whatever happened he could not live long.

For all his new boldness he did not dare leave the shelter of the cave mouth. He stayed there for a long time, sniffing the air like his mother's old dog, closing his eyes and letting the wind buffet him and blow away the last remnants of the cellar's stink from his nostrils. He let the breeze and brine take his breath away and blast him clean. He hoped that from a distance his own silver sheen might be seen as a rock pool or some portion of the great sea.

There were no boats in the cove which surprised him, though perhaps there were as many savagely sharp rocks below the sea as on the shore. It was quiet too, apart from the screeching of the gulls and his own personal honour guard of birds singing what sounded like 'To be free, oh, to be free!' in three-part harmony. It was almost as if they understood. Luckily it was so windy that Tommo could scarcely hear them. Their pure voices simulating human words frightened and disturbed him. He wished they'd find some other fugitive to bother; they acted like some huge aerial signpost, signalling his precise position to anyone with the wit to notice them and an ear for their eldritch song.

The sea had its own sound. At first all he could hear was the crashing boom of the great waves as they bombarded the rock only to be broken into a surging torrent of white water, spindrift and spray. Then gradually he thought he could hear a small, persistent voice crying 'Help!'

Tommo tried not to hear, but the sound was so piteous he could not but investigate. He began to rub the hemp rope that bound him against the sharpness of a nearby rock. It quickly became obvious that it would take a long time for the strong rope to fray and the cry for help was very insistent. He gave up and sighed. His hands shook but he tried not to notice. For a moment there he had been perfectly happy, now he had to move again, struggle again. Stumbling unsteadily, he followed the voice to the furthest edge of the cove. It was difficult to keep his balance when he could not freely move his arms and he fell once quite badly and skinned his knee. He carried on anyway to find the source of the voice and found a place where rock was replaced by soft, pale orange-pink sand. At first he thought there was nothing there but wind-blown sea grasses. Then, as he got closer, he could see the washed-up body of some large sea creature, bigger than a fish but smooth-skinned, even in decay – and very obviously dead. It was with some horror that Tommo realised that the sound emanated from this dead body on the beach.

'Who is it? Who is calling?' Tommo asked in a small voice that was whipped from his mouth almost before the words had formed.

'It is Deep-diver of the Dolphin People. Let me die!'

Tommo approached the body cautiously. It was very dead, though still intact and smelling of the sea.

'I don't understand. Where are you?'

'Here,' the voice answered and Tommo wondered if

perhaps it were not a real voice at all, but something in his head – perhaps a side effect of the quivers.

'I can't see you,' Tommo said, suddenly frightened. It was bad enough that the sky was filled with birds that sang with human voices without his own head being filled with voices too.

'My body is dead, but something keeps me here – a command not to leave the shores of the Protectorate. It traps me here. I yearn to be free.'

Tommo did not know what to say, for if that were true and not just something invented by his own sickness and imagining, then it would be a terrible thing.

'What can I do?' Tommo said forlornly. The idea of being trapped in a dead body was making him feel queasy. He hoped it was not true. The wind was cold on this part of the beach and it cut through his clothes, as he imagined Akenna's gutting knife might do, when she found him missing from her secret cave. Tommo shivered and his hands quivered. He thought to himself that it would be hard to find a creature less likely to be of use to a dead dolphin, or indeed anything else, in the whole of the Protectorate. He would have laughed except that would have seemed disrespectful to the dolphin's plight – whether it was real or something Tommo had himself imagined.

'If you can hear me, then you have power. Be merciful, use it and let me be free.'

Above Tommo the birds, which had briefly flown out of earshot, began to keen, 'Be free! Oh, to be free! How I long to be free! Free me!' There seemed to be more of them and they had developed an extra layer of harmony, a bass voice, that carried through the air like the nightly curfew bell.

'Oh, shut up! All of you. I can't help anyone. I'm dying and I'm powerless and my sanctuary band just turned black.' It had too, though he'd only just noticed it: the silver spellstone runes had glowed more brightly and then faded into nothing so all that remained was a damp pig-leather bracelet that had been poorly cured and still smelled of swine. He must have been wrong about how long he'd been travelling. Unga's udders, he really was doomed. He rather suspected that now anyone could kill him at any time and be regarded as doing the Sheriff a favour.

The dolphin responded with grave and incomprehensible politeness: 'I'm sorry to hear that. I am unhappy to have diverted you from the current of your choice.' Then it started its haunting, piteous cry again. 'Help!'

The birds above echoed it in exquisite four-part harmony. 'Help him! Oh, help him to be free. Oh, to be free!'

Tommo covered his ears with his hands but it made very little difference. Perhaps the sound was inside his head and he was in an even worse condition than he had feared. Then he realised that he ought not to have been able to cover his ears with his hands because they had been tied firmly together with Akenna's workmanlike binding. He ought to have been bound, but it seemed that somehow now he was free.

'You see,' said the dolphin's soundless voice, responding to his unspoken thought. 'You have power.'

'I don't know how . . .' Tommo began, addressing his words to the head of the yellowing corpse. Above him the birds formed themselves into the symbol for 'Listen and learn' as they had when he lay dying in the ditch. He thought back to the good student's litany, just in case the birds were actually attempting to communicate something useful, and remembered a fragment of a phrase from *The Book of White Urtha*:

> Let he with pity so be moved
> To ease the sufferer's burden.

He took a reluctant step forward and rested his trembling hand lightly on the dolphin's yellowed, flaking skin. If the dust had any power, he would learn of it. He felt a bit foolish, even though his only witness was the demented avian chorus, but he spoke the words aloud anyway, just in case.

'If I can give you freedom, if I can ease your burden, I give it gladly.'

He felt the dolphin give a deep, reverberant sigh and then suddenly he was silent. The birds were not. They started singing so loudly and so joyously that Tommo feared that anyone in the vicinity would be drawn to their wildly inventive anthem. He hurried back to the cave, only pausing to wash his hands in the saltwater of a rock pool to remove the sweet odour of the dolphin's dead flesh. He could not quite believe he had succeeded in setting the dolphin free. He could not quite rid himself of the impression that the whole thing had been a kind of fever dream; he had the quivers after all and was probably not entirely sane.

CHAPTER SIX

Fallon, the self-styled Protector of the whole Island of the Gifted, sat back in his elaborate chair, which was not quite, but almost a throne, and looked unseeingly at the bustle of the great hall, which was almost, but not quite a court. He no longer noticed the proportions of the room, the richness of the tapestry hangings, the vastness of the stone fireplace, nor the splendour of the huge glass mirrors of spellstone wielder origin that gave the illusion of infinite space contained in this one room. There were paintings too, done with such a wondrous eye for detail that they seemed to have the life of Unga within them. Statues of gold and semi-precious stones dazzled the eye and impressed the Unga-given-breath out of Fallon's visitors. He ought to deal with the many and various petitioners who had come to the hall for judgement, for favours, for the sale of information, but this one new piece of information troubled him so deeply that he could no longer concentrate. A lad had claimed sanctuary in the name of Gildea.

Fallon called over Lord Awnan of Brinden, his overworked factotum, whose father had once had Fallon flogged for the theft of a mouldy apple.

'Awnan, send them away – tell them that something urgent has come up and I am indisposed.' A follower of Gildea had claimed sanctuary and no one had dared to do that since Fallon had become Protector.

'But, your honour, Lord Coman of Hay has been waiting these three days, and the deputation from the brotherhood of fishers are . . .' The young man's voice trailed away into a whisper.

'You heard what I said. Unga-under-all, just do it, Awnan,' Fallon said coldly. Such moments of casual command still gave him pleasure after all these years. Lord Awnan's father had been the first to die of the blue pox and was blamed in many quarters for bringing the plague with him from his journeys overseas. It was a very satisfactory rumour which still blighted the son's marital chances, and was not entirely without foundation because Lord Awnan the Elder had been with the High Priest, Gildea, on the trip to the smoking mountain where the spellstones had been discovered. It was undeniably true, though he would deny it to the last, that without Gildea's discovery of the spellstones and his recognition of their power, even Fallon's malevolence could not have conjured the blue pox.

Fallon barely noticed as his elaborately equipped, and generously paid, guards cleared the great hall in moments. He ignored the cries of 'Lord Fallon, Protector, My Lord!', just as many years ago Lord Awnan the Elder had ignored his complaints that he was hungry and it was only a small and damaged apple. A follower of Gildea had claimed sanctuary and that must mean something: a challenge, a call to arms, a rallying cry to whoever still lived who might oppose him? Could that be true?

He had ruled to the best of his ability for almost seven years and in all that time had never forgotten his origins. No, he never ever forgot that he was one of the people. It made his position all the sweeter. He did his best and yet there were still complaints from mealy-mouthed cowards who could not see how much better he ruled than the lily-livered Convocation of magicians, physickers and women. Unfortunately he could not kill all his critics, though he had done his best. He called Awnan over and asked with a sigh, 'So? What are the complaints?'

'The brotherhood of fishers complain that people are eating cheap birdmeat not fish. The bread you gave to the poor of the North Barra Marshes was gratefully received, but has so reduced the value of the local farmers' grain that there are riots in Dunreel.'

Fallon sighed. He ought not to have intervened in North Barra. He ought to have learnt that lesson by now. Early in his Protectorate he'd promised free bread for all so that many of the fields did not get planted. When he had discovered how costly bread was in terms of spellstone power, he had tried to affect the weather so that a later planting was possible, but with all the power of the spellstones he had been unable to prevent the floods or the famine from which the north was still recovering. As for the birds, he had been having them killed ever since they had begun flying round his own tower in suspiciously large numbers. His instinct told him they were a threat so he had acted.

'We'll have to send troops off to the north then – for the sake of the peace.' He would have liked to dispatch troops to finish off the fishers too. They had ever been an ungovernable mob of hard-drinking smugglers, free-mouthing whoever was in power. At least there was nothing new to threaten him in this current crop of complaints against his rule.

Awnan was watching him intently, waiting for his next instruction or maybe for a sign of weakness.

'Smooth it over – use that old Name charm,' Fallon said. 'Offer them some refreshments in the ante-room. Unga's heart!' he snorted. 'I will see them tomorrow. I can't have them believing that the Protector fails to protect.' Awnan's expression was veiled. Sometimes Fallon wondered if Awnan hated him; he certainly hated Awnan. Fallon had one of his pages bring him his decorated map of the Protectorate. It showed him the full extent of his territory, from Kincable in the far west over to Oldtithe in the East, from the northernmost point of Cartdoney to the south-ernmost tip of Kinroyal. It showed him clearly enough that this lad Tommo, from his starting point at Tipplehead, east of the Spine, could not escape from the broad Borough of Tippo within his allotted time – at least not without thaumaturgical or some more practical aid. That was it, though, did he have aid? Was he part of some bigger group plotting against Fallon? There was no obvious reason why the news of the apprentice's escape should make his innards twist and quake.

It was his instinct again. He should be done with fear; his position was almost unassailable. The power of spellstone magic kept the whole Protectorate hidden and forgotten, lost to those lands overseas that might have designs on an island which harboured true thaumaturgy.

Fallon chewed at his fingers which were already raw. He had bought up most of the spellstones in the Protectorate and he had used the power of the stones to infect most of the Priesthood of the Inward Power and the Convocation with the blue pox. In doing so he hoped he had destroyed all natural thaumaturgy. Why then did he feel so vulnerable? For all that he paid the army and his spies, his street runners and his gafferboys, his bullymen and his sheriffs, his court agents and his assassins, his tax collectors and his tax enforcers; for all that he kept his dungeons full and his torturer and executioner in work, he was still vulnerable.

Once at the beginning of his Protectorate he had taken the testimony of a woman, a priestess of the Inward Power, one with secret sight and strong will who had survived longer than anyone expected on the wheel. Urtha's udders, but she had been a tough old sow and betrayed no one, until at her dying breath she had told him that he would never suppress thaumaturgy. She had smiled a death's head grimace at him and said that she had seen it: she had seen that an agent of Gildea would be the death of him. His advisors, the few remaining country Names, his spellstone wielders and his spellgrinders had laughed and made light of it, calling it the only revenge of an anguished woman and nothing but an empty threat. Those few thaumaturgists still living at that time explained the vagaries of secret sight and how the future was a castle with many rooms, only some of which would one day be built. He believed none of it, but perversely never doubted the priestess's threat. Fallon was no fool and thought they were all against him, because they were, and no one with Inward Power ever owned to it again. He rewarded his friends with spellstone gifts of wonder and he punished his enemies, usually fatally, and kept his guard up waiting for the time when an agent of Gildea might appear. Was Tommo such an agent?

He could have him killed. That would be easy – he could snuff out a life like the light from a candle. He needed to know if the boy was truly an agent of Gildea and if there were any more lurking out there who had somehow eluded his spies.

His reverie was interrupted by the tall, angular and untidy presence of his Chief Spellstone Wielder, a sorry excuse for a man with the bare minimum of Inward Power necessary to wield the spellstones effectively. He wore the gold hat of his office as though it were the round felt hat of a common soldier of the guard and seemed always to be apologising.

'My lord,' he began, 'if you would excuse me. I have

learnt something of the greatest importance to my lord's happiness.'

'Oh, what is it now, Kalen? Don't tell me you have rearranged the garden again. These wonders are all very well, but there is business to deal with.'

'Exactly, my lord, and there can be no business closer to my heart than my lord's happiness.'

Fallon eyed the Chief Spellstone Wielder suspiciously. He was not fool enough to believe that Kalen held him in particular esteem. Fallon kept Blathnaid, Kalen's daughter by his first wife Alissa, as a 'guest' in the high tower of his Fortress of Summer, her welfare the hostage to Kalen's loyalty. Fallon raised an eyebrow and indicated that his taster should pour him a drink.

'My lord,' the Chief Spellstone Wielder persisted, 'the Lady Vevena remembers her father.'

Fallon spluttered and nearly spilled his drink. 'She can't. The spells placed on her were invoked by Gildea himself, at my request.'

'Nevertheless it is clear that she does remember Haver-snatcher.'

Fallon thought for a moment. 'And how does this improve my happiness?'

'Her father was the most effective at hunting down those with Inward Power, was he not? If you fear that there are those abroad again with the talent, might it not be a good thing to put him to work again, releasing him from his cell and thereby earning Vevena's gratitude?'

Fallon sipped his wine thoughtfully. So Kalen knew about the boy, Tommo, and his own fear of thaumaturgical conspiracy. That was to be expected – the fortress was a hotbed of gossip. He would be more concerned had Kalen not been so eager to show him what he knew. The man was a fool, but it was not a bad suggestion and, try as he might, he could see no way in which such a move would be to his detriment.

'And how would my releasing Haver-snatcher benefit you?' Fallon asked, after another long, calculated pause. He did not believe that disinterested advice existed – every advisor had their own profit to gain. Kalen blushed and stammered and eventually revealed that, as everyone knew, some vestige of Inward Power assisted in the wielding of spellstones and he didn't want any young pretenders snapping at his heels. Satisfied, Fallon sent the fool away. By Unga though, it was not such a bad idea. It would be good to see his greatest friend again, to remind him of how unequivocally he, Fallon, had won in their joint bid for power. Success was all the sweeter when it was contrasted with failure and there was no greater failure in all the land than that of his former Witch-hunter General, Vevena's father, known to all as Haver-snatcher.

CHAPTER SEVEN

Haver-snatcher was sleeping when they came for him. He slept a lot, trying to preserve what strength was left to him against a time when he could use it. The others were quiet when the guard came and unchained him. It was torture night again. They'd heard the screams for the last few hours. Fallon was clamping down on some poor Urtha-abandoned folk worried about some minor threat to his position. Haver-snatcher felt so weak he had to lean against the damp wall for support. His feet were almost numb. No one expected him to be next – he was, after all, Fallon's oldest friend. The spellstones mounted on the walls to prevent the use of natural thaumaturgy gave enough light to see by. They showed him the look of near despair on Breen's face. They had been chained just feet apart for the last five years.

'Urtha keep you, and may your death be easy,' Breen muttered under his breath so that the guard wouldn't know who to kick. All that meant was that he kicked each of the chained men in turn.

'Shut up, dog turd! I tell you the stink in here would kill you if you were even half a man,' the guard said. No one made the obvious rejoinder because it was the guard they called Lun, the one who was as handy with his fists as his feet. The others, his cell mates for too long, turned weary, tragic eyes towards Haver-snatcher. They did not need to speak.

'When we meet next – look out for me. I'll be the one enjoying the joys of Unga,' he said as carelessly as his galloping heartbeat would allow. It was an old tale in the farmyard of his youth that fear alone could stop a heart; he almost wished it were true.

Lun pushed him forward and he almost overbalanced. Breen's manacled hand stretched out to save him and he contrived to pass him a small fragment of rock painstakingly carved with the rune for 'peace'. The gift made Haver-snatcher tremble: the years here had softened him – he did not understand how.

Once out of the cell, Lun did not lead him across the narrow corridor to the inquisition room, but instead pushed him towards two smartly liveried guards.

'The Protector himself wants you – maybe he'll do his own bit of inquiring. Get out the hot irons, eh?' Lun laughed nervously, but the other guards did not so much as smile. 'You wouldn't think he was known as the most handsome man in the Protectorate to look at him now, would you?' Lun continued, apparently blind to their contempt. Haver-snatcher knew Lun was an imbecile, but he seemed blissfully ignorant of the fact.

'Come with us,' the taller of the two guards said. As

Haver-snatcher staggered after them up the steep stairs that led to the keep, the guard wrinkled his nose.

'Ah,' Haver-snatcher thought, 'I smell and I have lost my looks – do I care as long as Fallon lets me live?' Even that small boon did not seem likely.

Walking made Haver-snatcher dizzy and breathless. He felt worn out and feeble, a dried-up husk of his old self. Even so, the guardsmen, so bright in their scoured and polished plate that they made Haver-snatcher's eyes hurt, kept their hands within reach of their swords. He had once had a reputation that kept brave men fearful in their beds.

He caught a distorted reflection of himself in the guards' armour – a huge, shambling, grey giant, scarcely human. He could not imagine what they were afraid of.

The castle beyond the keep was all new. He could barely discern the outlines of the old King's winter fortress in this fanciful creation, stuffed with objects without obvious purpose. Fallon's spellstone wielders had been busy, for no ordinary builders could have produced the strange ceiling of the ante-room, shaped like the inside of a bell, or the ornate statues and brightly coloured glass that cluttered the patterned floors of seemingly endless passageways.

It was a shock to see his old associate dressed like one of the aristocratic Names, all in velvet and lace. He was as squat and ugly as ever, a toad with mismatched eyes, one blue, one brown, and teeth like the crags of Cartdoney. They had been lads together, in the days before Haver-snatcher got his name and Fallon his lust for power. It took all Haver-snatcher's strength to speak to his enemy as he always had, with a snarl that bordered on contempt.

'What in the name of Unga-under-all d'you want now?' he asked, hiding his trembling under his bluster.

'It is good to see you too,' the most powerful man in the island answered. 'I trust you've found my hospitality to your satisfaction?'

Haver-snatcher noted that Fallon had learnt the fine words that went with his clothes, but he was not taken in. Fallon needed him for something, he just couldn't imagine what.

'Sit down – share a goblet of wine with me.' Fallon signalled to one of the servants who hovered around. One brought a chair, another a rug with which to cover it – to protect it from the filth of Haver-snatcher's clothes.

'Why now – after all this time?' Haver-snatcher said, trying not to fall into the chair with exhaustion. He had barely walked ten steps in his dungeon, and the journey to the great hall had sapped what little energy he had managed to husband.

'There are things that only an old friend can do,' Fallon said airily, as if their friendship had been regularly maintained by a shared pot of black-bitter in a comfortable snug.

'And what of the old enemy?' If he was going to be killed, Haver-snatcher would rather get it over with.

'I have no old enemies.' Fallon flashed his feral grin which turned him from a toad to a wolf in the space of a heart's beat. 'The old gang are all gone – dead from the blue pox or the hangman. You, my friend, are the only one from the old days still living.'

'Why didn't you finish me?'

'Sentiment maybe. I don't know. I thought I might need you.' He sounded honest which made Haver-snatcher deeply suspicious. 'You were always so successful at whatever you attempted.'

Haver-snatcher's laugh sounded hollow in his ears. 'Which is why I've slept with the rats while you sit here in rich man's velvet, is it?' He took the plain goblet of wine the servant offered him and gulped it down, barely tasting what was probably a fine vintage. He would have preferred a pot of black-bitter.

'There's a boy ran from a spellgrinder's cellar,' Fallon began. 'Claimed sanctuary in the old High Priest's name. I want to know what that's all about. I fear we missed a few with the gift of Inward Power. If we have, I trust to your unfailing nose to hunt the witches out. When you know all there is to know, I want the boy, and anyone else who might threaten me, dead.'

Haver-snatcher drained the goblet and crammed the pastry he was offered into his mouth. His stomach felt so empty, he was not sure it could take the wine. He feared that he might vomit on the polished marble and fine, woven rug.

'What do you want? Hanging, cutting, spiking, splitting, throttling, garrotting –' he said with his mouth full.

'I'll leave that up to you,' Fallon interrupted, as though unwilling to be reminded of the sordid details of their shared past.

'And why will I do this for you?' Haver-snatcher answered, wiping the grease from his fingers on his tattered tunic. He examined the filth on his hands as though Fallon's answer was unimportant, though he had a fair idea of what it would be.

'I could have you killed as easily as –' He snapped his fingers and three guardsmen lowered their pikes in Haver-snatcher's direction and took a step forward. Fallon lifted his hand casually and they retreated. 'And if that doesn't worry you as much as it might, never forget your girl is never more than a footstep away. Do you want to see her before you go?' Fallon grinned again at Haver-snatcher's discomfort. 'Guard, tell my wife I need her here. There's someone she'll want to see.'

'There's no need for that. I'll do what you want,' Haver-snatcher said quickly, but Fallon waved his beefy arm in command and the guard scuttled out to do his bidding.

Vevena was wearing her midnight blue nightcoat embroidered with precious stones which flashed rainbow-coloured in the candlelight. Her dark-blonde hair was unbraided and fell in loose curls to her slender waist. Haver-snatcher knew that she took after him with her regular features and glacial, violet eyes.

She wrinkled her nose in disgust at Haver-snatcher's

unwashed smell, the foul taint of the dungeons he carried with him.

'Father?' she said, and Haver-snatcher turned reluctantly to look at her.

'Vevena!' Haver-snatcher could not keep the tenderness from his voice, even though he tried. Vevena was so much better at behaving like ice. He willed her to keep the tears he could see glistening in her eyes from falling. Let Fallon believe she despised her old man.

Her mouth worked silently for a moment as if she struggled to say what was in her heart.

'I must dress. I think the emerald satin would be best,' she said at length, coldly, and turned from her father so proudly and quickly, it was as if the moisture had been no more than the glint of a candle's reflection in the white of her eye.

'Unga-under-all take my heart, but get away with you, old man,' Fallon said loudly for the benefit of Vevena's retreating back, 'and don't come back until your daughter has something to be proud of. Remember what I've said, for the sake of your daughter. I have my eye on you.'

Haver-snatcher watched as his child walked away with head held high. Whatever else he had failed to achieve in life, he was proud of her, even bewitched and betrayed as he knew she had been; he would not let her down. He would find a way to set them both free. He copied her straight-backed gait, though Unga alone must have given him the strength, and walked proudly out of the fortress, ignoring his heavily armed escort. Only when the guards had seen him clear of the main gate did he allow himself to collapse. Fallon was a fool to let him free.

CHAPTER EIGHT

It was a long time later that Akenna returned, long enough for Tommo to have fallen back to sleep where she had left him in the cool dampness of the cave. Akenna brought with her a lantern which threw strange shadows on the uneven rock walls. When Tommo first woke he was so disoriented that he believed he was back in the cellar.

'You found the food then?' she said briskly, as she checked his bonds. To his consternation they were still intact, which meant that the whole episode with the dolphin had indeed been a dream: he had no power after all.

'You didn't go out, did you?' she asked, giving him one of her sharp looks that made Tommo think that she could gut a fish just by looking at it. Tommo shrugged in a way that he thought suggested that such a thing was clearly impossible, but Akenna's keen eye remained hard. 'Loosey Lanecroft said she saw a shining man the colour of the afternoon sea down by the cove. Everyone thinks she's soft in the head, as all the Lanecrofts are. Struck me that she could be right.' She paused and with some effort Tommo said nothing. There was something about Akenna that made it very hard to lie, so he opted instead for not telling the truth, or indeed for not telling anything at all. It was a strain. He wanted to blurt out the whole extraordinary story. Luckily she spoke herself then, so there was no silence for him to long to fill.

'Da's snoring by the fire. I put some mother's comfort in his beer – he'll sleep a while. Here, you'll need these.' She threw some strange black garments in his direction. They stank of old fish and oil; it made him gag. He held up his bound hands and, with an irritable clicking of her teeth, she pulled one end of the rope and the knot disappeared as if by the power of a spellstone.

It was quite difficult to struggle into the too large, reeking garments in the restricted space available, particularly as the shaking seemed now to extend to his arms.

'You sure you're up to this?' Akenna asked. 'You look poorly to me, right enough.' Tommo had no idea what she'd do if he said he wasn't up to it, and he wasn't sure he wanted to find out. She was fierce as the most vicious apprentice and fuelled by a kind of fury which made her every movement an act of suppressed violence.

'You have to follow me and when we get to our curragh – you'll push us out.' Tommo nodded dumbly. Akenna was his only chance of escape and he wasn't about to antagonise her by questioning her about what she seemed to think passed for a plan. She picked up a large sack to which she had sewn two looping leather straps which she secured over her two shoulders like a harness. It was a neat arrangement, leaving both arms free. She extinguished the lantern and led the way, swaying slightly under the weight of her load.

Outside the sea had calmed and only by the keenest observation could Tommo detect where the darkness of the sky met the darkness of the sea and the faint gossamer line that divided them. The moon was not bright and he did his best to extinguish his own brightness, covering his head with the hood of the stinking oilskins in the hope that he and Akenna would be invisible to anyone who might threaten them. Tommo was not even sure who that would be – the other fishers, agents of the Sheriff, Akenna's father? The list seemed to be growing. At least, thank Urtha, the birds were silent and he heard no voices in his head but his own questioning himself on the wisdom of following this skinny girl across bone-breaking rocks in the dark.

She led him well. She did not falter and, as long as he followed her pathway, neither did he. They crossed the rocks keeping the sea always to their left and the steep, dark wall of the cliff to their right. He saw the black squat shapes of small cottages hunched in profile against the sky and the occasional golden glimmer of firelight seeping through the cracks of shutters: it made him wish for the warmth of a homely fireside, for the comfort of his never-forgotten, lost home. When they passed the headland, the rocks fell away and the neighbouring cove was sandy in so far as he could see its outlines at all. This had to be Bentree Harbour: it was filled to capacity with boats of every size. Most were humble curraghs, one or two larger vessels had sails. A couple were huge, strange craft the wrong shape and size to have been made by anything but spellstones. They looked as out of place in the harbour of humble craft as all such spellstone works ever did, like a diamond among rocks or a pig's turd in a plate of buns: they made him feel uncomfortable.

Akenna picked her way between the vessels as nimbly as ever.

'Hide!' Akenna hissed, scarcely a moment before he heard voices. Two men talking at the shore line.

'I tell you there's no way I can get them stones offshore. Unga-under-all but I would if I could. If I could get out of the Protectorate, I'd still be smuggling the old contraband not hiding these witch stones. They make my skin crawl to touch them.' The voice was gruff and agitated, the kind of voice that seemed to Tommo to be filled with the possibility of violence.

'Well, the Sheriff's man will be here tomorrow. You get them "witch stones", as you call them, offshore or hidden or we're both for Fallon's fortress – probably in pieces.' The second voice was harder to place but it was this second man who walked away first, marching abruptly, his heavy feet crunching on the gritty sand. Tommo wanted to sneeze, but instead held his breath waiting for the second man to leave. To his consternation the first speaker continued to stand there for a good while. This bulky shadow figure lingered on the shore, while he took a leisurely nip of something from a hip flask and stared out at the dark sea. Tommo's leg was beginning to cramp before the man spoke again, this time to himself.

'Unga's arse!' he said before stomping back along the sand in the footsteps of his companion.

Akenna waited several long heartbeats before creeping forward along the shoreline. She seemed to have an instinct for danger because twice more she flattened herself to the ground just before Tommo's less acute senses warned him of the presence of people.

There was a building overlooking the harbour that though shuttered against the night appeared to be some kind of drinker's snug and was clearly the source of much of Akenna's concern. Men walked to and from it with some regularity. Every now and again the door opened and Tommo could hear raucous laughter and the odd snatch of a ribald sea shanty of the type rarely heard in the town. It seemed that there was no night curfew here, far from the Sheriff and his bullymen. No one came down to the shore again and eventually Akenna reached her father's curragh. She paused only to untie it from its mooring post, a thick piece of weathered timber deeply embedded in the sand, then clambered aboard.

'Push!'

Tommo's feet sunk into the soft, wet beach and he had to wait for his hands to stop trembling for a moment before he could bring his strength to bear on the boat and push it from its sandy bed. Unfortunately, he did not have a huge amount of strength to bring to bear. He was thin and badly malnourished as apprentices did not justify generous feed-ing and his time starving on the road had not helped much either. Although he heaved with all that was in him, he could not shift both the boat and Akenna's weight.

'Push!'

Akenna's whisper seemed louder than a shout to him and he almost despaired. He dare not admit his weakness or he feared her knife might flash against his throat. He paused to take a deep trembling breath. He was a man, near enough, and Akenna must weigh less than he did, she was so slight and skinny. The curragh was made of nothing but bowed timber and waxed skin and must be lighter than the grinding wheel he'd lifted often enough. He gathered his thoughts and his strength, and did not forget that the stories might perhaps be true and that there may yet be some power in the grind-dust. He tried again. He didn't think it was the dust that helped him, more that he got the knack of the thing, because this time the boat lurched suddenly forward and he felt the water take its weight. The cold water was up to his knees, soaking his breeches and the tattered remnants of his shoes. The boat was surging forward and Akenna was urging him in a noisy whisper to 'Jump aboard!'

It took all the strength that he had left to drag himself over the high side of the curragh while Akenna cursed him for rocking the craft, then helped him with her wiry arms, strong as the hemp rope she'd tied him with and scarcely thicker. He collapsed gasping into the bottom of the curragh. He would make it: he was leaving the borough and the Protectorate, and it would not matter that his sanctuary band was black and that he had just run out of time.

CHAPTER NINE

Neither Tommo nor Akenna spoke for a time. Akenna was busily using an oar as a pole to negotiate her way through the many obstacles in the harbour mouth. There were boats moored everywhere in an apparently haphazard arrangement. Akenna's narrow face was closed, focused on the task. She seemed to Tommo to be enormously skilful. He could do little to help, having never even been in a boat before. He liked it though, liked the sense of being embraced by the sea, liked the way the small craft rode the swell of the tide as if the broad back of the vigorous water rippled powerful muscles beneath them. He could have fallen asleep there, so bone deep was his exhaustion – but Akenna of course would have none of it.

'Having a nice rest are we? Very much the country Name at his hearth with his dogs and all, aren't you? Take an oar and look lively or the tide will bring us back where we started.'

Tommo's whole body was afflicted by tremors, but that was another thing he had no wish to share with Akenna. Somehow he gathered himself together and sat up. The boat leant ominously to one side and Akenna cursed.

'By Urtha's belly and the wrath of Unga-under-all, have you never been in a blessed boat before – you turd-headed landlubber!' Although they were by now some distance from the shore, she still whispered, which made her words seem, if anything, more aggressive than if she'd screamed at him.

'No,' he said, simply because it would be clear to anyone, particularly someone as competent as Akenna, that he was totally and literally at sea. To his surprise she didn't shout at him, but instead secured her oar somehow and sat beside him and spoke in an unexpectedly frank, confiding tone.

'We were lucky back there. Old Garth, the big bloke, the smuggler, he would have killed us if he'd seen us spying on him. He's a drinking crony of my da's and as nasty a bit of manflesh as ever slung a hook. It's as well we're going tonight. If Old Garth says the Sheriff's man will be here tomorrow, you can be sure of it. He's bribed every legman from Tipplehead to Bentree.' She gave him a quick sideways glance. 'I'll show you how to row, but if you can make us go further and faster with – you know – your grind-dust thaumaturgy that would be good. It's wearying work rowing and you look done in already.'

Tommo felt done in already, but also guilty at misleading her. 'It doesn't work like that,' he said, more abruptly than he had intended. Akenna's face, which in the light of his glowing skin had for a moment seemed open and eager, closed down again.

She lifted the pair of oars that had been lying at the bottom of the boat and slotted them into their places in the paired notched holes in the boat's side and demonstrated what to do. 'Pull hard when the oars are in the water. The sea's getting heavy and we'll need to pull away fast. There's always a chance that one of the men from Old Ma Rainer's drinking snug'll see us. If we're spotted, they'll come after us. My da's got friends enough from there, as he's as generous as a man can be with no cares in the world and no heirs to build a business for. He talks up a good revolution too, though he stumms-up fast enough when the Sheriff's men come calling.' Her voice was bitter, but Tommo, being unable to offer her any comfort, decided to keep silent and save his energy for the rowing.

It was difficult to get both oars in the water at the same time, and more often than not they bounced off the waves and did not even enter the water. Spray drenched him and Akenna cursed quietly under her breath. Her own efforts moved the boat forward efficiently enough, but the waves were high and even Tommo, ignorant though he was, could see that to make headway he needed to pull his weight at the very least. He tried. He tried until the sweat ran down the inside of his rough shirt and all his muscles trembled with more than just the quivers.

After a while Akenna shouted out, 'We can stop now and eat.' She threw something, maybe the anchor, overboard and slumped forward over her oars. It was less dark than it had been and the sky above the horizon seemed suddenly more grey than black. Akenna passed him some food – fish, of course, though fresh rather than salted – and they ate in silence. She passed him some black-bitter in a small waxed sack. It was sour enough to make him shiver but quenched his raging thirst.

'Where are we going?' Tommo asked when he had finished his meal.

'There's an island a way off from here – Tisket – no one lives there any more, but there's shelter and enough sheep and fish and seaweed to keep us fed.'

'Is it still part of the borough?'

Akenna shrugged as though it mattered little to her. 'It's a fair row for my da in a borrowed boat, that's all I know, and when we're rested we can carry on to the far island which is a bigger place altogether. From there, so they say, you can row to the Better Land and a new life, though we'd need a bigger boat and more hands.' Her tone had thawed almost to the point of being friendly.

He did not press her for more details – an island a little while away was as good a target as any for the time being. He shivered, this time from cold. The wind was getting up and the day was no lighter. Akenna glanced at the sky anxiously and hauled up the anchor.

'We're going to have to row hard now,' she said, suddenly terse and businesslike. 'The weather's getting up.'

The boat started to rock alarmingly as the waves lapped over the bows. One wave unexpectedly slapped Tommo full in the face and took his breath away. He tried to follow

Akenna's lead and keep in time with her, for that was the way the boat moved best, but the water was so choppy his oars seemed as useless as a one-wheeled cart. He could not believe they were making any progress at all towards their destination and when he glanced back over his shoulder all he could see was the white-crested waves bucking and rearing like the unbroken horses in the paddocks near his childhood home. The wind blew his hair from its binding and the rain began to lash him with icy cords.

'Hold tight and keep pulling!' Akenna's voice reached him in small, scattered bursts of sound and he more or less guessed at what she was shouting. He had no choice but to hold on and keep pulling, though all his efforts seemed to be at best keeping them where they were. Several large waves soaked him completely and soon he was up to his thighs in water as the waves broke against their small vessel and drenched it. It would not be long before they began to sink.

'Bail!' Akenna screamed against the roar of the wind and began frantically scooping out water using a bowl, lashed to the underside of her seat. There was a bowl under Tommo's seat too, but his hands were so numb he could not untie the knot that held it there and he instead pulled it free. His shaking hand lacked Akenna's desperate speed, but he did what he could. Every few moments they were engulfed again by saltwater.

'Keep going! Don't give up!' Akenna screeched her defiance against what to Tommo looked like hopeless odds, which was a pity – for a moment there he'd thought he stood a chance. He kept bailing anyway, there was something about Akenna which made him do what she asked. Then a huge wave, bigger even than the rest, swept over their bow as another rolled the curragh over and he was dumped into the icy water. The breath was knocked out of him by the cold and then by the next wave, which submerged him and abandoned him to total blackness. He flailed his arms in panic, never having learnt to swim. He did not know which way was up – all was cold impenetrable blackness. He opened his mouth to scream and took in a mouthful of saltwater that he could not spit out. There was no air or sound, only the black and terrible underbelly of the beautiful sea. So this was how it would end – not in the hangman's noose, not in the cold mud of a roadside ditch, nor quivering and trembling his way in disease, but here in the darkness, drowning.

And still his life did not flash before his eyes. Instead something swift and strong pushed him upwards, catapulted him to the surface, where he emerged gasping and choking, gulping air and water in equal measure, coughing himself back to life. Something unseen but powerful pushed him on to the upturned boat, just visible in the wild waves. He grabbed it with the whole of his trembling body and clung to it as tightly as any limpet to its rock. There was no sign of Akenna. He was certain that she would be able to swim; someone that indomitable surely would not drown? With the fragile security of the boat under him, he took in several lungfuls of air. Somehow he was still alive.

'Akenna!' he yelled, though his voice seemed pitiful in the tumult of the storm. Lightning cracked the sky and in the brief brightness he thought he saw Akenna's head, a tiny ball bobbing on a distant wave. 'Akenna!' he screamed with all the power he could manage.

He did not know if she heard or not. It was too dark and what with the rain and the grey waves filling his vision it was hard enough to breathe let alone to see; he held on as tightly as he could to the boat and to hope.

CHAPTER TEN

Tommo was not sure of what happened next. The huge waves continued to lift him to vertiginous heights and then drop him suddenly. He clung to the upturned curragh and closed his eyes – it was less terrifying that way. He kept calling out for Akenna but he did not think that she heard him.

Perhaps he slept or passed out, he did not know, but when he opened his eyes he was back on land again, in the cove of the dead dolphin, beached like something dead himself but still breathing, still living on the wet sand. The sea was calm, lapping the rocks as softly as his mother's cat used to lick his knee. It was still early in the day, and the sky was a clear, pale wintry blue. The rain had gone and the sun shone weakly, so that the grey-backed sea glistened in the light, like it too was sprinkled with grind-dust. Had the storm been another quiver dream? He was racked by a spasm of coughing and struggled to his knees. The battered shell of the curragh lay beside him, proof the storm had been real. Fresh seaweed and flotsam littered the beach and the dead dolphin had gone.

'You're alive then.' It was Akenna's voice. He blinked

and saw her silhouetted against the sun so that he had to squint to see her.

'So are you.' He could not disguise the surprise and pleasure in his voice. 'How?'

'Urtha's Holy Folk of the Sea, the dolphins, brought us back. Or we'd both of us have been with the spindrift on the white shore,' she said. 'I'd heard that the folk did that sometimes to pay debts to fishers who helped them, but I never believed it.' She sounded shaken. 'I've never known a storm come from nowhere so fast without warning. We'd have drowned – easy – if the sea folk hadn't come.' She sat down beside him and he could see her properly. She was pale and battered, her bruised eye closed and her face scratched. Her hair hung, stiff with salt, like rats' tails round her shoulders.

'We can't stay here. Too close to home. My father'll kill me – skin me more than likely and use my hide for a new curragh. I've scuppered his boat and that means no more haverlings for Old Ma Rainey. Cover yourself up, for Urtha's sake. You're twinkling like the Protector's diamonds.' She sounded exasperated and Tommo was impressed that she still had the necessary energy.

'Oh no, just what we need – the blessed birds are back.'

So Akenna heard them too. A flock of the singing birds perched on the nearby rocks, their small human faces squinting against the light reflecting off the sea. There were more of them than there had been before, of that Tommo was sure. Perhaps there were as many as twenty singing: 'Oh rejoice for life! Oh rejoice for life!'

The sound made him shudder – it was so odd. He could not work out why they had been made nor why they still hung around him. Still, it was none of his business what people chose to do with spellstones.

Akenna got to her feet. 'Can you walk?' she said, more accepting of his weakness than he had expected. He got shakily to his feet and wrapped himself in the battered oilskins she'd given him. He nodded as much to himself as to Akenna – yes, he could walk.

'There are other fishing villages beyond Bentree Harbour and I can maybe get work, find another boat. If we cling to the coast, we'll find another village straightaway, but we'll be spotted by the fishers. If we take the trade road, it'll take longer and we'll be spotted by everybody else . . .' Her voice tailed away, for once indecisive.

'If I'm seen at all, I'll be hanged,' Tommo said gloomily and held out his wrist with the damp remnant of its pig-leather band. 'It's been eight days – I have no sanctuary rights. I think anyone could hang me.'

'Well, we've both got our problems,' Akenna replied sharply and Tommo wondered if she was debating whether to leave him behind. He knew he would not find the determination to keep going without her. Perhaps if she believed that his thaumaturgical powers had called the dolphins she might keep him with her.

'I expect the dolphins came because I called them,' he said, rather too tentatively for someone who was claiming thaumaturgical powers.

'Maybe they did and maybe they didn't,' Akenna answered, 'but you weren't too quick about calling them. They only just saved you. I thought you were as good as dead. Why didn't you say you couldn't swim?'

It had not occurred to him that anyone would have thought he could, but he could not find the energy to answer so he shrugged. It was fast becoming his characteristic gesture.

They walked on in silence for a while, Akenna electing to leave both the coast and the trade road behind and cut across country. The rain had made the fields muddy and Tommo's now bare, blistered feet were soon cold and sore. Most of the land was useless for much besides sheep grazing, the grass being too poor for cattle, and there were many foul-smelling bogs along the way. Akenna was limping, and toying with her beads, but she had set her mouth into a tight line; if she could keep going, then so could Tommo. The ensorcelled birds followed them, though mercifully they flew at a height that made their song little more than a distant bird-like chirruping.

'I think there's a shepherd's hut somewhere near here,' Akenna said. 'I used to run away to play there when I was small. We can catch our breath there and then drop down into Kullen's Cove. It's not much compared with Bentree Harbour, but there are boats there and fishers.' She did not pursue the thought. Boats and fishers might not do Tommo much good. He, at least, still had to get away from the borough.

The shepherd's hut was close by. Akenna seemed

surprised. 'It felt like a long way from home. I ran away and stayed here overnight once, but then I got hungry and went back. I don't think Da noticed I'd been away.' She smiled grimly. 'I should have pushed on and not gone back.'

The building, if you wanted to flatter it with such a title, was less of a hut and more of a covered sheep pen – a low ring of stones no more than the height of a toddler, covered with a rotting timber roof. Inside it was damp and dark. There was a hearth but no chimney, which might not have mattered given the state of the roof. Anyway there was no wood or turf to burn.

Tommo did not care. The quivering in his limbs was getting worse and exhaustion overwhelmed him. All these close brushes with death were wearing him out. He lay down on the bare packed earth and fell immediately to sleep.

He woke to the sound of voices.

'We were walking and took shelter here. By Urtha, it's a way-shelter for any poor traveller, boy or man, and everyone uses it hereabouts. The shelter has never belonged to nobody.' Akenna sounded aggrieved, aggressive and very likely to bring trouble on them.

A man's voice answered. 'Look, lad, I'm here on the authority of the Sheriff of Tipplehead to check that there's no spellstones hidden here. If you'll just come on out into the light, I'll have a quick look round and then be off. Now am I going to have to force myself in?'

Something in the man's voice brooked no argument and even Akenna was obliged to back down. Tommo scrambled to cover his gleaming flesh with his clothes. He was shaking badly, but he no longer knew whether it was from fear, from cold or from the quivers. He felt feverish. He struggled to sit up and tried to focus on the figure who crawled towards him.

'Come on outside so I can have a good look at you and be sure you're not some spellstone smuggler.'

Tommo crawled unwillingly out. The sunlight seemed blindingly bright after the darkness of the hut. He shrunk inside the oilskins, hid his sanctuary band as best he could and tried to disappear. Perhaps if he made his already small and undernourished frame smaller still, the man would not notice him. He hardly dared to breathe in case he drew attention to himself and tried to think tiny, insignificant thoughts, though quite what good that would do he wasn't sure. He hoped the man was as dazzled by the sun as he was. Akenna shot Tommo a desperate look, though what she expected him to do he couldn't imagine. In the far, high distance, birds circled and sang 'Danger!', as if he didn't know. He hoped the Sheriff's man was both blinded and hard of hearing too because the birds sounded loud to his ears.

In spite of his threat to have a good look at them, the Sheriff's man merely glanced at Akenna before crawling back inside the hut. He didn't look at Tommo at all. Akenna looked like she wanted to run, but Tommo shook his head. There was nowhere to run to in this bleak windswept country: the vegetation was sparse, the trees stunted and bent, and the only possible hiding places were in the bog-pitted fields or the ditches, dug to stop sheep from wandering too far. He had noticed neither bogs nor ditches anywhere close to the hut. Akenna did not acknowledge his signal, but had obviously come to the same conclusion. Instead of running she merely played with the dark beads round her neck and touched her gutting knife in a gesture that was both nervous and dangerous.

After a very few heartbeats the man re-emerged from the tumbledown hut with a grunt and Tommo withdrew even further into his oversized cloak.

'No. No spellstones there. Well, better to be safe than sorry, lad. You might as well get back to your rest, though why you're resting on such a fine day, blessed by Urtha, is beyond me. It's up and off you've got to be, if you want to get on.' With that not altogether comprehensible remark he was up and off himself. Akenna waited until the Sheriff's man had disappeared from view and then sagged to her knees as if in prayer to White Urtha.

'Tommo? Tommo?' she whispered. 'How did you do that?'

'I don't know what you mean. How did I do what?'

She turned to look at him and at last met his eyes. She looked both frightened and awed, an odd mixture of expressions for her normally impassive face.

'Don't act stupid, of course you know,' she said angrily. 'Don't think you can pretend the idiot with me. You were right about the grind-dust and the thaumaturgical power. How did you make yourself disappear?'

CHAPTER ELEVEN

It seemed that Fallon expected Vevena to be pleased with him. He had released her father.

It was at first difficult for Vevena to remember that, because her father was a threat to Fallon. She knew that and whatever Unga-cursed spell she was under knew that too, because every time Fallon spoke of her father her mind was diverted to flowers, as if she had ever given a pig's arse about them. As the day wore on, it seemed clear that Fallon wanted her to know all about his renewed friendship with Haver-snatcher. He spoke of the time when they were boys together in the days of the old King before the Convocation came to power. He spoke of the time before all the deaths and the chaos wrought by the blue pox, when he was young and wild and wicked and Haver-snatcher was his friend. He reminisced about the days when thaumaturgical power was treated as a blessing of Urtha, when the talented were respected, honoured and trained by White Urtha's priests in thaumaturgical chapels throughout the land. The more that Fallon talked about Haver-snatcher, the more Vevena remembered her father and his imprisonment and all he had taught her, until even in her hazy ensorcelled state it seemed to her that something of the power of the spell was weakening, that her mind was clearing just a little. If Fallon wanted her to talk about her father, who could be harmful to him, she must do it, for not to do what Fallon desired was also harmful to him. For whatever reason her sharp, inquisitive mind was a little more awake and a little less obsessed with floristry and jewels, with haberdashery and couture.

So it was that when she was sitting in the enchanted garden on a seat woven from entwined golden and silver roses, which had just sprung up besides a stream of bubbling sparkling wine, she noticed a dense flock of birds flying around the disused north tower.

Her violet eyes were as keen as they were lovely and as she stared she noticed something suspended beside the topmost turret of the tower, something that flashed blue in the clear sunlight, that glinted like the jewels with which she was all too familiar. 'Sapphire, larkspur, freedom,' she muttered to herself. As far as she knew there was nothing to attract birds to the tower, it was unsuitable for roosting and contained no source of food. There were birds in the tower. Her husband killed birds. Birds in the tower might be important. She tried to make herself remember that, to hold on to that thought . . . briar roses are prettier in embroidery than in reality. They are too prickly for a posy. Perhaps she should wear the cream gown embroidered with turquoise and coral birds, and wear her hair in a towering bun interwoven with sapphires. She did not look towards the tower again, but this time she did not quite forget what she had seen. That evening, as she dressed for the feast, she did not wear the gown with the embroidered birds, choosing instead a plainer one and a cape trimmed with feathers, and she remembered why.

They ate some kind of goose stuffed with a chicken, stuffed with a pigeon, stuffed with a lark and everywhere that Vevena looked it seemed she was reminded of birds. Feathers decorated hairstyles, jet earrings shone like beady eyes and men talking with their chests puffed proudly out looked like robin redbreasts displaying their plumage.

She could not escape the imagery of birds nor their ubiquity in conversation. There was much talk of the bird-catchers and their impact on the land. Someone joked that their feast, consisting so entirely of birds, was poor man's fare, as the peasants ate pheasant and lark like the old aristocratic Names since the bird-catchers had come. Vevena felt as if she were emerging from a kind of a sleep. She knew that Fallon hated birds, but she could not remember why. She would have liked to ask why her husband had seen fit to introduce the bird-catchers, but as she formed the question in her mouth found herself asking something else entirely, something so irrelevant and inane that she could see it confirmed the opinion of her companions that Fallon had married a beautiful idiot. She discovered she did not mind. She was Haver-snatcher's daughter and she would find advantage where she could. If Fallon's court thought her an idiot, all the better, for idiots heard what wise men did not.

Vevena woke suddenly in the second quarter of the night to find bright moonlight illuminating her chamber and an image of birds inspiring her dreams. She had dreamt of the old man who'd given her a toffee, locked in a cage in the tower. Birds of all sizes hovered round his head and plucked jewels from his ears and mouth, then turned to flowers in the air.

She had the strong sense of having glimpsed something important; flowers meant danger and danger was good: anything dangerous to Fallon was good for her. It was a clear, cold night after a day of bright sunshine and clean winds. She dressed rapidly in her fur wrap and warm, soft shoes. Dolina lay snoring on her pallet by Vevena's bed; she slept heavily for a spy, but then what danger could a woman with a pretty head full of flowers possibly pose? Vevena carefully slipped off her marriage chains, which clinked and jingled as she moved. Like everything else she owned, they were expensive, heavy and liberally encrusted with precious stones. When she was free, she would wear no jewellery, no gold, no silver, no gems – they were symbols of her slavery. The thought startled her. It was the first time in her ensorcelled state that she had been able to recognise so clearly that she was not free.

The fortress was still a fortress in spite of its many embellishments. Guards still patrolled the corridors and kept watch over the great hall and the Protector's bed chamber, guarded the dungeons and the gardens and the mews. Vevena had chambers of her own, as befitted Fallon's Lady and wife in a three-heir dynastic contract of unspecified duration. Her rooms were guarded of course, though not constantly, and it was easy enough to wait until the guard had moved away to another part of the fortress before slipping out. The door did not creak. Such sounds annoyed Fallon and he had once insisted that his spellstone wielders silence all creaking doors and clanking armour so that his voice should be more clearly heard. It was a pity the magic had not extended to her own chains but she surmised that he liked to hear her noisy jingling progress through the fortress, liked to be reminded that the daughter of his oldest friend and most feared rival was his.

Vevena had no clear idea of what she was going to do. She tried not to think because her thoughts were untrustworthy. She let her hidden self take her, dimly aware that she knew things her thoughts could not access. She allowed herself to consider the garments of the other ladies at the previous night's feast and to decide that she disliked too sumptuous decoration as a general rule and that the shade of green favoured by Lady Corwen made her look decidedly bilious. Such inanities got her as far as the staircase to the north tower, which was guarded.

When she was a girl her father had taught her to fire an arrow and if memory served, which given her state of mind it might well not, she had been pretty good at it. She remembered days throwing pebbles in the stream near her grandmother's house on those rare times when Haver-snatcher came to see her. She wondered if she could still throw as well as she had as a child. She challenged herself to hit the silver statue of White Urtha, may the merciful lady forgive her impiety, a good way down the corridor. She was, as ever, overburdened with rings. The signet ring she wore on her little finger was particularly splendid with a diamond much the size of the pebbles she had thrown as a girl. She weighed it carefully with her hand. She must tell her husband about this innocent game she had enjoyed so much with her father, who was his friend. How clever she was to hit the statue and disturb the guard who saw the diamond gleam in the moonlight streaming silver and sharp as an arrow from the narrow window.

How funny it would be if she could slip up the stairs while this guard was momentarily entranced by the gem – which would surely make some girl very happy – and hesitated between retrieving the jewel and checking on its source. Hide and seek – surely she had played that as a girl with Haver-snatcher, and if she hadn't she should have.

She ran, as if she were a child playing hide and seek, up a flight of bare stone steps to the topmost room where a spellstone wielder and a guard were playing jackaroo by spellstone light. They leapt immediately and guiltily to their feet. One bowed deeply while the other saluted.

'My lady.'

'The wards are still in place, my lady,' the spellstone wielder, a novice in a pale blue hat, said anxiously, as though she had every right to be there. She had never been there before, she was sure, but the novice was clearly so startled by her presence that he had to say something. She felt quite giddy with the sudden realisation that she was not as powerless as she thought . . . though her current gown went rather ill with her shoes, being of a slightly different hue to the rich red of her robe. Unga's arse! She hated all these thoughts of robes. She was doing no more than playing a game, a game of pretend of the kind she used to play with her father of whom Fallon approved: there could be no danger in that.

'I checked the prisoner not an hour ago, my lady, and he was sleeping.'

Vevena nodded. 'May I see?' she said brightly in a little girl voice, which led the guard and the novice spellstone wielder to exchange a surreptitious look. The guard led the way to the narrow, shuttered window. Beyond the window, suspended in midair without visible ropes or chains to hold it, was a cage. It was constructed of multi-faceted spell-stones, threaded like beads on a chain of finely worked metal; it glowed with an unearthly blue light, lighter than sapphire, darker than aquamarine, but with a similarly luminous quality. Inside the cage a gaunt man rested his head against the bars and slept. His mouth was open and he dribbled slightly for he was old. Although the night was cold and Vevena shivered even in her fur, he had no blanket and the wind tugged at his clothes and beard, though he never stirred.

'White Urtha at her mother's breast!' Vevena said, which caused the novice to look pained and the guardsman to look slightly shocked – it was not a ladylike oath. Vevena was so stunned she could say nothing more. It was the old man with the toffee who, even she knew, was supposed to be dead: Gildea, High Priest of the Inward Power.

CHAPTER TWELVE

Akenna refused to accept that Tommo did not know that he had made himself invisible.

'It's the grind-dust – like I told you. It does strange things.' He felt light-headed and very tired. The last thing he wanted to do was to argue with Akenna. He wanted to eat something and curl up back in the shepherd's hut and sleep. He had escaped with his life once more, but sooner or later his bizarre luck would have to run out and then it would be the gallows for him after all.

'Come on. Let's go,' Akenna said at last when it was clear he was going to tell her nothing more.

'Where are you going?'

'Into Kullen's Cove. We've no food, my supplies went with the curragh, and if we have to walk out of the borough you're going to need some food.'

'But the Sheriff's man is going that way – he'll see me and that will be it. I don't know if I can do that disappearing thing again because I don't know how I did it the last time.' He ran his shaking hand through his long, white hair and sank to the ground. It was easier there. He was too tired to stand. 'You'd better go on without me.'

'No.' Akenna's mouth was set into a thin line. The bruise on the side of her face was turning a yellow-green and it made her whole face look ill and sickly. She pulled him to his feet and once more her wiry strength took him by surprise.

'You're not getting rid of me,' she said firmly, 'not till you've told me how you do that thaumaturgy. Now you'd better tidy yourself up if we're going to get any food out of the villagers. Maybe you could wash in the sea?'

Akenna looked extremely disreputable. Tommo had little doubt that he looked worse. Akenna began to pull her fingers through the knots in her matted hair, but it didn't make any appreciable difference. He was about to do the same when he caught a fleeting look of concern on Akenna's face. It was so uncharacteristic it disturbed him.

'What? Do I look like a scarecrow or something?' he said.

'You're shaking all over,' she said gruffly.

'It's just the quivers,' Tommo said, more light-heartedly than he felt. She was right; he was a lot worse – perhaps his body would settle somewhat if he ate something.

Kullen's Cove was no more than a few low, lime-washed cottages, a communal well and a twisted track that led from the dwellings to the sea. Tommo had never been anywhere that did not lie on the trade road before.

'Won't they chase us away?' Tommo asked. He could not imagine such a small community welcoming strangers of any sort, least of all two skinny, ragged fugitives. Akenna shrugged and started shouting at the top of her voice.

'Workers for hire! Will gut, fish, smoke, net mend or caulk. Good workers for hire!'

Her voice was piping and strong and rang with a certain confidence. Tommo had no idea what she was offering to do, but had no doubt that she could do all of it. A middle-aged woman peered out of the door of the nearest cottage and gave Akenna an appraising look.

'Let's see your hands, lad,' she said less put off by Akenna's appearance than Tommo might have expected. Akenna stepped closer to the woman and showed her calloused hands, reddened and chafed with heavy work.

'You can handle a curragh?'

Akenna nodded. 'Been fishing all my life, can set my hand to everything, and I'm quick too.'

The woman nodded. 'Why d'you leave your place?'

Akenna managed to look suitably saddened yet stoic.

'Boat sank in a storm night before last – old skipper drowned.'

'Aye well – it was a proper blaster of a storm that one. What about him?' She cast her sharp eyes in Tommo's direction.

Akenna didn't hesitate. 'He's a good worker, missus, though not so skilled. He can row and he's strong for his size.'

Tommo did his bit to look strong and hard working, and for a moment contrived to get his shaking limbs under control. He hoped the oilskins disguised his glowing skin sufficiently. The smell of baking coming from the cottage was so strong it was making it hard to think of anything but his hunger.

'My man's sick just now and my son could use some extra hands. You'll want something to eat I suppose?'

'That would be a blessing, missus. We've been on the road since the storm and we've worked up quite a hunger.'

'You'd better come in then – under the usual terms?' Akenna nodded her agreement and the deal, whatever it was, seemed to be done. The woman seemed to lack the expected fear of strangers, but then maybe Akenna was not such a stranger being a fisher too.

Tommo understood her apparent carelessness the moment he got inside. 'Her man' was a giant of a man, black-bearded and sullen, sipping his black-bitter from a sizeable bowl by a good fire. He looked up at them with dulled eyes and Tommo thought he grasped the nature of the man's sickness. A look of understanding passed between Akenna and the woman, whose plump arms under her marriage chains were patterned with bruises.

The woman gave them a porridge of oats and barley sweetened with blackberry preserve, and very good it tasted. She had a loaf standing and another in the cook pot over the fire so when they'd finished she gave them a generous hunk of bread spread with butter. She carefully gave them a small spill of salt in their palms and a drink of well water.

Tommo was overwhelmed because it was clear it was not

a wealthy house. There was just the one small room with a dresser dividing it in two, a hen coop underneath it and a chest.

'We've got plenty of pot-bread at least. We trade flour for the fish you see,' the woman said proudly, as if she'd understood his furtive glance around the room to be disapproval.

Akenna ate quickly and gave Tommo a hard look to tell him to do the same. He did his best but the porridge was difficult to manage with his arms shaking so badly. The woman affected not to notice and busied herself with sweeping the dirt floor. The man of the house did not even look in their direction.

'My boy's with the boat,' the woman said. 'He'll show you what you need to know – you can leave with the tide.'

Akenna nodded. 'May Unga-under-all take me if I betray the salt bond,' she said, and shook the woman's hand.

'May the tides be kind,' the woman replied and saw them to the door where the birds were waiting.

'Urtha's udders and all the hosts be damned!' Akenna said the moment that they were out of earshot.

'What?' Tommo asked. He had the strong feeling he'd understood less than a quarter of what had gone on in the house.

'She bound me. I can't take her boat. I accepted shelter and water and salt. I have to give her a fair day's work in return.'

'What do you mean?'

'It's not spellgrinder's magic. It's the old kind, older than anything. If I break faith with her now, I'm cursed. I'd hoped that we could borrow her boat and take it over to Tisket. Oh, Unga-under-all take her!'

Tommo greatly appreciated the thought – in trying to get to Tisket she was thinking of him, he was sure. Even so he wouldn't have been easy in his mind about robbing a poor woman with a drunken husband – seven years in the spellgrinder's cellar hadn't succeeded in undermining his early training in the spiritual path to Urtha.

'But you're not in danger, are you? You don't need to get away. Surely your father won't know you're here?'

She pulled a face. 'Word will get around. All of us hereabouts fish the same seas. I've even seen her man before. He drinks at Old Ma Rainey's now and again, though whether he's at Ma Rainey's or not, I reckon he drinks as hard as Da.' Akenna looked morose. He remembered the bruises on the woman's arms and changed the subject.

'Well, we have eaten and I'm no longer cold – that's enough for now. I'll just have to keep an eye out for the Sheriff's man.' He put on the most optimistic face he could find. 'I'm surprised the woman gave us work, looking like we do,' he said, by way of making conversation.

'People always do what I want,' Akenna said and grinned briefly so that Tommo wasn't sure if she was joking or not. By and large it seemed to be true. He found himself doing what she wanted all the time. 'It's hard – fishing,' Akenna continued. 'Folk are forever getting themselves drowned and the like. Only another fisher understands. It binds us. Business is hard now. Fish isn't worth much at the moment – the Protector has taken it into his head to kill all the birds. Don't know how he missed this lot.' She indicated the growing flock carolling noisily above them – too far away for Tommo to hear the words. 'He's made the spellgrinders ensorcell rabbits so that they jump into snares. He thought it would help the poor, but it hasn't helped us.'

'Why did the woman want us to fish then, if the fish aren't worth anything?'

'You are a city boy, aren't you? She'll eat the fish and she'll need to give away even more for her salt and her bag of flour.'

Their conversation took them to the beach and to the boy sitting by the boat, checking the nets. He looked younger than Akenna.

'Your mother sent us. Are you ready to go?' Akenna asked. She put a swagger into her walk and somehow gave off a general air of cocky certainty. The boy looked at them with the same hard, calculating look that Tommo had seen on Akenna's own face.

'Is the shaky one coming?' he asked doubtfully.

'He's an extra pair of hands,' Akenna replied. 'Let's check the boat.'

When she was satisfied that all was as it should be, Tommo and the boy pushed off and Akenna used a single oar to punt the curragh out of the shallows and into the sea.

Tommo found that he was less nervous of being back in a boat than he ought to be. He checked the sky constantly, but it was a cloudless, cool blue disturbed only by the birds flying high above. They made the formation for 'Be aware!' and 'Danger!', but he didn't take too much notice. He had been in danger so long he was beginning to get used to it. Besides, they were obviously ensorcelled and who knew what they meant by it?

CHAPTER THIRTEEN

'Do you ever fish over by Tisket?' Akenna asked the boy as they rowed. 'There's bream there and pollock and fat fish – you'd get money at market for fat fish.'

The boy shrugged. 'Can't get so far as Tisket. Didn't you know? We can't fish further out than the Black Rock and no craft can come in neither. We can't trade no more and we're stuck with what we can make from the fishing.'

'What do you mean?' she said and the boy looked at her with all the contempt of a younger child discovering he knew more than his elder.

'Fallon's got a spell on the whole island. Everyone knows that. Nothing can come in and nothing can go out – not by sea at any rate. The birds still fly – them that's not meat for the table anyway.'

Akenna looked startled, then understanding gradually dawned.

'Your da's a smuggler?' she asked and the boy scowled his reply.

'My da was a trader in fine goods before Fallon's spells.'

Akenna nodded her understanding. 'I knew the trade had

dried up but I didn't know it was because of those Unga-cursed spellstones. Still, if you get your hands on some of those they'd be worth more than a pot of black-bitter at Old Ma Rainey's.'

The boy shot her a rapid glance, as if uncertain how much she did know. Tommo, remembering the conversation he'd overheard by the shore and the threat of the Sheriff's man busy searching for spellstones, wondered if spellstones were indeed the boy's father's trade these days. Tommo was watching Akenna intently to see whether she was going to interrogate the boy further, so he saw the precise moment her face changed: he saw the shadow of fear cross her face. He didn't think it was possible for her to get any paler, but Akenna's thin face blanched white as the spindrift on the waves.

'Akenna? Are you all right?' he asked, following the direction of her eyes. He didn't know what he expected to see: certainly not two remarkably ordinary-looking men in work clothes walking along the coast road talking.

'It's Old Garth and my da,' she whispered, so that the boy would not hear her. 'I'm going to have to swim for it.'

'No, wait!' Tommo stood up to try to stop her. The curragh bobbed slightly and Tommo reached for her, but it was too late. In a moment Akenna had shed her outer garments and dived soundlessly into the still water. The irate boy pushed Tommo forcefully back into his seat.

'What in Unga's name did he do that for?' the boy said, steadying the boat with practised ease. 'Stupid lubber.

We've got to fill the nets by dusk.' He sounded aggrieved. Overhead even the birds were temporarily silenced. Tommo hadn't even realised that they were still singing until they stopped. The sudden quietness felt very ominous, the only sound was the water lapping against the side of the boat. Where was Akenna?

Tommo expected her to surface right away but she did not.

'I don't know what she – he did that for. He hasn't . . . he hasn't drowned, has he?' Tommo found it difficult to get the words out, he was so afraid for her. He had a sudden memory of the power of the sea dragging him downwards into the icy depths, from which he would never have escaped without the dolphins' help.

The boy laughed humourlessly. 'He's a fisher, isn't he?'

'Yes, but even fishers drown,' Tommo said, his fear making him thoughtless.

The boy's face darkened. 'He's just wag-skallacking, and we've got fish to catch. My ma'll have his neck when I tell her. He'll get no work if he doesn't take it serious.'

Now was not the time to explain that Akenna was a girl, now was just the time for watching the dark water, willing her to re-emerge. Tommo found he was holding his breath, he let it out in a frightened sort of gasp. How much breath could Akenna's slight frame hold? Tommo noticed that the boy also searched the flat, unbroken sea for any sign of Akenna surfacing. There was none.

'Can't you go in after him?' Tommo asked desperately and got a cold, quelling look for his trouble.

'You'll just have to work for two,' the boy said. Out of the corner of his eye, Tommo thought he saw something surface briefly and then disappear. It could have been the sleek, grey head of a dolphin, but he hoped most earnestly that it was Akenna. The birds began to sing again overhead. He could not hear their words, but he was almost sure that they had been worried for her too and had seen that brief breach of the water's smooth back as he had. Perhaps they were singing with relief – if that wasn't too unlikely an emotion for even human-faced birds to feel.

Tommo kept his expression as neutral as possible and concentrated on following the boy's cryptic and not very helpful instructions. He could not see the men who had so terrified Akenna, but he had little time for looking. It took all his energy to do as he was told without rocking the boat and spilling them both overboard. Tommo was clumsy and found that his shaking interfered with even the most basic of tasks. Eventually the boy lost patience.

'I'm going back in. The light's dying and as a fisher you're not worth a crab's claw on a day of plenty. Why that fisher teamed up with you beats me.'

'We're related,' Tommo lied. 'I'm sorry he ditched us – he's very nervy, um . . .' and there Tommo's ingenuity ran out.

He helped the boy drag the curragh in and unload their measly catch. The boy looked miserable and it seemed clear

94

enough to Tommo that he faced a beating for his poor afternoon's work. There was nothing Tommo could do about it.

'Can I take a couple of the small ones?' Tommo asked as the boy began to walk homeward. 'I've nothing else to eat.'

The boy shrugged. 'You might as well, two of them scraps aren't going to make any difference.'

Tommo took two small fish gratefully and put them into the pocket of his oilskins. He would have to work out how to gut them without even a knife. As he raised his hand in thanks his oilskins slipped back to reveal the damp pig-leather band and his own silvery wrist, growing brighter as the light faded.

'Get away from here real quick,' the boy said flatly. 'You won't want to see my da mad.'

He spoke in a very level voice, but Tommo saw in his eyes the same merciless toughness he knew all too well from the cellar.

'I'm going. Don't worry.'

He felt exhausted, lost and, without Akenna, hopelessly demoralised. He turned his back on the boy and walked up the road the way he'd come.

'If he lives, he'd wash up at the Burrows Bay. Follow the coast road,' the boy said flatly, taking Tommo by surprise. He'd expected no help from that quarter.

'Thank you,' Tommo said. 'I'm sorry if we brought you trouble.'

The boy pulled a face. 'Trouble is what happens round here. You'd do well to get away.'

Tommo nodded miserably. It was not just apprentices who had it tough on the Island of the Gifted. He walked on a few paces in the direction of the sea to show that he appreciated the boy's advice, but he wasn't at all sure that it was the right course. Would Akenna stay by the coast having seen her father on the coast road? The decision was taken from him a moment later when, glancing back up the road, he caught a glimpse of the Sheriff's man heading down towards him, towards Kullen's Cove. Tommo walked as briskly as his tired and trembling limbs would take him and it was fortunate that he was so weak or he would perhaps have followed the urging of his frantically beating heart and run for it. Instead, he headed for the bay and the coast road trying to look like a man with every right to be there.

The light was failing and he was worried about falling, worried about lighting his steps with his own eldritch light. He tried to weigh up which was likely to happen first, his falling and breaking his neck or his discovery by the Sheriff's man. The birds were silent – perhaps they slept, he had no way of knowing – but he could have done with some singing, however other-worldly, to comfort him on his lonely walk. In all the confused days since his escape from the cellar he had not felt truly lonely until that moment. It was extraordinary how much he'd come to rely on Akenna.

He walked for as long as he could and then he stumbled a little bit further. He would have crawled if it would have helped him find Akenna, but there was no sign of her. Perhaps he and the birds had been mistaken and she'd drowned. Perhaps she'd found some other safer road. Perhaps she'd been glad to leave him behind. If he was honest with himself, he could have expected nothing more. What good was he? A dying apprentice condemned to death, slowing her down, making her look bad, making her more noticeable. She had only done what anyone would have done, what any one of the apprentices would have done, except maybe for Ahurn and he was long dead.

There came a point where he could no longer stumble, when he fell every few paces and lacked the strength to pick himself up. It had something to do with his knees, which had started trembling as badly as his hands, but were obviously more necessary to the whole business of staying upright. He was too tired to seek any shelter but lay down where he fell. He wrapped himself in his reeking cloak and slept.

CHAPTER FOURTEEN

Tommo did not sleep for long. He woke to the sound of the waves crashing against rocks, the wind howling in his ears and salt on his lips. It was cold, he was very thirsty and he found that he had been lying on a stone.

It was still no more than the second quarter of the night and he knew that if he were to survive he had to find warmth and shelter. It was a struggle to get to his feet, but he did it.

His knees still shook, but at least they would support his weight. He lowered his hood so that he had enough light to see by and staggered forward on the uneven path. He could hear no following footsteps but the waves were loud. It didn't much matter in any case for if he did not move on he might well die of the chill. When he was a child his mother had found an itinerant physicker dead from the cold, slumped with his pack outside their gate. It had made a huge impression on him and caused his mother to have a bell fixed to the gate at the far end of their path so that they would know should anyone call again. The physicker had looked peaceful enough, but Tommo was only fifteen and he was not yet ready to embrace that fate.

He had not been staggering for very long when he noticed that the shadowed mass of the cliff to his right was folded and twisted along itself in a way that made the existence of caves a possibility. The wind was so wild it was pulling at his hair, giving it a life of its own, and while it was very invigorating in its way, it was also making his ears hurt. He opened his cloak further to give himself more light, and then felt the chill wind cool his body still further. He had to get out of that wind. Thank White Urtha for her timely grace that he saw what he was looking for soon after. He scrambled up the rocky scree and dragged himself through the mouth of a small cave. For a moment he thought he'd gone deaf: the roaring of the wind and the violent crashing of the waves both stopped at once, as if by the power of a gifted spellstone wielder. He would have collapsed with relief but for his very strong presentiment that he was not alone, a belief confirmed a moment later when he felt the point of a knife against his neck. So this was his end then, may Unga take him quickly and Urtha grasp his soul.

'Who are you? What are you doing here?' a male voice said.

'Oh, just stick him and be done with it,' said a second. 'We're not having a ceilidh, by Unga's three balls.'

Tommo swallowed with difficulty. He would have liked very much to disappear, but he did not know how.

'Hurry up! He's glowing like the North Star. You'd see him for miles around and it wouldn't surprise me if the Sheriff's man's given up sleep for his mission.' The speaker spat when he mentioned the Sheriff's man and Tommo really believed it was all over until he heard a voice he recognised.

'You'd be a fool to kill him – he's a thaumaturgist.'

'You know this bag of bones, Akenna?'

She was alive! Was the blade's pressure against his neck lessening?

It was hard to breathe when you knew that every breath might be your last, but hearing Akenna's voice had given him hope.

'I met him on the road,' Akenna said casually. 'I kept him alive because he could be useful. You've got to be a fool not to recognise a bit of luck when you see it.' Akenna's tone was so cool, so dismissive that he felt he'd been kicked in the stomach. He knew that she'd not liked him, of course; he'd known that all along.

'Are you calling me a fool?' The hand that held the knife against his neck trembled slightly as if with rage.

'Course not, Da,' answered Akenna. 'I was just saying. Gifts from Unga's table don't fall our way that often.'

The pressure on Tommo's neck eased and he was flung bodily against the sandy floor of the cave, so hard he was amazed to discover that he had broken no bones.

'Can you work the spellstones, bag of bones?'

A large, booted foot kicked him, so that Tommo's reply came out as a most unmanly squeak. 'Yes, yes, of course. I was a spellgrinder.' He didn't say he was an apprentice, but he didn't have any breath left with which to be honest. He had rarely been more scared.

'Akenna's right, Naal. If it comes to a fight, we could use a lad who can wield a spellstone. The gallows aren't that appealing to me right now and if we're brought before Fallon, from what I've heard, we'll be a lot worse off alive than dead.' That speaker must have been Old Garth. He was chewing on something and waving around the bottle in his hand. Tommo's frightened brain was gradually beginning to make sense of the scene before him. The two men were sitting sharing a bottle of something and tucking into bread and fish, while Akenna lay tied up beside Tommo so close they could touch if she'd had the mind to. Her eyes were hot coals of fury and her face was caked in blood. She did not look at Tommo but at her father, and Tommo was surprised that Naal didn't fall down dead from the focused hatred that burnt in that look.

Naal's reply was incoherent as he grabbed the bottle from Old Garth and took a deep swig.

The business seemed to be settled; they would let him live.

There was something not quite right about the cave, though, now that his ears had adjusted to the absence of wind and his eyes to the limited light from his own body and the storm lantern that the men had just relit. He could feel it low down at the base of his spine: the buzz and living pulse of spellstones. His trembling was worse too, but terror will do that to anyone, apprentice spellgrinder with the quivers or not. He surreptitiously sniffed the air and his heart sank. The smell confirmed it. It was as if he was in the cellar again: the air was tainted with the familiar scent of misery. There were spellstones here he was sure of it.

The men proceeded to ignore both Akenna and Tommo while they ate and drank their fill. Tommo waited until he was sure enough that he could speak in a steadyish whisper and then murmured, 'I thought you were dead. What happened?'

Akenna turned her head away from him so he almost could not hear her low whisper.

'I panicked when I saw Da and I swam for the next cove. I knew there were caves along here where I could hide. Unfortunately, Old Garth knew about them too and that's where he'd stashed the spellstones he'd managed to get hold of. Da thought I was trying to steal them as well as his boat and let me have it. I think he might have killed me if Old Garth hadn't been here. He's all right for a smuggler. He doesn't beat children. They're leaving at dawn to get the spellstones inland. There's a chance for you – they're going north to sell the stones away from the borough.' Tommo almost laughed with relief: it was all right she didn't hate him, it was just a ruse.

She turned then to face Tommo and he could see that she was fighting back tears. 'He will kill me one day,' she said. 'Can you not teach me thaumaturgy? If I could disappear just long enough to get away . . .' her whisper tailed off as Naal yelled.

'You two better keep your gobs shut or I'll paste them shut with this.' He waved his meaty fist in the air and Tommo felt his stomach churn with fear. He could understand why Akenna had to get away, but he couldn't work out how.

He tried hard to be positive and count White Urtha's blessings, as he used to do when he was small and afterwards in the cellar where he had to use his every measure of imagination and ingenuity to find any blessings at all. First he wasn't dead, second Akenna wasn't dead, though he didn't know if she was fit enough to walk, third there were spellstones around and he knew enough about their grinding and their testing to do something with one. He wasn't exactly sure what, but he could work that out later. That was it. No, there was a fourth thing: the men were drinking and by the smell it wasn't black-bitter, but some kind of brandy. It reeked of the stuff they used to clean the turnknives. If you were daft enough to drink that, which some apprentices were, unconsciousness was swiftly followed by paralysis. For most such apprentices it was the last thing they ever did. If Naal's brandy was anything like that stuff, all he had to do was wait until the men slept, stay awake and be ready. Even a quiver-afflicted, renegade apprentice spellgrinder could do that, couldn't he?

CHAPTER FIFTEEN

Fallon listened to his wife's handmaid with every appearance of boredom.

'I'm sure she did not leave her room under my watch, my lord, sir. I'm a very light sleeper.'

'Well, by Unga-under-all, leave it she did and the experience has made her most unwell. If she leaves your sight again for so much as an eye blink, I will find you a new chamber in my dungeons. She is so upset I think it wiser to keep her among familiar faces or I wouldn't be granting you a second chance. Give thanks to Urtha and Unga both that I have not separated you, soul from body.'

The girl left the hall, as shaken as anyone he'd ever seen. In fact Fallon was confident there was no harm done. Vevena, having seen Gildea in the north tower, collapsed with shock. The apprentice spellstone wielder, lacking instructions on what he should do in the event of the Protector's wife collapsing on his watch, had called on Kalen who had seen that Vevena was safely returned to her bed. She quite obviously remembered nothing of it – when she came round she was babbling about larkspur.

Kalen waited in the shadows now, his grubby nightshirt partially unlaced, his gold hat of office awkwardly askew and a blanket wrapped round his gaunt shoulders against the bone-numbing cold of the vast hall.

'Tell me what happened one more time?' Fallon asked, more from his habit of checking any story several times, than from concern.

'From what I can gather Vevena somehow found her way into the north tower and wanted to see what the men were guarding, but she had no idea who he was. The guards and my man thought you must have sent her. I think it was just one of her whims.'

'And how did she get past the guard on the stairs?' Fallon was inclined to agree with Kalen, but saw no reason to let him know that, until he'd sweated a little longer.

'It seems the guard heard a noise, my lord, and while he was investigating Vevena slipped past him. I assure you, my lord, she is still ensorcelled and, as far as I can gather, was playing some kind of a game.' Kalen's unctuous tone irritated Fallon.

'My wife is not a child nor a soft-headed idiot, Kalen.'

'Certainly not, my lord, but the thaumaturgical curse upon her is so powerful and far-reaching that sometimes it results in peculiar behaviour, which, while not in any way dangerous or sinister, particularly to your person, is a little hard to understand.'

'The guard has been dealt with?' Fallon demanded and Kalen paled.

'Your Captain had him summarily beheaded, my lord.'

'Good. I understand the prisoner is close to the end.'

'Your torturer could get nothing from him, sire, nothing but groans,' Kalen looked sickly, as though the business distressed him, but then he lacked backbone. 'And both your physicker and I agree that he has lost the power of speech.' Kalen's voice was, as ever, hesitant and apologetic and Fallon wished, not for the first time, that there had been some other candidate for the job of Chief Spellstone Wielder. It was his own fault of course. Fallon was so nervous of those with the natural thaumaturgy he himself lacked that he had made sure the blue pox killed all those with any significant power, or strength of character, and what he was left with was, well, Kalen and his guild of milksops.

'What of the birds?'

'They still come to his cage, my lord. They come to him and then fly away, but none of my men have got any closer to discovering why.'

'The order to kill all birds in the Protectorate is being enforced by your guild as well as that of the bird-catchers?'

'Certainly, my lord.'

'Then when he is dead – it will be over,' Fallon muttered, as much to himself as to his servant. How could a man believed dead have much of a following? All his very considerable intelligence network had discovered nothing but a half-cooked spellstone smuggling ring, and the story of Tommo. He had no doubt that the Sheriff of Tipplehead would deal with the former and Haver-snatcher the latter. For the first time he began to believe that he had been fearing shadows all these years. Perhaps his position really was unassailable. Perhaps he could rest easier and devote more time to being the just and reasonable ruler he aspired to be.

'My lord?' Kalen asked, confusedly, and Fallon wondered for a moment how much he had spoken out loud. It was the third quarter of the night and he was tired.

'Gildea is an idiot. A lack-wit, a turd-headed imbecile dafter than a spring hare, as White Urtha is my witness. He has told me nothing of any use in all the years he has been at my mercy. When he is dead I will have to give up trying,' Fallon said, and he knew his voice betrayed both his exhaustion and his frustration. 'Each day he has grown less himself, less able to tell me what I wanted to know. He had secrets, Kalen, I know he had secrets. I knew him and there was more in his head than I could find out in a lifetime, and now it's all gone – all of it; he told me nothing.'

Kalen looked as though he was struggling not to yawn. 'Go to bed – there is nothing further to be done,' Fallon said.

He followed Kalen out of the great hall, but paused before entering his own bed chamber. Vevena's violet eyes opened as he entered her room. Her face was caught in the light of a moonbeam so that even Fallon, who prided himself on his pragmatism and lack of sentiment, was enraptured by her inhuman beauty. She looked like a creature of pure spirit, a child of White Urtha, unconnected with the world of meat, of flesh and blood, sweat and anguish, separated from Unga's realm to which Fallon's ugly human body so obviously belonged. He sent the handmaid away. She scuttled gratefully out of the room, obviously terrified of what he was going to do. Perhaps she perceived the truth – perhaps it was written on his face. Fallon wanted to hit Vevena very hard. He wanted to despoil her perfection, bruise her white skin, force some emotion into those cold eyes, but he could not. He would not while the slightest chance remained that she could be his, that she might see that part of him belonged to Urtha too. Vevena, as Fallon was quick to recognise, was his one great weakness, just as she was Haver-snatcher's, and he could not bear her to be damaged in any way.

Fallon sat down on the edge of the high bed. It was made from lilies trapped under delicate-seeming spellstone glass, draped in sheepskins and fine furs, in wool woven with gold thread. Vevena's pillows and silk-quilted cushions were stuffed with goose down, scented with her favourite essence of the sun-warmed flower meadows of her childhood home. At least that is what Fallon thought her favourite scent would be, if she ever deigned to confide in him. When she moved, the bed would play harp music, such as the Kings of the Island had once paid good havers for. It was one of his many gifts to her for which he received no thanks and no acknowledgement. Fallon's weight on the glass bed caused a sudden trilling phrase of melody that startled him in the silence. He touched Vevena gently on the smooth curve of her white cheek. She could not pull away because of the thaumaturgical curse, but she flinched and her cold eyes grew icy. He kissed her on her lips, which were often described as full and generous, but were in fact mean and closed, and as unresponsive as those of a corpse. This was the best that all the spells in the world could do. She could not move away or hurt him by any action; Fallon had never realised inaction could also be a weapon and a source of power, not until he'd met Vevena.

'Dear one,' Fallon said softly. 'Your daddy's gone ahunting for me, because of you. He will help me to root out my last surviving enemies because of you. He will not oppose me for love of you. Does that make you sad, you chilly, vicious beauty?' It was funny in a way and Fallon should have laughed, but he could not: he was too weary. Vevena made him feel hopeless. Even through the dampening effect of the curse, he could feel her barely suppressed hate; it wore him out.

'I should have Gildea killed. He cannot speak to me now,' Fallon mumbled aloud. 'You should be pleased for me my ice-rose, my diamond-hard wife. When your father has got to the bottom of this business with the spellgrinder's apprentice, I think it will all be over. Gildea is no threat. If he still has any followers, other than the apprentice, I will know about it. That old witch who foretold that Gildea would be my undoing will be proved a liar and I may just declare myself King – King Fallon has a ring to it, don't you think?'

He sighed. It was what he had always wanted, but King Joran ceded all royal prerogatives to the Convocation, chosen by the people, and it was as the people's Protector that Fallon ruled now.

Vevena's mouth remained closed. But for the gentle rise and fall of her chest she could be dead. She did not look at him, not even when he took her hand in his and kissed it.

It was warm, which always surprised him. Surely her blood should be as cold as her soul.

Anyone who saw how he'd come to power from such poverty with only his will and wits should be impressed. Vevena was Haver-snatcher's daughter – she knew what he'd come from. How could she not love him when he loved her so much?

He let her hand drop back lifelessly on the bed. She still did not look at him.

'I will win, Vevena,' he said quietly and left the room.

CHAPTER SIXTEEN

Tommo was woken by a combination of dawn light striking his face and Naal's boot striking his thigh: the latter was more violent. His first thought was that he had failed Akenna. He should have been able to get her away.

Old Garth and Naal were not morning people. They grunted rather than spoke and man-handled Tommo and Akenna out of the cave without so much as a sip of water. It was a relief in a way because the cave stank of stale farts, male sweat, brandy, spellstones, and fish – Tommo had forgotten the two small fish he had hidden in his pocket the previous day.

In the grey morning light Akenna looked deathly. Her face was covered in blood and it seemed likely that her nose had been broken: the eye that had been blackened earlier was now puffy and had closed entirely; blood stained her thin, colourless hair. Tommo felt desperate on her behalf. What if he had it in him to do thaumaturgy? What if he could do it, but never discovered how? He tried to wish very hard that Garth would trip, fall and bang his head on a rock, but although Tommo imagined the accident as fully as he was able, Garth remained remarkably sure footed. The only person who stumbled was Tommo himself – he was having trouble with his knees again and only remained upright through fear and force of will.

Old Garth had taken the lead along the narrow cliff path, followed by Akenna, whose hands were still tied together, then Tommo and Naal brought up the rear. Naal stepped on Tommo's heel from time to time as if to remind him of his presence. The wind had died down overnight and everywhere was swathed in a damp veil of grey mist that made his face wet. It hid the contours of the rocks and swallowed up the sea so that if someone told him he'd died and marched to the limbo lands of Unga-under-all, Tommo would not have argued, except that he had been led to believe that the dead and disembodied felt no pain and he ached in every limb. It occurred to him that if he and Akenna could escape their captors in the mist they would be truly invisible even without the advantage of thaumaturgy, but then his natural common sense reasserted itself – they would be free, invisible and very dead unless they could avoid falling down the cliff by luck alone. Tommo's luck was of such an erratic kind he would prefer to wait for a better opportunity, for surely one would come.

They had walked for some unmeasured and immeasurable time when the mist began to lift and Tommo saw the welcome face of the sun. It was pale and wan as a winter moon, but it was at least there. A little later Tommo was pleased to see that they still had their avian escort. He didn't know why the sight cheered him as the birds were likely to get them into yet more trouble, but his spirits lifted.

They walked in silence and Tommo had no way of communicating with Akenna.

He followed her stiffbacked, limping walk trying to infer from that how she must be feeling: not good if his own state was anything to go by – not good at all.

Old Garth eventually called a halt to their slow progress and allowed them to rest by a craggy outcrop of rock overlooking the ridge-backed sea. They had the spellstones in a sack. Tommo could hear their low buzzing in his skull; it made him sick, like having bees in his bones.

'We need to eat, Da, if we're going to walk,' Akenna said, through swollen lips. By Unga she looked terrible.

'We're not walking. The cart'll come and take us north so you can shut that gob of yours or next time I'll break your jaw.'

Tommo didn't have to be a genius to recognise that the cart would take him out of the borough, that so long as he kept his head down there was a chance that he would be free of the threat of hanging. He took a surreptitious glance at Garth and Naal and wondered if they'd let him live if he did as he was told: not a chance. Then there was Akenna. Naal would kill her in the end right enough, whatever she did. He sat for a moment gathering strength. He tried to catch Akenna's eyes but she would not look at him. She was perhaps ashamed to be so weak in front of him. He stared at her and eventually she glared at him in response. He signalled with his eyes to look up because the birds had obviously come to Tommo's own conclusion. They had made the rune for 'Be fleet of foot' in the sky.

Unfortunately Akenna merely scowled and it occurred to Tommo that perhaps she had never learnt to read. Garth and Naal never raised their gaze, but produced another bottle of something from the sack which held the spell-stones. There probably wouldn't be a better opportunity.

Tommo did not give himself time to think too much. He shuffled along the ground, little by little, until the sack with the spellstones was in reach. The two men obviously thought both he and Akenna were too weak, too cowed and too cowardly to be a threat and did not even look in his direction until he put his hand in the sack. Then Garth turned and saw him.

'You'll not filch any of our food you Unga-cursed thief,' he said and Naal raised his hand to cuff Tommo, but by then Tommo had his fingers around a shard of spellstone and pulled it out of the sack. It was a spoiler, a reject, a portion of spellstone that had sheared off from the rest. Even so Tommo could feel the pulse of it through his fingers and the familiar nausea that touching spellstones always induced.

'Get your hands off that!' Naal said and lunged towards him. Akenna, watching Tommo intently, put her foot out so that Naal fell, sprawling on to the ground, gasping for breath and clearly winded.

Old Garth made a move too, but Akenna had made a remarkable recovery.

'I wouldn't Garth, he knows how to use that spellstone. You wouldn't want to be turned into a rock or a pile of fish guts, would you?' She sounded so confident that Garth stopped and stood very still.

'Now Garth,' Akenna said. 'First you are going to put down your knife and then you are going to untie me.' Akenna got unsteadily to her feet and placed one foot on the back of her father's neck. 'If you move Da, I'll break you – don't think I wouldn't. There may not be much of me but there's enough to send you to Unga's waiting arms.'

Naal spluttered something but he too kept very still. Garth did what Akenna demanded while Tommo merely held the spellstone shard and tried to look like he knew what to do with it. He had pulled his hood back so that his long white hair blew in the wind and the strange silver lights dancing under his skin were clear for Garth and Naal to see. He may not look terrifying but he was certain he looked strange and magical – dangerous, if you didn't know how close he was to fainting with fright. He kept his hands steady with an effort – he must not betray his weakness when Akenna had done so much to convince them of his strength. Akenna then used the ropes to tie up both her father and Garth. Neither of them moved a muscle to hinder her. When she had finished, she emptied their sack on the ground. There was a pot-loaf, a small hunk of cheese, a few apples, a storm lantern, candles and tinder, a bottle of brandy and three or four spellstone spoilers. None of them was big enough to be very useful, though one was sizeable and of a yellowish hue – it might have been worth something had it been properly ground. Akenna left the spell-stones on the ground, and wiped her hand on her tunic after she'd touched them. She returned everything but the bottle of brandy to the sack, before picking up Garth's knife and sheathing it in her own empty belt sheath.

'Want a drink, Da?' she said. 'Open wide.' She then proceeded to pull Naal's head back by his hair and pour most of the brandy down her father's throat until he was gagging and choking.

'Akenna?' Tommo said anxiously. Akenna was scowling with concentration and her eyes were dark with a kind of fury that was terrifying to see. Akenna gave Naal a little time to swallow before giving him more brandy. It splashed on the grass and the air was filled with the fiery smell of it and still she kept pouring, while Naal spluttered and swallowed the greater part of the bottle.

'I wish it was poison,' Akenna said. She smashed the bottle on a rock and waved the jagged edge at her father. 'I can't think of one good reason why I shouldn't finish you with this.' She waved the bottle so close to his face that he flinched. Even then his eyelids drooped a little as he was clearly struggling to focus.

'Akenna, love,' he slurred.

Akenna turned to Garth. 'Tell him I didn't do it when I could have, Garth. Tell him I could've killed him easy as looking at him and I didn't. D'you know how many times he's beat me and how many times I've watched him lying on the floor dead drunk? By Unga's arse and all the demons under all, d'you know how many times I could've finished him and didn't?'

Garth shook his head and mumbled something Tommo couldn't hear. Naal swayed a little and then slumped unconscious on to the grass.

'Keep him from coming after me, Garth, or I'll see him dead one way or another.' Akenna's voice broke, but her eyes were dry, and she was all business when she picked up the sack and turned to Tommo and said, 'Come on then, spellstone wielder, let's go!'

She was trembling, though, trembling almost as badly as he was, and she gripped the broken bottle so tightly he was afraid it was going to shatter in her hand.

CHAPTER SEVENTEEN

Akenna did not say anything until Naal and Garth, and the cliff where they'd left them, had disappeared from view. She couldn't run because of her injuries, but she moved more quickly than Tommo could easily manage. Suddenly she stopped.

'You didn't need to come after me, not after I abandoned you in the boat,' she said.

'I . . . I was afraid you'd drowned,' Tommo replied, panting to get his breath.

'Thank you,' she said awkwardly. 'I wouldn't have got away on my own.'

'I'm glad I could help,' Tommo answered, uncomfortable with her discomfort.

'No, I mean it,' she said. 'I thought I was done for. I'd almost given up.' She swallowed hard and Tommo looked away, certain that she wouldn't want him to see her distress. 'They would have killed me too,' he said, 'and I'd never have thought of bluffing like that.'

'What d'you mean?' Akenna's voice was as sharp as it had

ever been, all other emotion cut away by the razor edge of her curiosity.

'Well, I mean I can't do anything with a spellstone, but make it sparkle a bit and hum. That's how we tested them in the cellar. The better ones glowed brightly in the colour which showed us their power – yellows are best and then the whites and pinks. I don't know how to turn someone to stone or into fish guts.'

'But how were you going to get away?'

Tommo shrugged. 'I don't know. I hoped I'd come up with something.'

'Against Da and Old Garth you just hoped you would come up with something? By Unga's udders, Tommo, you're either braver than a cornered rat or mad as a hare in springtime,' and she started to laugh. Tommo couldn't help but join in because it seemed she'd not been bluffing at all and if she'd known how useless he was they'd still be back at the cliff top and still prisoners. Then when Akenna's laughter turned to sobs and he struggled against the choking lump in his own throat, he decided it was a good time to change the subject.

'We should walk further,' he said, still grinning so that she didn't realise that he'd noticed her crying. 'We should get further away from Kullen's Cove, your da and the Sheriff's man. Maybe we could find some high ground and take turns to keep a look out. We both need a proper rest and something to eat.' He did not dare ask her if she still wanted them to stick together, he preferred to assume it.

She had her back to him and so merely nodded and began marching onwards still dragging her right leg a little, but setting a blistering pace nonetheless – he already had enough blisters to notice. He didn't much want to know what Naal had done to her to make her limp. He was well used to hard treatment himself, though latterly his skill with the turn-knife and knack of determining the best form for an uncut spellstone had kept the spellgrinder off his back and earned him a measure of respect from the apprentices. His memory of his lost family life was of warmth and love; it seemed to him infinitely sadder that Akenna had never known that at all. He might have said something ill-judged and stupid to that effect but he was distracted by the sudden swooping arrival of the flock of human-faced birds.

Their numbers had been growing steadily without him noticing and now included every variety of bird from small brown hedge thrushes, to huge white gulls and black ravens. At first Tommo had thought that each bird wore a different face, but he could see now that this was not the case: they all wore the same face at different stages of life. Some of the birds bore the face of a baby and others that of an old man. It was thaumaturgical power of a most unnatural sort. He did not like the gleam of what might almost be intelligence in the tiny faces, the incongruity of human necks on feathered bodies. Each face had the same prominent features: a large nose and eyes the impossible-to-describe colour of the sea. By Unga-under-all, they were an uncanny sight. They started to sing, some hopping around their feet, others flying round Tommo's head. They were all singing slightly out of time with one another so it was a little hard to work out the words, but it sounded like 'Rejoice!'

'I'm not sure how we can hide with that lot shrieking their unearthly dirges wherever we are,' Akenna snapped. Although Tommo thought their song beautiful in a chilling kind of a way, he could hardly disagree with her sentiment, mainly because he had not the breath to speak. He had a stitch in his side and was panting for air: he had to stop. He bent double in agony. Akenna was also clutching her stomach.

'By Unga's children but you reek in that cloak,' she said in a normal-for-Akenna voice, fiddling with her beads again. She pulled a face. When he took out the two small fish from his pocket, her face split into a lopsided but genuine grin. 'Let's build a fire here and cook them. We're safe enough. I don't think Da will be up to moving for a while,' she said.

'But if the cart comes –' Tommo began.

'They'll have to stick to the road,' she finished.

Tommo did not know where they were, but Akenna smiled at him.

'I know where we are. We'll be all right here for a little while. We can't be seen from the road and Garth may decide it's better to get the Unga-cursed spellstones hidden before the Sheriff's man comes than waste time looking for us. The Sheriff's man would have them both hanged for smuggling spellstones.'

Tommo took the shard of crystalline stone from his pocket and looked at it critically. It was unmistakably a spoiler. Sometimes if you miss hit a spellstone badly, the whole thing shattered into twenty or so slender fragments, more lethal than tempered steel. They appeared in the records as spoilers and were used to sharpen the turn-knives. They were not supposed to be sold. This one must have been bought from some dishonest spellgrinder, but he doubted the ill-made thing could have much power – it had barely four facets. He did not want to look at it too closely – they drew you in did spellstones, got you fascinated by their light and shape and subtle colouration, by the way they seemed to hold living fire in their inner heart. He put it quickly away.

'They were just fragments of spellstones – not the real thing. They didn't have much power even if I'd been able to wield it. I can't see how they could be worth much.'

'Tommo – no one but Fallon and some of the Names and high-ups have even seen a spellstone. He could sell those fragments for any number of havers. It isn't what they can do that matters, it's what everybody thinks they'll do that makes them worth three or four times any cargo of smuggled brandy Old Garth's ever owned.'

'Have you truly never seen a spellstone before?' he asked.

She shook her head when Tommo had half expected her to lie. He hadn't known her long but he got the impression she didn't like admitting to either weakness or ignorance. 'How do you grind them?'

That was a question. How could he convey to her the terrible, oppressive wretchedness of the spellgrinder's cellar? He couldn't describe the stench, the fear and the spell-stones, which made his whole body resonate to their pulse, which made him sick to the marrow of his bones. 'Well, when you first start they don't let you touch the stones – they have you turning the grinding wheel all day,' he began, hesitantly. 'When you're ready to start on the stones you practise on the easy ones – small stones that just need tidying up. You hold them and you feel their pulse, a kind of beat inside them, a heartbeat of some inhuman thing, and you shape them with your knife. The wheel rotates them and you hold your turn-knife in such a way that you scrape away the surface to uncover the shape underneath. The noise used to raise the hairs on my neck and made all my teeth ache right down to the roots.' He paused and tried unsuccessfully to suppress a shudder. 'You don't cut the stone so much as grind away at it with the turn-knife so that the dust gets everywhere. You get to know somehow how each stone should be – they seem to tell you what shape they ought to be, how many facets they should have and where. And as you grind their edges with the turn-knife their colour grows. To start with you can hardly see it, but when you shape the stone right it gets clearer and more vivid. That's how you know you're doing it right. The more powerful ones are bigger and have more sides and you cut them so they're all even. It hurts you somehow to do it. They kind of bewitch you so sometimes you don't want to touch them at all.' He shivered and the day seemed colder and bleaker than it had before, as if he'd brought the darkness and pain of the cellar with him into the open air.

Akenna didn't look at him but simply said, 'I don't like them – they feel wrong, bitter, evil,' and rooted in the sack for the tinderbox. She was right, they did feel wrong, but few of his fellow apprentices seemed to notice.

He held the spellstone in his hands and shut his eyes. With a little effort he could make the stone shoot small sparks of yellow fire, like a fountain in a rich man's garden. The air was suddenly full of sizzling sparks of light like tiny fragments of shattered glass.

Akenna looked unimpressed. 'And that's it, is it – spellstone magic?'

'Well, I'm no spellstone wielder.'

'That's sure enough,' she retorted and began trying to light the tinder in the box with her flint. Tommo could take a hint and, putting away the stone, he got up with some difficulty and dragged his quivering limbs around the immediate vicinity to see if he could find any dry wood or any sign of Naal.

With a fire lit, Akenna demonstrated how to gut a fish with predictable efficiency. He was sure it was harder than she made it look. While they waited for the fish to cook, they stuffed their empty bellies with bread and cheese and the sweet tartness of apples. It was worth struggling on, Tommo thought, as he chewed on the stale bread. He might not be a great thaumaturgist or powerful spellstone wielder, he might be shaking with the quivers and weak as a week-old fledgling bird, but he hadn't given up. He was still fighting to stay alive and it was still worth living for the taste of bread, the sharpness of the cheese, for the warmth of Akenna up against him on the grass and the sound of the birds singing overhead with their own particular type of joy. He could make out what they were singing now: 'Rejoice! She lives! She lives!' And that was, after all, something to sing about.

CHAPTER EIGHTEEN

Haver-snatcher had used all his remaining strength to stagger to the crowhouse at Tipplehead. The old crone who lived there, in what had once been an orphanage dedicated to Urtha, wept to see him. Haver-snatcher was unsure whether her tears were tears of joy that he still lived or tears of anguish at the state of him. She wasted no time talking, but began at once to try to heal him. She made him a bed before the fire and fed him raw eggs mixed with milk, sweetened with honey and brandy. He did not know how long he lay there for the old crone kept the shutters closed against both the bitter cold of the night and the bright cold light of day. He slept easily and relaxed completely as he had not done in years. His back unknotted and his chest uncramped and he breathed freely at last. She never left him alone. She pottered around the room muttering and cursing, never hurrying, but never still. He would have liked to watch her go about her old familiar and still mysterious routines, but his eyes would not stay open. He suspected she dosed his nourishing drinks with mother's comfort.

The moment came when she gave him a plate of rabbit

stew instead of his invalid's eggs and opened the shutters. He did not know which day it was nor how long it had been since he had slunk back home like some beaten old scarfaced tomcat.

'You'd best make your way to Bet's bathhouse today. You've slept the best part of three days,' his mother said. 'The stink of you will put off an honest woman and tell a dishonest one more than you need her to know.'

He nodded, enjoying the taste of meat, vaguely aware that the stench of the dungeon was still in his nose.

'You can chop me some wood too – I've used all my stores keeping you cosy and I'll want something back for all that good food I've put inside you.'

The old crone flicked the dirt floor with her broom and tidied a stray lock of yellowing, grey hair back into her straggly bun. The light from the window showed him both how much and how little she'd changed. Her pale, faded eyes looked at him steadily, but with trepidation.

'Tell me, my heart's ease, is she still alive?' It was the first question she'd asked him and her eyes searched his face for signs of dissembling, just as they had when he was a boy and she'd been the biggest and meanest thing in his life.

'I saw her, Ma. She's ensorcelled. She doesn't know which way's down, but she's still alive.'

The old woman wiped tears from rheumy eyes. A small bird had flown in from the street and perched on the dresser. Haver-snatcher was surprised to see that it bore the face of a human boy. His mother ignored it.

'You have to save her, Har. You have to save my Vevena. I'll not let you loll around here no more. You've got to get her.'

She was right of course, but he felt weaker than a half-drowned kitten. To please her he ate two more hearty helpings of rabbit and barley broth, chopped wood halfway into an early grave and subjected himself to three havers' worth of hot water and a scrubbing at Bet's bathhouse. Bet's son, with a crippled leg, but a steady hand, shaved him, cropped his mane of matted, lice-infested hair and, with the finest toothcomb made, spent the better part of a morning's work ridding him of nits. With the filth of the dungeon washed away he felt like a man again; a skinny, grey-haired, feeble-witted shadow of his former bull-like self, but a man nonetheless.

'Well, you'll never pass for handsome again, but with your looks a ruin maybe you'll amount to something,' his mother said when she saw him later. 'There's some cleaner threads in the chest – you can burn those rags whenever you like.' He saw by the look in her eyes that, clean and shaved, his appearance was a greater shock to her. He was much wasted. He was still tall enough to have to stoop to keep from braining himself on the supporting timbers of his mother's cottage, but his arms ached merely from the morning's log-splitting and his soft hands had blistered easily. He had seen himself in a looking glass and his short hair was iron grey like his mother's skillet, his face was a skull, his flesh hollowed to the bone. Only the strange violet of his eyes remained unchanged.

'You'll be killing Fallon then?' she said conversationally.

'If it were that easy, do you think I would have been wasting in a dungeon these seven years?' His words came out more sharply than he had intended but she ignored his response, as she had always ignored what she hadn't wanted to hear.

'Anyway,' Haver-snatcher said, by way of changing the subject, 'how have you fared while I've been away?'

'I'm alive, aren't I? I've found a way. My orphans went a long while back when the Convocation stopped paying. Some went to their grave when the pox came and some to Unga's house of the flesh. A couple saw me right, sent Old Nan the odd gift through the really bad times. I can't complain. These days I do a bit of secret seeing and old time merciful wife work. I still do the odd spot of thieving and fencing, but I'm not much for that game any more.'

She looked old and tired, Haver-snatcher thought, and tried to calculate her age, a task made more difficult by his ignorance of his own.

'I'm sorry I wasn't here.'

'Don't be – by Urtha's white breast, you'd have got me into bigger trouble than I've managed on my own. How are you going to beat that Unga-cursed Fallon and save Vevena? Tell me that and I can die happy.'

'I'm still thinking,' he said defensively. 'I've got to get some backing. It's not going to happen overnight.'

His mother's face clouded. 'The old gang are dead, Har. Fallon's got his spies hard at it. They watched me for years in case his enemies came to my door. There's no time to get any backing unless you can strike a deal with the Hand of the Island, but to be honest they're not up to much, and as you finished many of their relatives they might be a bit suspicious of you.' She spoke flatly and Haver-snatcher wondered if she really expected anything of him at all. 'Why'd Fallon let you out now?'

Haver-snatcher shrugged. 'He still thinks there's some kind of plot, a gang under Gildea, folk with thaumaturgy out to topple him. I'd hoped he might be right.'

The human-faced bird flew down from its perch on the dresser to sit on his mother's shoulders. It had golden curls and eyes the colour of the sea. She fed it absently with a few crumbs from the pot-loaf she'd been cutting.

'The Hand is the only game in town, but they don't do much besides talk – and drink. They wouldn't keep me from a sound night's sleep, and as for thaumaturgy,' she pulled a face, 'there's not many with Inward Power left in these parts or I couldn't earn a crust with my bit of talent. By Unga's arse, boy, what did you promise Fallon?' Her tone reminded him of her strong right arm and, though her strength had withered with age, her power over him had not.

'I said I'd track down those with Inward Power. There's some boy he wants me to find – an apprentice.'

'The one who sought sanctuary in the market?'

'Yes. How did you know?'

'Not much happens in Tipplehead that I don't know –

my girls still call and the world is full of gossips. Anyway I saw him and I'd be surprised if he survived the night. He was a spindly little thing, ill-fed and white like he'd been milling flour. You'll find no challenger to Fallon in him. If you want there to be a revolution, reckon you'll have to start it.' She buttered him a slice of bread and handed it to him.

'There's no witches left?'

'You could take me, then at least I might see my Vevena again.'

'He'd think I was up to something. You tanned his arse too often for him to have forgotten you. Is there no one else?'

'Sibeal. She lay low when the blue pox came – saw no one. Her husband left her years back – she was in a three-heir dynastic, but never got with child. She earns enough doing the odd bit of power work, nothing to frighten the horses or to threaten the Protector. How would it help you to put her away? If you're going to betray my friends, do it to finish Fallon or not at all.'

He finished the bread and took the second slice she offered him.

'I have to think. Where is Sibeal?'

'Out Bentree way, a few hours from the Macalley road, south of Footsore. You know, Dan the smith bought some land out that way years back. Died before he set a foot there.' Strangely Haver-snatcher did remember Dan the smith and the farm he never saw.

They had used it as a base for smuggling for a while in his youth before Fallon got his taste for politics.

'I'll leave tomorrow. Vevena is hostage. Pray to Urtha that I get some inspiration for I've not an idea in my head.' He watched as his mother absently patted the tiny head of the child-faced bird. 'What is that?'

'Oh, I'm hiding him from the bird-catchers. He's some leftover from Fallon's cursed magic I've no doubt, but he's company and he sings to me sometimes.'

The bird smiled and so did his mother: the strangeness of that sight disturbed Haver-snatcher greatly. His guts told him that the bird was significant, but he could not imagine why and on that further issue his guts were predictably silent.

CHAPTER NINETEEN

Tommo must have dozed off, Akenna by his side. When he opened his eyes, the fire had burnt out and it was beginning to rain. He could not see the birds. He had to shake Akenna to wake her.

'Akenna, we have to go! We both fell asleep. We have to get away.'

The fire had scorched the grass so hiding the evidence of their presence was not very feasible. The rain made the charred ground smell of wood smoke like a ghost fire.

Akenna struggled to her feet, but she looked pale and very unsteady. It was clear to him that she could not walk far.

'Do you know of somewhere we can go, maybe a shepherd's hut where we can hide or a physicker who could give you something for those cuts?' Tommo was no expert but he didn't like the look of the abrasions on Akenna's face. They were turning yellow and pus was beginning to ooze from one of them. She felt hot too, as though she might be feverish.

Akenna looked at him wearily, through glassy eyes. 'There is someone who might be able to help – a merciful wife, Sibeal. She was a priestess of the Inward Power when there was such a thing. The women went to her when they had problems and she saved Merrison's arm when everyone said he would lose it. My father took me to her once, but he wouldn't think to look for me there.'

'How far is it? Do you know the way?' Tommo tried to keep his shaking voice under control. His hand had gone into a kind of spasm and its shuddering was making it hard for him to concentrate.

'I always know the way. It isn't out of the borough, Tommo. It's not far at all if we were fit, but in this state it might take us a while.' Tommo picked up the bag with the remaining food and the spoiler of a spellstone, and followed Akenna. He had given up on escaping the borough. It was too late for that. The rain soaked his face and ran down his neck even with his hood up. He ought to have been miserable, desperate even, but when Akenna staggered a little and he gave her his arm, she took it with all the appearance of gratitude. He was not alone and that was something, an important something. It surprised him that her weight when she leant on him was negligible: she was nothing more than skin and bone and raw, bloody-minded determination. In his mind she had become something altogether bigger.

It cheered him a little when he saw the birds flying in formation high above. He could not read the runes they formed for the rain and the cloud and his own blurring vision. It was good of them to try and communicate, he supposed, if that was indeed what they were doing. It probably didn't matter as he wasn't sure how much longer he'd got left. It would be enough to get Akenna safely to Sibeal's place.

They huddled together against the weather and lurched and stumbled their erratic way across the rough ground. It was poor grass, not much good for grazing, even worse for tilling, and not much good for walking either. Tommo lost all sense of time, lost his sense of anything but the next stretch of ground in front of him and of Akenna, head down against the rain, clutching his arm as they struggled to take one uncertain step after another. They walked on and rested in a relentless rhythm all that day. It was warmer to keep moving and probably safer. Finally, when they were in the middle of nowhere in particular, Tommo's strength failed and he stopped and sat down where he was.

'Come on. I don't think it's too much further now,' Akenna said, her voice shaky with exhaustion. 'When I came here before, with my father, we used the cart so we didn't go cross-country, but I'm sure it's just over that hill there. I remember the shape of the mountains and that lightning-blasted tree over there.'

She pointed to a solitary tree, scarred and splintered so that it was shaped like a star, and helped him to his feet. 'Why did you go to Sibeal with your father?' Tommo asked, to take his mind off the prospect of a still longer progress of shaky, awkward footsteps.

'I was always in trouble back then and Da thought I might have some thaumaturgical gift.' She sounded embarrassed. 'I don't know why – I haven't. I think he wanted rid of me, and Sibeal has a cousin in our village who said that she was on the look out for a girl-child to help her. It was a long way and Da got very angry when she said she wasn't looking for anyone. I think he was hoping she might buy me. I suppose I'm lucky that he didn't know about spellgrinders needing apprentices or he'd have sold me off to them.'

Tommo turned his head to better see her expression. Akenna was not the kind of girl-child who would take well to being rejected. 'Why didn't she want you?'

Akenna shook her head. 'She didn't say – well she told Da that she'd had a few tough months and couldn't afford another mouth to feed. It might have been true because I think the Protector's people were taking away the priests of the Inward Power at that time, the ones who weren't dead of the blue pox anyway. It was round about when the High Priest was taken and few of the fishers dared go to someone like Sibeal any more. Da never cares much for what people think – I think he enjoyed going against the Protector. He'd have taken any chance to get rid of me. At the time though, I thought she didn't take me because I had no thaumaturgical gift. She did give me these beads though – I don't know why. Maybe she felt bad about not taking me.' The beads were clearly important to Akenna as she fiddled with them constantly. They were dull, cloudy spellstone, the type Tommo thought of as 'dead'. He didn't much like the necklace, but he doubted Akenna had been given many presents. He didn't say anything for a while, mulling over

Akenna's words. He'd still been with his mother when the High Priest, Gildea, had been taken.

'Are you sure that the Protector's men didn't take this Sibeal too?'

'No, I'm sure they didn't. Her cousin never stops talking and if the Protector's men had taken Sibeal we'd have heard of nothing else when we were gutting but the whole sorry eel's tail of "Poor Sibeal".' She was silent for a bit, getting her breath and then continued, 'Da got something from her for his leg – she didn't even charge, she was that keen to get rid of us. Da's leg was hurt in a fishing accident a long time ago. He claimed that he only drank to dull the pain, but I don't think any pain needed that much dulling. For a while though, after he had Sibeal's brew, he was much better, less angry, and he didn't drink so much. He didn't beat me neither – even though he still had me to feed and care for – so I think the brew worked. Some say Sibeal would have been elected a priest of the Convocation one day if it hadn't all fallen apart. She's supposed to have secret sight.'

'As long as she has a fire, I don't care,' Tommo said, and could not help himself from adding, 'is it much further?'

'There, can't you see the chimney?' He thought at first that Akenna had imagined it, as sick people sometimes did, but then he too saw a thin coil of smoke the colour of pewter dribble from the chimney top and disappear. 'You'd better stay out of sight, looking like you do, until I know it's safe.'

He must have looked bad if she looked better. He

watched as she limped across the uneven ground. The sky was the colour of slate and the land looked hard and grey and unyielding; he found it hard to imagine that anyone living there would be any more generous. Above him the flock of birds circled and sang. He lay on his back and watched them. The quivers were bad. He wondered how much longer he'd got. Most of the apprentices died when they could no longer eat, many gave up trying long before that and died of hopelessness and fear. Strangely, he did not feel hopeless, just tired; exhaustion had become a familiar weight, heavy as a grinder's lathe stone.

The birds' song reached him from a long way away. 'Danger! Danger!' they sang. He was getting used to their music and the sound no longer chilled him as it had once. It was almost comforting; the harmonies were so rich and complex. It took a long time before the meaning of the words began to filter through his meandering thoughts. Danger.

He shambled to his feet, no longer doubting the wisdom of the birds, and he saw Akenna standing next to a tall woman with grey hair. Was she the danger?

But one of the baby-faced birds was perched on her shoulder and Tommo took that as a good sign, an indication that she was not a danger to Akenna.

'Call your friend and get inside – we haven't got very long,' Sibeal said, with an anxious glance around the barren, windblown fields that surrounded her cottage. Akenna signalled for him to follow and he hurried after them.

'I think Akenna's cuts have gone bad –' Tommo began, but Sibeal interrupted him.

'That's the least of your worries,' she said. 'One of Fallon's men is coming here to take me. He will be here very soon – I know – and then it will be up to you.'

'We don't know what you are talking about,' Akenna said and Tommo was glad to see that her injuries had blunted neither her wits nor her sharp tongue.

Sibeal only glanced at her. 'The birds are important. They are attracted to thaumaturgical power and gather in the greatest number wherever the Inward Power is greatest. It is too difficult to explain and there isn't the time, but you must keep them from the bird-catchers. Everyone of them is important and you have to take them all to the Fortress of Winter. It is the only way we will overcome Fallon.'

'We don't care about overcoming Fallon,' Akenna said bluntly. 'I just want some salve for my cuts, a bit of shelter until we're fit again and then we'll be away.'

'How can you be so stupid?' Sibeal said aghast. 'Only you have enough power. You are our only chance.'

Akenna was about to answer when there was an incredible cacophony of tuneless antiphonal singing from outside.

'Hide!' Sibeal commanded, and turning to Tommo, looked him squarely in the face.

'You must promise by White Urtha and all that lives in the spirit that whatever happens you will remain hidden.' Tommo was so taken aback by her intensity that he nodded dumbly. 'Right. Up the chimney,' she said briskly. He was about to protest because a fire roared in the grate, but Sibeal waved her arm and suddenly the flames went out, extinguished as if doused by an invisible bucket of water. It was the first demonstration of real thaumaturgical power he had ever seen. He glanced at Akenna but she just shrugged. She looked too ill and beaten to have an opinion. Looking at her all argument died on his lips. He hoped Sibeal had a better hiding place for her.

The walls of the chimney were quite cool and because Tommo was thin, and desperate and generally keen to stay out of trouble, he found that he could climb the chimney quite easily. There was even a ledge a little way up, just wide enough for him to rest his feet on. He hated the smell of soot and the sudden heat as Sibeal relit the fire. He concentrated on the small not quite regular square of sky above. He did not know the nature of the danger that was coming, but he saw one of the birds with the face of an old man perched on the top of the chimney.

'Fly away and hide!' he whispered, never expecting to be heard. The bird looked back at him, then flew away. He didn't know if that was mere coincidence.

Tommo rested his back against the chimney, his trembling hands pressed against the wall in front of him for balance, his feet wedged against the wall on the narrow ledge. He had to struggle not to cough as wood smoke filled the chimney. This was a new and totally unexpected prospect – being burnt or smoked to death. He wondered if it would hurt more than death of the quivers.

CHAPTER TWENTY

It felt good to be in the open air again. For all that she pretended powerlessness it seemed that the old crone could get him everything he needed. He didn't ask what favours she had called in or what threats she had made, and he didn't care. All that mattered was that somehow he found himself with a horse, a purse of havers, a good warm, waterproof cape and a sword. Haver-snatcher was in business again. Of course, he had doubts about the strength of his sword arm, but at least he was no longer imprisoned, no longer at his old friend's mercy.

He had no plan and that was a kind of a freedom too. In the dungeon in those early years he'd come up with a thousand ways of usurping Fallon and a hundred thousand ways of killing him slowly for what he'd done to him. Now, when all the old gang who might have helped him were dead, with so many of his contacts gone and his spirit all but broken, nothing seemed so easy any more. It no longer seemed that he could shake the world and shape it to his own will. Somehow in those long years he had learnt to be afraid, if not for himself then for his girl, his Vevena. Fallon had his heart and it made Haver-snatcher vulnerable.

It was a long, wearying way from Tipplehead to Sibeal's place even on horseback and Haver-snatcher did not hurry. He savoured his freedom and the freshness of the wintry air; he relished the pleasure of choosing when to rest and when to eat. Little by little he remembered the man he'd once been and wondered that he'd ever been so bold. He knew that he carried a bit of the dungeon with him as he rode, that no wind, however fresh, could blow away the memory of those years or of the men he'd shared them with, particularly Breen who had given him a token for peace. He had grown weak and sentimental.

There were few signs that the power of spellstones had been much used in the country. He saw an apple tree made entirely of glass, and a wayside shrine to Urtha in which her image had been fashioned from running water, but nothing else attracted his attention. Fallon had apparently more or less abandoned his schemes to magic away the problems of the Protectorate and focused instead on the ridiculous embellishment of his fortress. Haver-snatcher could not decide if that were a mistake or not. Every attempt Fallon had made to wield spellstone magic for good had cankered and ended badly. Fallon's world without power but crammed full of spellstone artefacts lacked grace – something no one had much valued until it had gone.

Each day of riding and good eating made Haver-snatcher stronger, or at least he hoped that the pain in his aching and chafed limbs was a sign of growing health. In the various snugs and common-houses where he stopped to buy food and the odd pint of black-bitter, he made himself as invisible as a man of his stature and ravaged beauty could be. He kept his ears open and his mouth closed. A brief dalliance with a fisher's daughter just along from Kullen's Cove brought him faith in his restored manhood. She also told him an elaborate tale of the mysterious disappearance of Naal, Old Garth and the Sheriff's man, lost chasing smuggled spellstones. Naal's skinny, foul-mouthed witch of a daughter had gone too. Haver-snatcher listened to the local gossip with all the appearance of boredom while hanging on every word. He could not help being heartened by the thought that Fallon's grip on the kingdom was a little less secure than he had believed, though a good deal stronger than he'd hoped.

There was surprisingly little talk of the apprentice who had escaped and demanded sanctuary. When Haver-snatcher contrived to drop the subject subtly into conversation, the consensus seemed to be that the boy was dead. Disappointingly Fallon's fears of a conspiracy were obviously unjustified. Haver-snatcher had hoped to learn more. The people were not happy. In the days of the Convocation the thaumaturgists had been at the heart of village life, doing whatever healing and finding work was needed, adding their power to help building and mining, mending and fixing, as well as being regarded as good sources of advice. The spellstone objects that Fallon had made were not available to the ordinary people. They were a poor substitute for the many practical skills of the priests of the Inward Power and those other lay people with thaumaturgical gifts, who also used their gifts in the service of White Urtha's path. Haver-snatcher had known about that before he had been imprisoned, and as Fallon's Witch-hunter General he had done more to rid the country of thaumaturgists than anyone else. The situation hadn't eased in his absence, especially as Fallon's sheriffs were over-mighty and heavy-handed. There was a real opportunity for the right man to sow some real discontent, but it would take time and Haver-snatcher did not have too much of that. He feared that if he did not return to Fallon quite soon, Vevena might be in danger. His only option was to buy himself more time out in the borough by earning Fallon's trust, by giving him something he wanted. The witch Sibeal was the only thing Haver-snatcher had to offer, though it wouldn't please the old crone. The apprentice would have been better. He toyed with the idea of walking into a spellgrinder's cellar, buying a boy and producing an apprentice's body for Fallon's inspection. One boy was much like another – but it was too risky. He did not yet know enough about Fallon's spy network, but he knew his old friend and he was cautious and canny. Fallon would have his eye on Haver-snatcher – more likely many eyes – informing, checking his reliability; he could not play any obvious games just yet.

He just had to ensure that he would get his chance later.

Sibeal's cottage was easy enough to find, not least because a flock of some hundred or more birds flew above it. He hadn't noticed the lack of birdsong on his journey.

The sight of so many birds all together swooping and wheeling like leaves in the wind reminded him suddenly of what he had missed on the road. Watching them fly almost brought tears to his eyes. He had become foolish in the dungeon, sure enough.

Fallon had ordered bird-catchers to trap all the wild birds. Haver-snatcher knew that, but he didn't understand why, and the borough folk who spoke of it were not much wiser.

'He thinks they lay spellstone eggs,' one old man hazarded, 'and if everyone had spellstones he'd be a dead duck.' Another had whispered that they were the souls of the dead of the blue pox come back to haunt Fallon. Even Haver-snatcher, who would believe almost anything of his old friend, would not believe that Fallon thought that.

Haver-snatcher was not much afraid of natural thaumaturgical power. The spellstones, however, scared him witless. Long ago, when Fallon first started making powerful thaumaturgists use them, Haver-snatcher had seen a man lit from within, burning horribly like a torch, at a spellstone wielder's command. No one with that kind of power still lived of course – all the really talented thaumaturgists had died of the pox – but sights like that stayed with a man and made anyone who valued his life a little wary. He was pretty sure Sibeal had no spellstones, and his mother had assured him that her secret sight foresaw no difficulties with this merciful wife, whose gifts were scarcely more considerable than his mother's own. Still, if she knew that he was coming, she might have laid a few traps and it would pay to be wary.

Haver-snatcher felt the familiar quickening of his pulse, the rush of blood, the excitement of the hunt and the possibility of a kill. He had missed it and had forgotten how much he missed it. It made him feel alive again. He almost smiled. Haver-snatcher dismounted carefully and strapped on his sword belt – more for the look of the thing than anything else. He should not need his sword to capture one old woman, even one who was a merciful wife, a soothsayer and a herbalist.

He strode forward to the narrow front door. It was poorly made and he could have kicked it down in an instant even in his much weakened state, but perhaps a softer approach was better.

'Merciful Sibeal, I've come from Old Nan with a message for you.'

It was true enough in its way, though the message was that blood was thicker than water and that Old Nan would sell her best friend for small change if it suited her son. The door swung open in well-oiled silence, but there was no one in the room. It was gloomy indoors. The only light came from the fire burning in the grate and a small trickle of dusty sunlight that escaped through the shutters across the window. He could see that the single room was neat enough, with only the most basic of furnishings: table, truckle bed, dresser and chair. Herbs were neatly stowed in labelled jars on the dresser and hung in fragrant bunches from the low rafters. He had to duck his head to walk inside.

'Hoy, Sibeal?' he shouted.

No good householder would leave a fire burning un-attended. Sibeal's kind of cottage fired easily and burnt like a haystack when it caught. He knew she was there, he could hear an echo of his own breathing. He held his breath, but she also held hers. He sniffed the air: baking, herbs, wood smoke, fish and sweat – fear-sweat, he knew the reek of that too well.

'I know you're here,' he said, trying not to show that he was disturbed by her absence. He'd learnt to suspect the unexpected. His hand crept instinctively to the hilt of his sword.

Sibeal shimmered into view in front of his eyes, as if she was made of smoke. There was empty space and then suddenly there was Sibeal. Startled, he took a step back, then hated himself for such a display of weakness. His heart thumped like a battering ram, worse – like an old man's heart which might burst. He made himself take that step forward, forced his voice into evenness and calm. The hand that held his hilt was slippery with sweat.

'My ma said you had the Inward Power,' he said, almost managing to appear nonchalant, but then he spoilt it by swallowing hard, so she knew she had him scared. Unga's arse, he would not be beaten by a witch.

'Your ma doesn't know the half,' said Sibeal and dis-appeared again. There was no warning; one moment she was solid enough to touch – to hurt – the next she was gone. Haver-snatcher hated being made to look a fool, hated it more than anything. He felt the heat of his anger burn, felt his neck flush. He shut his eyes. Ma reckoned he had a little bit of talent of his own, no great thaumaturgic power, but a little something that gave him an edge. He could feel that Sibeal was by the door watching him – he covered the distance in two large strides and his hand made contact with something fleshy and soft. He punched hard with his fist and Sibeal was there before him again, bent over and fighting for breath. She did not let that stop her – all credit to the old sow – she hit him hard across his nose with her open palm and her hand was hot as fire, burning and blinding him. He cried out with the unanticipated pain and sensed her run from him, out of the door, and his fury knew no bounds. He did not need to see to know where she was. He was quick still, in spite of everything. His old instincts were not blunted, and he was big. His hands found her throat with ease and closed round it. He didn't know why he had thought his strength was gone. He could crush her windpipe easily, break this woman in two with as little effort as he'd need to snap kindling wood.

Something screamed, 'No!' Something small hurtled towards him. Something small, he didn't see, tackled him low so that his legs buckled under him and he fell. He roared, struggling back to his feet, flailing his arms wildly until his meaty fist made contact with the unseen something. Something cracked and a young girl's voice cried out incoherently, and then, before he could reorientate himself and finish her, the air was full of birds, screeching with almost human fury, scratching him with razor talons, biting his ears with what felt like teeth, pulling his hair. He covered his eyes with his hands so they could not pluck out his blessed eyes. He could do nothing else.

He heard Sibeal shout: 'Don't be foolish, Akenna! Run!'

Haver-snatcher could do little against the weight of birds attacking him, but he found that Akenna's neck with a lucky swipe of his hand. He would wring it like he might a chicken for the pot. His fingers closed on something and he twisted, but it was only beads. He pulled, hoping to throttle her and he heard her make a terrible gurgling noise in the back of her throat as if she was choking, but, before she croaked, the thread broke and beads fell clattering on to the floor, getting under his feet, tripping him up. He heard the girl, whoever she was, scream, then felt her turn and run. Where she went the birds followed and he let his hands fall. He could see again, though blood streamed down his face from all the many scratches and bites.

Sibeal had not run, but stood still looking at him in what appeared to be shock. One of the birds perched on her shoulder and she raised a hand to shoo it away. He was reminded suddenly of his mother, but where her bird had borne the appearance of a young and golden-haired boy, this one wore an altogether more familiar face, the face of an old man with white hair and eyes the colour of the sea, the face of Gildea, High Priest of the Inward Power, as he had last seen him. By Unga's udders and all that lay down under, what did that mean?

CHAPTER TWENTY-ONE

Tommo had no idea how long he waited struggling to breathe in the narrow chimney. He struggled to cling on to consciousness. Akenna's loud, distressed voice brought him back to himself.

'Tommo! She's gone! He's taken her. I don't know why, but she stopped fighting and he took her. Come down!' He would have liked to, but there was the small matter of the fire below him to contend with. Luckily, Akenna seemed to realise that for herself for he had no strength to call down. He heard the hiss of water on flame and the chimney was filled with steam. He would have liked to let go then, but his arms had stiffened into a kind of a paralysis and he could not make himself move. It was not that far down to the fire – the cottage was a low, one-storey building, and yet he could not do it; he could not allow himself to fall.

Akenna's face appeared, peering up at him from the hearth.

'You've got to come down now, Tommo,' she said, more gently than he might have expected. 'The man came and took Sibeal away. He said he'd be back for me and the birds.

We have to get away from here Tommo – that bloke was trouble. He tried to strangle me with my beads, and the birds . . . the birds tried to save me!' Perhaps it was the way her voice cracked as she spoke or the look of panicked appeal he thought he could detect in her shadowed face, but he found himself doing as she asked and coming down. He managed to let go of the wall, to let his arms fall and then the rest of him followed. It wasn't very graceful, he tumbled like a scarecrow dropped down a well, but he made it to the bottom more or less intact: he only grazed his elbow on the way down, skinned his knee and dislodged a damp cake of soot which got in his eyes. He landed awkwardly on the steaming wood, but he did not think anything was broken. His whole body shook with a shivering so violent he did not at first believe it could be the quivers. Akenna offered him her bony hand and helped him wordlessly from the fire. Without its light the cottage was as gloomy as his spirits.

'W-W-What now?' he stammered.

Akenna opened the shutters to let the sunlight in. Tommo could see the red mark around her neck, livid as a rope burn, where Sibeal's abductor had tried to strangle her. She too was lucky to be alive: fear and worry had pinched her face into a taut mask.

'We're not doing so well are we?' he managed to say.

'We're alive,' was Akenna's only answer and his self-pity seemed to galvanise her into action. She started searching the shelves for something, opening jars and peering inside.

It was too much effort for Tommo to turn and watch

her; it was almost too much effort for him to be curious enough to care. His whole body was convulsing as muscle after muscle went into spasm. Everything trembled and quivered so that his vision blurred and his bones banged and shuddered against the ground. By White Urtha, this must be the end, he thought, and then passed out.

He came round to find Akenna scowling over him.

'It's getting worse isn't it?'

'What is?'

'The shaking.'

'It comes and goes,' he lied.

'How long have you got before it kills you?' she asked. She was careful not look at him, but instead stared at her hand as if she had never seen it before.

'Days, maybe hours.'

'Is there nothing a leecher or physicker could do? There must be others around besides Sibeal.'

'I don't know – I never saw either come to look at the apprentices. There were always plenty more poor boys to take over their jobs.' He paused and then said what he needed to all in a rush. 'Akenna, why don't you go, leave me? Run before that bloke comes for you. I'm going to hold you back. There's no point in me trying to run – I'm going to die soon.' It was easy to say, much easier than he had expected, and he knew it now in his blood as he hadn't fully known it before. He could feel the quivers sapping his strength, making him feel old and feeble and very, very tired.

She didn't answer him, but got up and resumed her search of Sibeal's possessions. She checked the warming ledge by the hearth and peered into Sibeal's collection of crocks and pitchers. She was thorough, Tommo would say that for her. She checked every part of the cottage and found cat gut and twine, a small jar of imported wine, one of flour (infested with weevils), a sack of apples and one of roots (both past their best), a bolt of sackcloth, a rock of salt and a small mouldering lump of cheese under a cloth.

'What are you looking for?' he said at last, bemused by her odd reaction to being half strangled and then told she should leave him. Akenna's response was difficult to hear as she didn't stop her clattering investigation to answer him.

'Sibeal's known for her wisdom – she had the gift of secret seeing. If she knew we were coming, maybe she left something for us to find.' She sounded weary, demoralised, but as determined as ever. Tommo couldn't but admire her relentless energy.

'Why would she want us to find something – except maybe some salve for your cheek?'

'She said the birds gathered where there was most thaumaturgical power and it was up to you to save them.'

'Did she?' Tommo had been so relieved to finally arrive at their destination he didn't take in much of what she'd said. Akenna gave him a sharp sideways look and clicked her tongue like the old fishwife she would probably one day become.

'It can't be up to you if you're dying, can it? Maybe she knew of a cure.'

Tommo's laugh was more bitter than he had intended. Akenna's reasoning sounded mad to him.

'Maybe you're the one with the power,' he said. He found that he cared very little about power or even the birds, he just wanted to rest. He wished the fire was still lit, for his quivering felt like shivering and might be easier if his bones were warm again. As a child he'd loved to stare into the heart of the hearth fire and imagine a world of flame flourishing there: he would have liked to see that hearth world again. Sibeal had only waved her arm to light the flames. He copied her motion, slightly embarrassed that he was even attempting such fancy. His foolishness was rewarded by the sudden roar of a fine fire, despite the dampness of the wood. Akenna was suddenly all attention.

'How did you do that?' she demanded, but Tommo could not answer. He was shaking too much. To his surprise she left what she was doing. 'You can tell me later,' she said firmly, taking in his appalling state at a glance. 'You should eat,' she said and, without being asked, fed him small slices of cheese and apple as if he were a child just weaned. It made him feel grateful, sad and ashamed all at the same time. No one had ever tried to feed the sick apprentices. When they grew too shaky to feed themselves they died.

After she had fed him he sensed her moving around him, but it was too much trouble to twist his head and attempt to follow her with his eyes. It was hard to focus anyway. Every hour seemed to make his world smaller – warmth, food, the pleasure of sleep, that was it. The shaking made him tired. He felt the warmth. He felt the comfort of his full belly. He felt all resistance to his need to sleep forever melt away.

To his surprise he woke up. He rather thought he was going to be dead. What little daylight that had breached the cottage's defences had gone and the only light came from the dying embers of the fire. Akenna had finally abandoned herself to sleep and lay sprawled by his side, her mouth open. It didn't look like she had found any salve.

He managed to roll clumsily away from her and crawl outside. It took all his strength, but his bladder was full and he was not about to shame himself as the sick apprentices so often had. It was cold and the wind brushed the back of the wild grasses and set the treetops swaying. The air still bore the faint salt tang of the sea and he was full of regret. He did not want to die when he'd only just begun to live again. He rested his back against the cottage wall and slept.

Akenna found him there at dawn. He felt her warm fingers touching his face and neck, checking for a pulse. He heard her muttering under her breath, which was warm and smelled of apples. She half supported, half dragged him back inside even though she still limped from her own injuries.

'We have to leave,' she said firmly.

'G-G-Go – I can't walk!' he answered, struggling to control even his tongue. He knew his voice sounded slurred, but there was nothing to be done. His journey had ended.

'I'm dying,' he said, anger making it momentarily easier to get his words out.

'Y-Y-You must g-g-go,' he managed to say, though it was a struggle. He tried to fix her with his eye so that she would know that he meant it. It would mean the end of the warmth and the food and the companionship that had made the last few days a strange kind of pleasure, but he did not think any of those things would matter for much longer.

Akenna made him drink some warmed milk, which seemed to be past its best as it had a rather strange flavour. She was very gentle, for Akenna, and he understood her kindness as an act of Urtha-blessed charity before she left. He would have liked the moment of comradeship to last for a long time but he had to end it; it was wrong to do anything else and he didn't want to be wrong.

'G-G-Go!' he said, with what was left of his strength. It was hard to make out the expression on her face. The firelight threw strange shadows and the smoke made his eyes water and his vision blur. He thought for a moment that her face was wet, which seemed unlikely. Then, after a long stretch of time, she nodded.

'If that's what you want,' she sniffed and scraped back the matted tangle of thin hair from her face. It was odd how such an ordinary face had become so dear to him so quickly. The firelight softened the sharpness of her chin and cheek bones, made her look gentler and more childlike. She sniffed and wiped her nose on the back of her hand. 'I'll build the fire up,' she said. He did his best to smile, suspecting that the expression he managed to produce was anything but pleasant. His eyes stung and he longed to close them, as if sleep was an enchantment that he couldn't resist. He felt himself dragged down and under into unconsciousness as powerfully and as inevitably as the sea had pulled him under into its dark embrace: sleep took him before he could say good bye.

When he woke again his body was being jolted by some other force than its own inner eruptions. He opened his eyes and almost cried out. The ground was moving beneath his head. It was hard to make sense of the blurred shadows beneath him, but he thought he made out the basic shapes of rock and shale and wild grass moving beneath him. He thought he might be sick.

Akenna's voice cut through his fear. 'Whoa there!' she said. 'Tommo? Are you awake?' Akenna's wiry arms were round his back.

'Don't panic. You're strapped to the back of Sibeal's mule, like a dead man – it's the only way I can manage you. You slept a whole day and night.'

He was a dead man and she shouldn't have bothered. She should have left him in the warmth of the cottage to die. He didn't want to struggle any more. He didn't say anything as Akenna somehow manhandled him off the mule and he half fell on to the stony ground.

It hurt and that woke him up. He wanted her to look at

him so she could see what he thought of this for an idea, but she didn't look at him, she would not face him.

'You're not going to leave me on my own,' she said fiercely.

As his head began to clear, Tommo realised that he was wrapped tightly like a corpse in a winding sheet so that his shuddering limbs were tied tight to his torso. He could barely feel his extremities. Akenna had made him as warm as possible – only his face was exposed to the night air.

'I'm sorry about the mother's comfort,' she continued, while she busied herself with the mule. 'I found some in Sibeal's cottage. I hope it won't make you sick. I couldn't think of any way to persuade you to come with me so I decided not to try. I found the mule when I went outside – it must have been Sibeal's. Now I've rested I've got some of my strength back. I found something for my face.' Tommo could see it was plastered in a kind of white grease. 'I'm not leaving you, Tommo, and I won't let you leave me. You haven't told me what I need to know yet. I still need to know about the thaumaturgy. I always get what I want, Tommo.' She sounded scared somehow – she was talking far too much. She had said more words than he'd ever heard her utter before. Tommo couldn't decide whether he was grateful for her efforts or angry that she had ignored his wishes.

'We'll have to sleep rough,' she said, apologetically.

'Here we go again,' he thought. His head hurt from the mother's comfort, and his whole body ached from the jolting the mule had given his bones. Akenna rolled him roughly under the shelter of some stunted trees, as if he were a barrel of fish, and then joined him. It was dry, at least, and afforded them some shelter from the wind. She settled herself with her face against his padded back and he felt her warmth against him.

'Th-Thanks,' he said into the darkness, struggling with a tongue still thick from mother's comfort and clumsy from the quivers.

'We're not done for yet, Tommo,' she said softly. 'You're not dead yet'.

CHAPTER TWENTY-TWO

The Chief Spellstone Wielder felt his heart contract when he saw Sibeal; it had been so many years. She was terrified he knew, but hiding it well. He had hoped that she was safe, well out of the way of the court and the town, known only to locals who might call her in times of emergency. He had hoped such locals might be grateful enough to be loyal to her.

Haver-snatcher brought her in with much of his old swagger restored. His flesh hung on his monstrous frame: he had grown cadaverous in his long years of imprisonment, but his violet eyes were sharp and predatory. When he sneered at Kalen, Kalen's guts twisted. Haver-snatcher was an unpredictable new element in what passed for a plan. By rights he ought to be ripe for recruitment, but only a fool would trust Haver-snatcher to serve any cause but his own.

Sibeal was as pigheaded as ever. The years had been kind to her: Though her long hair coiled into her characteristically untidy bun was now virtually white, her face was unlined and still handsome. She did not show by even a flicker of an eyelid that she knew Kalen, for which he supposed he should be grateful. Nonetheless he knew that she saw him in his despised gold hat of office and he felt that familiar shame. It was the only way, he told himself, it was the only way that they had a chance. Kalen's guts tied themselves into six different kinds of knots as they took Sibeal down to the dungeon to await questioning. It would be bloody and painful, and he was not sure how much she had to tell. They had confided in one another once and she had a long memory. He dared not consider how much Fallon's inquisitors could wring and rack from her. He wished it were over. He was tired of the sickness in his stomach that made it difficult to eat and almost impossible to sleep. He was tired of the constant worry about his daughter, Blathnaid, whose life was hostage. He had been sure that Sibeal, at least, was free. By White Urtha, he was soul-stained and sick at heart.

There were things he had to attend to – ordinary things that kept him from hearing the animal cries from the dungeons. It was a while before he could legitimately visit the dungeon to fulfil his obligation to Sibeal and even then he dragged his feet. He was, in truth, the coward she thought him. He took a deep cleansing breath and focused his mind on other places, places where the air was sweet.

He had just enough thaumaturgical power to confuse all of them clustered round the dungeon's entrance: the guards, Fallon's spies and one of his own spellstone wielders – a weak man of almost no natural gift. He was able to convince all of them that he was not there. It took more energy than he had anticipated, but he was quietly pleased that service to Fallon had not quite sapped all his strength. It was the work of a moment to steal the key to the dungeon cell and go through the door.

Sibeal looked terrible, even in the dimness of the dungeon, lit only by the sepulchral grey-pink light of almost exhausted spellstones. She was battered and bruised. He noticed that she wore no marriage chains to indicate her status as a married woman and he felt a moment of annoyance. She was bleeding from her lip and her face was tear-stained.

Kalen didn't waste time on sympathy – everyone who opposed Fallon had to suffer. 'Well?' he said. 'What did you say?'

'Nothing,' she said, 'nothing at all, but that I'm a witch and worker of Inward Power. The power helped a little – I managed not to feel most of it.' She was trembling, an unnerving sight. Kalen knew of no one tougher than Sibeal. He did not want to talk about what she had been through. He changed the subject: 'Did they come to you as you foresaw?'

'Two came,' Sibeal said. 'Can you get me out of here?' She sounded more desperate than he knew she would have wanted, but being questioned by Fallon's thugs tended to reduce anyone's pride. Kalen shook his head. The presence of the spellstones sapped his power as they were meant to do. When Fallon had demanded that he protect the dungeons with spellstones, he had used the weakest he could find, knowing that only luck kept him from languishing in them. Weak or not he could feel the pulse of the stones like the drumbeat of an insistent headache. Working against the spellstones, not with them, was unutterably wearying.

'One of them was your boy,' Sibeal said, and the words sounded like a kind of revenge. He felt as if the earth shifted round him as she spoke and that suddenly he was standing on a high, precarious place: he had to hold on to the cold stone of the wall for balance. He was sweating.

'What do you mean?' He knew what she meant, but it could not be true.

'I saw him – the one with the greatest power. There is no mistaking his face, even though it glistened with grind-dust. He is yours – yours and Eavan's.' There was a certain bitterness in her tone.

'My boy died with Eavan and the baby long years ago, Sibeal. Don't reopen all that again.' He thought he'd die of grief when it happened, losing all of them – Eavan, Tommo and the nameless baby. As if the grief had not been enough, Sibeal had punished him for giving Eavan children when she, unlike his first wife, Alissa, had borne him none. She was wise enough to know it was not his fault that she was barren, but the gulf between her head and her heart was wider than the chasm that divided Urtha of the spirit from Unga of the flesh. This surely could not be the time for such cruelties? He refused to believe that she told him the truth.

'That boy is not my Tommo.' His Tommo had been

born in the fourteenth year after the death of King Joran the Illustrious, the fourteenth year of the Convocation, which, but for the fatal bout of cow's foot fever, would have made his own son almost sixteen. It had been his hope that the small, bright boy of his memory might also have been much blessed with thaumaturgical gifts. Even after so long, he had to swallow down a choking lump of loss in his throat.

He did not know what Sibeal was trying to achieve by bringing up all that again. Maybe it was kindness that made her change the subject or maybe the recognition that she had scored a direct hit on his heart.

'What of Gildea?' Sibeal asked. Her voice was harsh with thirst and suffering, but Kalen had little sympathy to spare.

'He has almost gone. When his time comes, I will try to have his ashes buried in the Sacred Garden of Memory. It is all I can do and I may not be permitted to do even that.'

'How will that help?' Sibeal's harsh voice was full of accusation. She had never forgiven him for becoming a spellstone wielder and it had completed the destruction of their relationship that his love for Eavan had begun. It was a source of regret to both of them that they had never been able to sever their association. He did not want to look at her.

'I have to go, Sibeal. I came to say I'm sorry Haversnatcher found you – it was not of my doing.'

'Your boy is sick, Kalen, he may not be strong enough for what is needed and I had no time to talk to the girl. I met her when she was a tiny child and gave her a necklace to hold back the blossoming of her great power. She may never learn of it now. It might be too late. I should never have meddled there . . .'

It was unlike Sibeal to be self-critical, she was one of those women who were always right – particularly when they were wrong.

'We will only know whether what we've done has truly been for the best when we have our new High Priest,' Kalen said soothingly. He could not really believe it. He had grown too tired and too fearful even for hope. 'I will get you free when I can.' He touched her hand and tried to heal her injured Urthene spirit as well as her Ungine flesh. He could do little, his power was weak and healing had never been his talent. 'I pray to White Urtha to restore your spirit and Red Unga to restore your flesh,' he intoned and she drew her hand away.

'I'm sure you will get me free Kalen, when you can and not a moment earlier. Think on what I've said. Tommo is yours. Trust me.'

That was it – he could not trust Sibeal. There was too much between them. There was no one he could trust. Almost everyone spied for Fallon and now that Haver-snatcher was back on the scene, and his daughter was somehow becoming more aware, everything could unravel. He toyed with the diamond he'd found on the soldier beheaded for failing to guard the stairs to Gildea's cage. It was Vevena's ring – she must have lured the soldier away with it. She should not have been able to subvert the curse.

It was Gildea's intention that no one should act. His plan depended on no one else having a plan – on letting thaumaturgy take its course. Only Gildea truly believed that keeping everyone ignorant of his intentions would allow the Urthene and Ungine elements of the world to find their equilibrium and restore him to power. Kalen's own faith was far from firm. He doubted that anything could release them from Fallon's yoke and the cursed spellstones he so loathed to use.

'Goodbye, Sibeal,' he said.

With a swift backward glance at Sibeal, he headed out of the dungeon still cloaked in his cloud of obscurity born of the inmost secrets of his hidden thaumaturgical power. He got past the guards all right. They didn't see him, but then he felt so ill with his stomach cramps and his nausea that he had to race to the kitchens to beg some of the stomach-settling potion he had called into existence for the Protector himself.

'Unga's armpit!' the cook said, patting his bony rump familiarly; she had known him a long time. 'Look at that. I've seen more flesh on a lark's wing. You're a disgrace to my provisioning – get the man some more breakfast, boys, or we'll all be out of a job!' Her cheery joshing sent kitcheners scuttling in all directions. She was something of a brute was cook and an unreliable ally to boot.

He drank the stomach-settling potion, which tasted as disgusting as such medicaments ought to, and managed what was probably a tight and joyless smile as he accepted a heavily laden platter of food. It would do the gut rot that had plagued him since the day he became Chief Spellstone Wielder no good at all, but he ate it anyway, for it was unwise to upset cook who had been known to stoop to poisoning if the price was right or her pride was offended. Mother of Urtha and all that was sacred, how had he come to get involved in all of this? He had neither the power nor the temperament for subterfuge. He wished for the umpteenth time that Fallon had admitted women into the spellstone wielders guild for then perhaps these burdens would have rested on Sibeal's shoulders, which, though narrower than his own, were better designed for such responsibilities. Fallon did not trust women and did his best to exclude them from positions of power, though he had failed in the case of the cook.

He thanked the kitcheners and flattered cook on the unerring perfection of her culinary offerings and slunk off to find some peace, some calm in the anthill that was the Fortress of Winter. The stench of the dungeons was on him and in his nostrils, and he could not forget Sibeal's pain-ravaged face or her words. Tommo could not be his son. His son was as dead as this Tommo was soon to be. The same thoughts kept repeating in his mind as if the ideas he most wanted to forget were being learnt by rote. There was no peace and calm for him anywhere in the fortress. Fallon's guards were everywhere; Fallon's eyes were everywhere. Even the walls of the fortress seemed steeped in the Protector's watchful malevolence holding him captive, trapped. In the end he left the fortress altogether and walked for a while in the winter garden, created from nothing by his own spellstone working and consequently as dogged by failure as all his other pursuits. The strange and exotic plants of spellstone origin only depressed him. There were no birds either. Fallon's bird-catchers had killed as many as they could before they could fly to Gildea's cage. He hoped that they had caught none leaving the tower. Fallon's paranoia would not allow them anywhere near his secret prisoner. Perhaps the birds survived? He sat on an elaborate iron-worked bench that bloomed with living metal roses and he held his head in his hands. He had not the courage to deal with such uncertainty.

It was so quiet in the garden, devoid of birdsong and the noise of palace life, even the farmyard sounds of the provisioning farms were muted and distant so he heard the flight of the great eagle before he saw it, felt the wind blown by the powerful down stroke of its broad and beautiful wings, felt it lift the hairs on the nape of his neck and send a shiver of foreboding down his stiff and brittle spine. It flew unhesitatingly to the High Priest's cage of spellstones, which hung like a blue jewel outside the white marble walls of the Fortress of Winter. Kalen felt his stomach clench and sickness rose into his mouth. He knew what the arrival of the great bird meant. He and Gildea had talked when they could in the long years of his captivity and Kalen knew that this eagle was what Gildea called his key, the High Priest's unifier, and that it was almost over. Kalen wanted to run to Gildea's cage, careless of all danger, of Fallon's spies and guards and his own spellstone wielders. He wanted to fling himself at the feet of his old mentor and beg for forgiveness – for all that he'd done and so much that he hadn't. Instead he started to sob, at first quietly, then more violently, finally he let his head drop into his hands so that his whole body was racked by powerful spasms of grief, for Gildea, for the Protectorate, for Sibeal, for Blathnaid, for Tommo and for himself. When he looked up the eagle had gone.

It did not take long for the hue and cry to start. Within moments a messenger arrived to inform him that Fallon demanded his presence immediately for, of course, Fallon knew where to find him. Reluctantly and with a sinking feeling of foreboding he followed the violet-liveried messenger across the gardens and the courtyard and through the carved ornamental portico of the Petitioner's Gate into the ice-white fortress.

Fallon was waiting for him on the decorative chair that was a throne in all but name, in the great hall that acted as throne room. As usual there were people everywhere – former aristocratic Names and high-ups trying to maintain their influence, advisors and assorted hangers-on. They parted before him, seeing his gold hat of office. He was feared by those who knew no better. He was aware that he ought to have brushed his dusty cloak and otherwise smartened up his appearance for he no more wanted to parade his shabbiness, than he wished to display his grief before this assembly.

'You called for me, your honour?' he said steadily.

Fallon's piercing mismatched eyes examined him intently and, as always, Kalen had to fight to stand his ground. Those eyes were the work of Unga-under-all, a visible sign of Fallon's affinity with all that was base and material and contrary to the life of the spirit, to White Urtha and to thaumaturgy.

Fallon spoke: 'There is news you should know. One of the bird-catchers might finally have hit one of the birds flying from the tower with his slingshot. Our guest of the castle walls is dead.'

It was hard to know what Fallon thought of that from his expression, which was, as always, alert, sardonic and watchful. Kalen did not know what he was supposed to feel either and, unable to take his lead from Fallon, kept his own face as neutral as possible.

'Would you like me to deal with the corpse?' he said.

'No. I want you to accompany me to view it for myself. He was ever a tricky character, Gildea. I would like to be sure that none of his clever machinations outlive his death.'

Kalen's mouth was too dry to answer and he hoped his face did not betray his fears. His only hope lay in the remote chance that Gildea's clever machinations had done just that.

CHAPTER TWENTY-THREE

'Hoy! Up and about! Hoy!' The strange harmony of the birds' chorus stirred Tommo to startled wakefulness. It took him a moment to remember that he was bound tightly in what amounted to a shroud, but even that could not daunt his optimism. The sky was a pale blue-grey and the birds' dark shapes formed patterns in the sky – the symbols for 'joy' and 'health' and 'wakefulness'. There were more of them than ever. He watched them flock, mingle and divide like tea leaves in a market-diviner's cup. Their music set the hairs on his neck erect and made his eyes water with what might have been tears: the sound was a kind of perfection.

'Unga-under-all but I'm as stiff as a salted mackerel,' Akenna said loudly in his ear, breaking the mood somewhat. 'I wish those blasted birds would stop their squalling. We're supposed to be in hiding.' Akenna dragged herself into Tommo's line of vision. She stretched and yawned and stared at the sky, then she smiled at him, an unguarded smile of real warmth that made Tommo feel unaccountably happy.

'You made it through the night, then. I half feared that you'd be a corpse and I'd have to bury you in some ditch.'

She grimaced. 'I dreamt you were a corpse in a winding sheet and . . . well, never mind.'

'No – tell me what happened.'

'I'm not so daft as to waste words on dreams.' She looked uncomfortable and the mask of Akenna the hard-faced fish-gutter was back again.

'I'd like to know!' Tommo said earnestly. He noticed that he hadn't quivered yet, not since he'd opened his eyes, and he didn't want to give himself time to think about the possibility that this was the final, terminal stage of his condition and death was imminent. He wanted Akenna to talk to him – any kind of cradle-croon would do – to keep the fear at bay.

'I got angry,' she said. 'I was furious that you'd died on me, after all my struggling to get you on that blasted mule. You're heavier than a half-starved spellgrinder's apprentice has any right to be. Anyway, you were cold as I lay against you and so I ripped off the sheet and your skin was all white and silver, like a butterfly's cocoon or something, and –' her voice dropped – 'and I tore at your skin with my fingernails. I pulled at it and ripped at it until you started to scream, as if somehow I'd got to the still living part of you. Under-neath you were all small and thin and dark, like all that white stuff that surrounds a chestnut when you break it open. I felt bad that I'd hurt you and you were angry, but I said at least you were alive, and then we had an argument. Stupid eh?' She looked away.

'I'm sure a market-diviner could learn a lot from that,'

Tommo said without stammering, but Akenna had disappeared from view, perhaps to see to the mule.

He could not move, he was too tightly bound, but surely he should be shaking by now and he wasn't. He could not help but hope. What if Akenna did have thaumaturgical power? What if she had the healing talent of the Inward Power, like Sibeal was supposed to have? He could not bear to hope, but the birds were still singing and still shaping the runes for 'health' and 'joy', forming and reforming the patterns with their flight. There were so many of them that he could not count them. Could it be?

'Oh, cursed Unga!' Akenna said angrily, as she stomped back from seeing to the mule. 'I picked up the beads from my necklace when that man broke it and put them in the sack, but there's a hole in it and they have gone.' She sounded upset, but Tommo was in no position to help her look for her beads, being trussed up like a bird for a baker's oven. Besides he knew the beads to be of spellstone origin, which was reason enough for him to dislike them. He didn't think it politic to mention that fact just then and something else more pressing was on his mind, not to mention his bladder.

'Akenna, can you get me out of this thing you've wrapped me in? I need to . . .'

Akenna needed no further encouragement and started undoing the swaddling blankets. His arms felt numb and the need to find some privacy to relieve himself grew more urgent. Still the shakes had not returned. He left Akenna, talking to the mule – at least it didn't talk back – and walked to the next clump of trees. He was far from steady on his feet, and he had pins and needles everywhere, Akenna having swaddled him as tight as any babe, but he could walk, his head didn't bob around uncontrollably and his legs didn't tremble. His skin was still lit as if from within with firefly sparks of silver but surely he could now see the healthy glow of his true complexion emerging. For all that he had spent the night in the open, he felt better than he had since he had sought sanctuary – how many days ago?

He was even well enough to consider his surroundings with some enthusiasm and to assess them as more than a burial site. They appeared to be nowhere. He could not see or smell the sea, there was no sign of the trade road, or even one of the drovers' ways that criss-crossed the country to join with the trade road. Though he peered in every direction he could not even see a homestead. He turned his head and with steady eyes identified the whitethorn, the mountain ash and the yew trees, names his mother had taught him, and the wild grasses: cocksfoot, purple fog and some others he did not know. Beyond them the foothills of the island's Spine stretched ahead of him. All round him the country was coloured a hundred shades of green and grey and brown. Tommo blinked back the tears that blurred his eyes. He did not know where he was and he did not care. He thought he might live.

If Akenna thought he looked emotional, she gave no sign. She barely glanced at him when he returned, as she was busy preparing some kind of breakfast from Sibeal's supplies.

'I don't know which way to run. Do you have any idea?' he asked her.

'I think we have to go north to the Fortress of Winter,' Akenna said grimly. 'Sibeal –'

'Why there?' Tommo asked, surprised.

'Where else?' she began. 'I can't stay near the sea or my da's friends will get me. I've never been further than Broadford, my whole life. Everywhere I know, Da knows better. I have to go somewhere he doesn't know.' That made sense to Tommo, but she surprised him by continuing: 'Besides, my da –' she hesitated – 'my da hates Fallon, all right? He's part of the Hand of the Island rebels, supposedly. He thinks I don't know. They've never done much – but they're dedicated to bringing back the Convocation and getting rid of the Protector.'

'But why should you care what your da thinks? He almost killed you.'

'I think he's right about Fallon. Sibeal said that we should take the birds to the Fortress of Winter – it was the only chance to get rid of him. I want to get rid of Fallon, Tommo.' She still didn't look at him, but was tearing hard pot-bread into chunks small enough to feed him with. There were now more birds, a larger flock than he'd ever seen before, and they were no longer singing in their weird harmony. Some had started to sing: 'Hungry, hungry, feed the birds'. At the same time as others were singing: 'Health' or 'Bread'. The sound was far from pleasant.

'What, by all that swims in the blighted sea, are those birds doing?' Akenna said crossly. 'I suppose I should give them some. They fought for me after all – and that's another thing. I owe it to the birds to do what Sibeal said . . .'

'Akenna!' The tone of Tommo's voice made her look at him.

'Tommo?'

'I think I can feed myself.' He saw her expression transform from irritation through astonishment to something that looked suspiciously like joy.

'You're not shaking?'

'I think maybe there was power in your dream.'

'Mother of Urtha, it can't be something *I* did. Maybe the quivers get better on their own if you don't die of hunger. It can't be.'

She rushed towards him as if to embrace him and then patted him on his shoulder in an embarrassed, manly kind of way.

'I can't believe it!' she said again, but anything else she might have added was drowned out in the insistent crying of the birds.

'Feed the birds! Feed the birds! Feed me! Hungry!' they demanded, their now discordant voices so harsh with need that listening to them was almost painful. Akenna gave them some crumbs, while they themselves gnawed their way through the tough bread. Tommo was worried he would lose a tooth to the chewing of it, though his teeth, like the rest of him, felt stronger than he had for a long while.

Akenna kept glancing at him surreptitiously, as though

she could not quite believe what she was seeing. After a while she said, 'I don't understand. It can't be me. If I could've healed folk, I'd have done it before.'

'Would you?' Tommo asked.

'Well, not Da, but maybe some of the other fishers.' She sounded doubtful and Tommo thought it a good time to change the subject.

'Which way do you think your da will have gone?'

She shrugged. 'I don't care. We can stay clear of him if we head north to the Fortress of Winter. He'll be busy enough keeping clear of the Sheriff's man.'

Tommo didn't feel inclined to argue. He would go where Akenna went – he was in danger everywhere, and he couldn't see that going north would be a worse direction than any other.

'We'll stay away from the trade road and keep going cross-country,' Akenna said, as she began gathering the remnants of their breakfast.

'How do you know where we are?'

'I always know where I am,' she said with such certainty that Tommo didn't dare argue with her. 'We're a day's walk from Broadford. We'll have to loop around a bit to avoid Gatesy and Clagg, but if we walk steadily we should make the fortress in two or three days. We'll be out of the borough when we reach Broadford.'

'Let's go then.' Tommo got to his inexplicably steady feet, unable to keep the grin from spreading across his face. Maybe he would live long enough to be hanged after all.

CHAPTER TWENTY-FOUR

Tommo's quivers started to return about midday. He didn't want to say anything to Akenna. It would have made them both so happy if she truly had thaumaturgical gifts: he would have been cured and she would have had the power she wanted so badly. Still, by White Urtha's great heart, his life thus far had schooled him to expect disappointment and to deal with it.

Akenna was lost in her own thoughts and didn't say anything about his sudden change in mood. Perversely he was a bit offended that she hadn't noticed, even though he was trying hard not to show his distress. Hope was the cruellest thing of all.

'Can we rest now?' he said at last, struggling to keep petulance and self-pity out of his voice. 'I can't go any further.'

'We'll stop then.' Akenna almost suppressed her sigh of frustration. Something had happened to her since she'd left Sibeal's cottage. She was full of energy and had even lost her limp. The bruise on her face was fading almost as he watched. She was eager to get on with her half-cooked plan to take the birds to the Fortress of Winter. The birds seemed to come and go as they pleased. Although they had followed them for a good while, if they chose to follow someone else Tommo didn't see what he, Akenna or anyone else could do about it. Taking them anywhere seemed a nonsense. Akenna hunkered down next to him on some dry stones on the muddy bank of the river. Tommo thought, from what he could remember of his childhood geography, that it might have been the River Url which flowed over Kimrick way. Urtha knew, and probably Akenna too, but he didn't feel like breaking through her shell of silence.

'If I have thaumaturgical power,' she said at last, as if she was carrying on a discussion they'd been enjoying for some time, 'why don't I know how to use it?' In the absence of her beads, she worried away at her fingernails, something he'd not noticed her doing before.

He shrugged. 'I don't know anything about thaumaturgical power, Akenna – so I can't say.'

It didn't seem to be the right answer. She scowled at him so that her face took on a pinched nasty look like a small dog on the attack. 'No – you can disappear and call on the Holy Folk of the Sea and light a fire with a wave of your hand. Course you don't know anything about thaumaturgy, like I don't know about fish. What is it? Do you just not want to share your knowledge with a fisher girl?' She sounded angry, and all the joy of his cure seemed to have gone. 'If I have power, why did it not come before when I needed it? Answer me that. Why didn't it come when Da was knocking Unga's bites from me? And why didn't Sibeal take me all those years ago? If she'd only taken me, Da wouldn't have beaten me and I might *be* somebody by now.'

'Oh, for Red Unga's sake, Akenna, you'd most likely be dead along with Sibeal, taken away somewhere.' He sounded crosser than he'd intended, but she did not notice even that.

'Sibeal's not dead. I'm sure she's not,' she said, missing his point.

'Akenna, think, for Unga's sake! Maybe the beads Sibeal gave you stopped your thaumaturgy – they were made of some kind of Unga-cursed, hotch-potched spellstone. If they did block your Inward Power, Sibeal probably did you a favour. I don't see what's so wonderful about thaumaturgy anyway. What good is it? It makes birds that can't feed themselves and any number of pointless things. It's kept me cooped up in a cursed cellar for Unga-under-all knows how long and the blessed grind-dust has given me the quivers, and for what? Who is one bag of corn better off because of thaumaturgy? You said yourself fish are worth less – so you were poorer for it. I haven't seen one good thing come from thaumaturgy yet and believe me I've been looking.' He was so angry and so weary and so upset that he had been foolish enough to believe for one moment that Akenna's non-existent thaumaturgy had helped him. He almost burst into tears – except that he hadn't cried properly since the first night he'd spent in the cellars, and a fine lot of good that had done him then. He felt the same pathetic prickling of tears in his eyes and nose now, a sensation he thought he'd never know again. Akenna turned to look at him, surprise in her sharp, dispassionate eyes.

'What, by Unga's arse, is wrong with you? Why are you so angry? Oh, by Urtha, no! You've got the quivers back, haven't you?'

He had to turn his head away from her, in order to answer so as not to shame himself. He wiped his face and nose roughly with a shaking, glistening hand. 'I knew I was going to die before. I'd got used to the idea, but for a moment there I thought I'd be all right. It makes accepting it harder. You see?'

He spared her one furtive glance, from the corner of his eye. 'So you didn't cure me – not really. Maybe it's just the way the quivers develop – you get a half-day off, once you get to this stage.' He knew he sounded bitter and childish and he hated himself for it. Akenna's mood had changed abruptly and she was suddenly gentle again. 'What if I had managed to cure you, but I wasn't strong enough to do a good job? What would happen if I used the spellstone? Would it make the thaumaturgy stronger? I've still got that – "spoiler" did you call it? You could show me how to use it.'

He should have remembered: Akenna was not someone who ever gave up.

'Akenna, listen to me. I don't know anything about thaumaturgy. Whatever happened with the Dolphin People and the fire was just something that happened – I don't know how. All I know is that I'm not going to get well.' He was pleased that his voice barely trembled at all and the lump in his throat was not so big that he couldn't get the words out. 'I faced it before and I'll get used to it again. Let's get on with this journey to wherever it is and get it over with. And please throw away the spellstone spoiler – they're evil things.'

Akenna pressed her lips together so that they made a thin, puckered line. He did not know what that meant, but she didn't look pleased. She did, however, throw the spellstone as far away from them as she could. She had a strong throw on her; Tommo was impressed.

By late afternoon they had reached the peak of the smallest mountain in the Spine, Camarty Hill. Below them Tommo could see the borough town of Broadford and beyond that the villages of the northern borough. Further still he could just make out the thin sliver of silver-gleaming sea. They had a different sheriff in the northern borough, who might not know of his crime, or who knowing might not care to do the work of a rival. Even Tommo, who knew very little from his sequestered years in the cellar, was aware that there was no love lost between boroughs as they all vied for the approval of the Protector, who seemed to delight in setting one against the other. He wasn't sure if that would make any difference or not.

Akenna shared the last of the apples with him. She hadn't spoken since he'd made her throw away the spellstone.

'It doesn't look so far,' he said as brightly as he could.

'Not if you walk as the crow flies. Skirting Broadford will take time. You can ride the mule if the shakes get bad.'

'I'm not as bad as I was, Akenna. I'm sorry I was angry before. I had thought it might all work out – you know.'

'I know,' she answered. 'I thought the same. We can't give up though, can we?'

Tommo thought he probably could. It would be easy when the quivers got really bad like they had at Sibeal's cottage, but he knew that wasn't what Akenna wanted to hear.

'No, we can't give up,' he said, softly.

'Good,' Akenna said. 'Then I'm going to walk into Broadford – they catch freshwater fish there and I've seen a few of the Broadford wives at market in Bentree. I can get a few havers for food there and then I'll meet you tonight on the Macalley road. There's a traveller's snug at Footsore Farm there where we can rest. It won't be completely safe. Da's stopped there before, I know, but if we're careful –'

'No!' Tommo said.

'What d'you mean, no?'

'I don't want us to separate,' Tommo said stubbornly and irrationally. He'd been telling her to leave him earlier – what was wrong with him?

'We need havers to live, Tommo. Don't worry – I'll find you. I'll know where you are.'

She pointed out the thin brown line that marked the Macalley road, then turned from him and walked away – her limp quite gone. More than half the flock of birds followed her, wheeling and swooping high above her head, singing loudly and discordantly, leaving him alone with the Unga-cursed mule. He wished she hadn't. He had changed his mind about dying alone – he didn't want to do it.

CHAPTER TWENTY-FIVE

Tommo led the mule down the steep slope of Camarty Hill.

The quivers hadn't yet reached his legs so, although he was tired, he made good time, only mounting the mule when he judged the ground was good enough and the creature wouldn't slip. He didn't much like riding the mule. Neither he nor the mule were well nourished and his bony behind bounced on the mule's bony back, but he decided it was sensible to conserve his strength – he had no doubt that there would be trouble at Footsore Farm and he would more than likely need it.

Two of the birds perched on his shoulder and more rested on the mule's neck. The mule flicked his ears but seemed to tolerate their tuneless refrain, which had reduced to 'Who? What? Where? Why?' It might have driven him mad, were it not that he was glad of the company: he missed Akenna's stiff-backed, bloody-minded presence.

He looped around Broadford walking through sheep country, taking care to stay away from buildings or signs of habitation of any kind. There would have been travellers on the Macalley road and it was better not to test the effectiveness of his cloak in hiding all his gleaming, sparkling skin from view. He reached the better grazing of the richer lowlands and cow country by dusk, and joined the Macalley road north of Broadford at dusk. He covered himself as fully as possible with Sibeal's blankets but even so he was the kind of traveller he himself would have gone out of his way to avoid.

It was easier walking on the metalled road and he and the mule trudged side by side. The birds on the mule's back had stopped singing and instead busied themselves with cleaning their feathers with their moist pink tongues, and dozing, their strange heads buried out of plain view. Tommo seemed to have been landed with birds from all of the five stages of manhood – from babyhood to senility – though none of them were very lively. They seemed almost depressed, as if missing the larger flock as he missed Akenna.

There were more people on the Macalley road as he neared Footsore Farm and, as it was not feasible to leap into a ditch every time someone approached, Tommo followed the birds' example: he kept his head down and pretended to be asleep.

Footsore Farm was well named. Even though Tommo had spent a fair part of the journey riding the mule, his feet were blistered and bleeding and caked with mud. In the fading light he could see the distant glow of the hearth fire and hear men's voices laughing and talking. Their voices carried a good way, blown by the wind, which also carried the tantalising aroma of some kind of hot meat. As he got closer he could see a crowd of drinkers gathered outside the small traveller's snug, which was a bit too snug to house that many people at one time. This would be a real test of his courage. He found that his heart was beating abnormally loudly and his legs, particularly his knees, had started to tremble again and probably not from the quivers. He felt slightly sick.

'Danger!' sang the baby-faced bird.

'Listen and learn!' sang old-man's face.

'Hush!' hissed Tommo. 'Unga's arse! You stupid dung-for-brains no-hopers – you're putting me in danger!' He found that the cellar curses came to his tongue all too easily. Rather to his surprise that silenced them.

'Hoya!' the men outside the snug called to him.

'Hoy!' he answered nervously, and pulled his hood down over his face.

'Grena, look at this one. I think he wins the "Footsore bucket for today".'

Tommo's feet were suddenly the focus of the most unwelcome attention of all the drinkers present. One of them whistled slowly through a gap in his teeth, his dark face was sympathetic.

'Now, I've not seen blistees like that for a good long while. Never you worry Grena will get you the alepot and her bucket of traveller's ease – we'll have you smiling in no time.'

The rest of the men echoed the sentiment. They all remarked on the exceptionally poor condition of Tommo's feet, the wicked sharpness of the stony surface of the Macalley road and the necessity for stout leather shoes for walking any distance in the winter. With all his other problems Tommo had barely noticed the pain in his feet and whatever Tommo had expected it was not kindness. He felt that prickling behind his eyes again.

A boy of about seven came to take the mule to the rough wooden stable next to the snug. Tommo panicked briefly about the birds, but they must have flown away while the men were talking. He hoped they'd have the sense to stay out of sight in a place which, if Akenna was right, had little to do with thaumaturgy and where bird-catchers were at large.

Grena turned out to be a woman of massive proportions and all-embracing hospitality. Within moments she had found Tommo a wooden three-legged stool of the kind his mother's servant had used to milk their cow. She thrust a large flagon of spiced black ale into his shaking hand, steadying him slightly with work-roughened fingers. Before he could argue she had lifted his muddy feet into an enamel bowl of warm water and used a sponge to rub away the dirt. She was gentler than he'd feared.

'You can tell a lot from feet,' she said enigmatically. His feet, free of their coating of sludge and blood, shone with the inner sparkle of grind-dust. Tommo tensed, ready for whatever she would say next, but she said nothing, only brought him another bowl, filled with a warm, milky substance that smelled of aromatic herbs, some of which he recognised from Sibeal's cottage. The warm liquid stung his open cuts and the tender skin beneath his blisters, but then soothed and relaxed him, which was quite an achievement, given his circumstances.

'I've no coin yet – I'm waiting for my friend,' he whispered awkwardly in Grena's ear.

'I know, lad,' she said. 'She won't be long neither.' Her uneven smile lit by the diffused glow from the fire transformed her face, which otherwise resembled a round loaf of pot-bread, into something beautiful. He could not help but smile back.

'I see you've got some of those pretty birds with you. I had a blackbird with the face of one of Urtha's own, but a few days ago he upped and went. You'll want to keep them hidden from the bird-catcher. He's after catching every last thing with wings. Some say he's even started on the bats and the butterflies. Tell them birds of yours to fly high and keep their faces turned to the skies.'

Tommo didn't really know what to say. He drank his fill of the spiced ale and felt himself drift off into a kind of a dream. He hadn't eaten much and the northern brew was more potent than its western equivalent. In moments he was asleep.

When he woke all the other drinkers had gone and the only sound was that of the snores of the sleepers in the snug. Someone had removed his feet from the chilled water and covered him in a blanket that smelled strongly of cats. He felt a firm hand on his shoulder and a shape the size of a mountain loomed before him. It took him a moment to remember where he was and a moment longer to recognise the intimidating form as belonging to Grena.

'You'll want to go now,' she said firmly. 'There's trouble coming for you and trouble's already come for your friend.' She pushed something into his hand – a cloth wrapping what felt like a sizeable hunk of bread.

'I've no coin –' he began.

'You can pay me when you come this way again, as you surely must,' she said. 'Go quickly. I don't want trouble here. Your mule is ready.'

He began to thank her, but she cut him short. 'Save your breath, boy. You'll need it and a better friend to you might have hidden you in the warm rather than sending you into danger. I do what I can afford to do. Now go on!'

He got to his feet and she thrust a pair of worn boots into his hands.

'By the Hand, may Unga's warmth keep you and Urtha's light guide you!' she said, softly. It was not an expression he had heard before. He put the boots on – they were not going to help his blisters but they had to be an improvement on walking barefoot on the cold and stony road. Tommo regretted that he had nothing to give Grena. So few people had been generous to him in recent years. He thought such kindness would have been worth his last haver, if he'd got any havers at all.

CHAPTER TWENTY-SIX

Fallon was surprised by just how relieved he was to see Haver-snatcher again, the more so as he had a former priestess of the Inward Power with him. He had thought they were all long dead.

'Sibeal, welcome to the Fortress of Winter. I understand that you know what is expected of you,' he said with a smile that could chill sunshine.

The woman nodded, calmly. 'I have known that for many years, Fallon.'

But Fallon was not interested in her response. He ignored her and continued, 'I usually find out what I want to know, but I imagine you know that already.'

'I know that you intend to kill me and that if you do that you will regret it for ever,' Sibeal answered with some spirit.

Fallon laughed with genuine mirth. 'That's a good try, witch, but I'm not so easily frightened.'

Sibeal's face did not change. 'Do not misunderstand me, Protector. That was not a threat to encourage you to keep me alive, but a true vision of the secret sight. There are many roads to the future. The one you walk that has me dead is the worst of all possible roads for you. I would be going against my calling as well as my own best path if I did not warn you.'

'And you want me to believe that your own survival means nothing to you?'

'I don't ask you to believe anything – the truth does not depend on your belief.'

Fallon nodded. 'Mother of Urtha that's true enough,' he muttered. His factotum, Lord Awnan, hung back anxiously: all the servants in the fortress were nervous of unpredictable thaumaturgy and the even more unpredictable temper of the Protector. Fallon let the dramatic silence stretch on. Silence was a powerful instrument. Most people fidgeted or blurted out anything to fill it, but Sibeal waited for him to speak quite impassively. 'Oh, take her away,' he said impatiently, breaking the silence first; he hated witches and all thaumaturgy.

Fallon allowed himself to relax a little. Haver-snatcher had come back. He was not causing him trouble in the country. He had done what Fallon had asked of him. Fallon had gambled on Haver-snatcher's love for his daughter, his first such gamble in a long time. If Haver-snatcher had escaped the Protectorate or betrayed him, Fallon caught himself wondering if he could have found it in himself to punish the proud, cold beauty he had married for the sins of her father. He was glad not to have been put to the test. Sometimes when Vevena gave him that look of scarcely controlled contempt and her pale eyes flashed he thought that killing her would be a pleasure. Other times, when she did not know he was looking at her, when the icy mask seemed to thaw for a minute, he wanted to know the woman hidden by the power of the thaumaturgical curse, and by her own compromised, but still powerful will. He feared that he had gambled too recklessly because if Haver-snatcher had not returned he would have had to punish Vevena as publicly and painfully as possible, and it would have broken his heart.

Fallon therefore greeted Haver-snatcher warmly and was even prepared to accept Haver-snatcher's excuses for his failure to bring him the escaped apprentice. Instead he poured him a generous measure of fine wine and dismissed all his other attendants besides his several bodyguards and Lord Awnan.

Although Fallon knew he ought not make any concessions to his old friend, he was so mollified by his return that he felt that he could afford to be bounteous and even had Vevena called for. She was dressed in a gown of rich, wine-coloured velvet embroidered with rubies and emeralds. Her face lit up when she saw her father and just for a moment Fallon got one of those tantalising glimpses of that other warm Vevena, the beauty with a loving heart. Her face closed down again the second she saw him looking at her.

'Father,' she said.

Haver-snatcher nodded in acknowledgement. 'I see you have adorned her loveliness in yet more riches.'

'As my wife she deserves nothing less,' Fallon replied pompously. 'Vevena, it would be best if you returned to your needlework.' Vevena's expression was veiled but was not warm. He could not help but watch her walking, the way her unbound hair swung shining like a shawl of silk. She was too much on his mind. Fallon got a grip of himself.

'Haver-snatcher, I meant to tell you. I visited the dungeons after your release. They were in sore need of cleansing. I had the remaining prisoners killed in a kind of winter clean. I thought you'd like to know.'

Haver-snatcher's face darkened and Fallon knew he had scored a direct hit. He wanted no allies of Haver-snatcher surviving incarceration. Haver-snatcher had perhaps harboured other ideas. 'Now tell me about the boy.'

Haver-snatcher took a noisy gulp of dark wine. It dribbled unattractively down his chin and he wiped it away with the back of his hand.

'Well, I would have caught and killed him –' Haver-snatcher hesitated long enough to wipe his face with the back of his hand and leant forward eagerly in his chair, like a man sharing an enthusiasm – 'but this is the big news: you were right. He is a thaumaturgist! I will need to go back with a cohort of men.'

'Oh no you don't,' Fallon answered, too quickly. He would not trust Haver-snatcher that far. 'You are sure that the boy has power?' Fallon said, disturbed his own Urtha-blessed guts had not lied. Fallon drummed his fingers on the table distractedly. His own lack of thaumaturgical skill was his greatest weakness. He had contrived to keep almost all the spellstone magic under his control, but he feared hidden thaumaturgical talent almost as much as he had always feared Gildea and his as yet undiscovered agents.

Fallon took a delicate sip from the chased-gold and jewelled goblet in front of him. 'Perhaps I should send out a spellstone wielder to trap him?'

'That might work,' Haver-snatcher belched flamboyantly and reached forward to take more wine. 'It might work,' he repeated, 'though I suppose you would have to trust the spellstone wielder. From what I hear most of them were minor priests in the Priesthood of the Inward Power themselves, so there's always a danger that they may be able to show the boy a trick or two.'

Fallon knew that Haver-snatcher was deliberately trying to unsettle him, and he had – mainly because it was true. Those with some thaumaturgical talent, former priests of the Inward Power, got better results when they handled spellstones. Almost all the registered spellstone wielders were indeed the least gifted former priests, whom the pox had spared. Fallon did not trust any of them.

There was a silence between the two men only broken by the persistent drumming of Fallon's fingers against the fine inlay of the table.

'He is still alive, isn't he?' Haver-snatcher said softly.

'Who?'

'Your old enemy.' The statement hung there as a kind of challenge.

Fallon shook his head. 'No. He died last night. He is already buried.'

'You did not allow him to be burnt then, to become one with the ethereal presence of Urtha?' Haver-snatcher sounded surprised. It was usual to honour the deceased by disposing of their body according to the tenets of their allegiances in life – burying those of Unga so the earth might feed on the body and burning those of Urtha so the spiritual realm might feed off the soul.

Fallon laughed. 'He was up to something with those birds that came to his cage. Every day they came and every day he grew weaker and his wits more enfeebled. Curse him and may Urtha never taste his soul!'

Fallon stopped his diatribe abruptly – there was no point in letting Haver-snatcher realise the full depth of his fear and hatred of Gildea. He signalled for Lord Awnan to call for some sweetmeats. He wanted Haver-snatcher to know just how far he had come, that he could have an aristocratic Name wait on him.

Haver-snatcher greedily stuffed a sweetmeat into his mouth and chewed it noisily. He scraped the delicate, gold-leafed chair, which had once belonged to King Braduff the First, back across the marble of the floor so that it set Fallon's stretched nerves on edge. Fallon knew perfectly well that Haver-snatcher's every gesture was calculated to annoy, to remind him that he too was an uncouth commoner with the manners of a street runner. When Haver-snatcher got to his feet to pace the room, Fallon noted his small half-smile of amusement as the guards suddenly jumped to attention. For some reason that annoyed him too.

'I don't understand. Why does it matter that birds came to his cage?' Haver-snatcher asked.

He still had a kind of unpredictable power about him that bothered Fallon. Haver-snatcher was like a great bull which, injured and maddened, might still charge. Fallon should have used the sense he was born with and kept him locked up.

Fallon gently rolled the red wine around the inside of the goblet to release the greatest flavour. He had left the gutter far behind and Haver-snatcher would not bring him back to it. 'It meant something, but Kalen claims he knows nothing that might help, for in all the writings of Gildea he never mentioned birds.'

'And you trust Kalen?'

The Protector laughed and dribbled a little, his lips were feeling slightly numb.

He had drunk more than was usual for him, as though the presence of his boyhood friend had returned him to the state of a callow youth who did not know when he had had enough. He cleared his throat. 'I don't think a wise man in my position trusts anyone,' he said pompously, 'though I have his daughter kept close, and fathers are so much more cautious where daughters are involved, don't you think?'

Haver-snatcher's expression changed. Fallon could see his great bull's neck, thinner than of old but still powerful, flush. Fallon shivered.

'And do you trust me enough to do your bidding in this important matter and root out this apprentice and his associates?'

'He has associates?'

'Certainly, but I need some kind of power to root them out.'

'You have your own wits, Haver-snatcher, let that be enough.'

'I need assurance that you will not harm Vevena.'

'Vevena is my legal wife in a three-heir dynastic contract, signed, sealed and witnessed. I will do with her as I see fit.' The wine was beginning to make him feel sleepy. He had been a fool to drink so much with Haver-snatcher there. Haver-snatcher had always been able to drink Fallon under the table.

'You have to give me your word that you'll keep Vevena safe.'

Fallon pulled a face. 'I don't have to do anything – I'm the Protector, remember? Besides I can't promise that – I need to ensure your loyalty.'

'Unga-under-all, Fallon, I have done nothing to deserve your poisonous enmity for a long while. Promise me you won't harm Vevena.'

'Oh, very well then.'

'Let Unga's curse be on you if you are lying,' Haver-snatcher said gravely.

Fallon sighed melodramatically. 'Yes, yes, I accept all the usual twaddle.' He spat on his hand, as did Haver-snatcher, and then they pressed their palms together as if about to arm wrestle, before shaking hands. Fallon surreptitiously smoothed his robe with his hand.

'When did you get so grand that you have to wipe a smear of good old swear-spit off your lily-like hands?' Haver-snatcher sneered. He was feeling wild and reckless. 'Now tell me when did the birds come to Gildea and how many were there?'

Fallon ignored Haver-snatcher's question. He was not so drunk as to tell Haver-snatcher anything of any importance. Why had he ever agreed to release him? Ah yes, Vevena. That plan had worked well: since he'd released Haver-snatcher Vevena could barely resist his charms. There was no avoiding the conclusion that releasing his old friend had been a mistake and if the worst Fallon got from it was a very bad hangover he would have got off lightly.

CHAPTER TWENTY-SEVEN

Haver-snatcher took another deep draught of wine and watched Fallon surreptitiously. He was unused to drink himself these days and felt himself becoming drowsy, which was most definitely not the plan. He glanced around the spinning hall at the richness of the wall hangings and rugs, at the elaborate carving on Fallon's chair and the well-armed soldiers standing to eager attention at every corner of the room. Although a vast fire roared in a grate the size of his ma's main room, the hall was not exactly cosy. He wondered whether Fallon had, in achieving more than he ever expected, somehow ended up with less than he might have wanted: a beautiful enchanted princess who hated him and the onerous responsibility of a Protectorate to rule. It was an odd kind of triumph. Fallon should have stuck to thieving and general villainy – this was a step too far. There were scrolls and scrolls of paper at Fallon's feet. By Unga's arse, Fallon had even had to read and reckon, skills which Haver-snatcher had picked up only in the dungeon when there had been nothing else to do. He watched the Protector fall into a drooling sleep. Lord Awnan eyed them both cautiously.

'Sir, I . . .'

'It's all right, man,' Haver-snatcher said, reassuringly. 'Does he never drink too much these days? When we were lads together back in the bad old days of the Convocation, it happened all the time.'

Lord Awnan looked uncertain, caught between his fear for his future when Fallon woke and his fear for his present in the face of the bulky presence of Haver-snatcher.

'Don't worry about it,' Haver-snatcher added, wondering whether it was entirely wise for Fallon to have surrounded himself with foppish weaklings like Lord Awnan. He was not at all sure that were he Fallon he could have put up with them. Haver-snatcher left the hall with a nod to the guards. He half expected the guards to follow him, arrest him, finish him – they were fools not to. He sighed and rubbed his face to wake himself up. He was getting too old for this game and the dungeon had taken its toll.

There was too much he didn't know – he was playing jackaroo with half the dice set missing. He calculated that Fallon should sleep for a while and that there should be time to see Kalen alone. He was challenged several times on the way to the Chief Spellstone Wielder's college – a set of rooms that overlooked the garden. Lord Awnan, too nervous to arrest him outright had sent guards of Fallon's personal cohort to shadow his every move and the ordinary guards were anxious to show that they too knew their business. However, Haver-snatcher was known to be an old friend of Fallon's, father of the Protector's wife and an honoured guest who had brought in the witch Sibeal; the guards given no direction from their superiors could find no suitable reason for restricting his access to any part of the fortress.

Haver-snatcher finally found Kalen in the garden. He did not seem happy to see Haver-snatcher if his pained expression was anything to go by.

'So, I brought in your wife, Kalen. Was it good to see her after so many years?'

Kalen looked startled, fearful, as if Haver-snatcher's reputation might be deserved.

'I d-don't know what you mean,' he stammered unconvincingly. Not for the first time Haver-snatcher was grateful for his ma's long memory and still sharp wits. She alone seemed to remember that Sibeal's husband had done rather well for himself and become Chief Spellstone Wielder.

'So what game are you playing and is Sibeal in it with you?'

'I don't know what you're talking about,' Kalen said, fingering the grubby fur of his cloak.

'I've seen Gildea's face on wild birds all over the Protectorate, Kalen. And Fallon tells me he is dead? This has the stink of thaumaturgy and my nose is as keen as ever it was.'

Haver-snatcher spoke softly. Cowards like Kalen often found that more threatening and he had the satisfaction of seeing Kalen suppress a shudder. He didn't do badly – most likely only an experienced interrogator like Haver-snatcher would have noticed. The shudder told him that Kalen probably knew, or had guessed, that it had been Haver-snatcher who had sought out all the most gifted in the Inward Power and informed Fallon, so that the blue pox would do its worst where it would do most damage.

'Tell me your game, Kalen, or I could expose your dangerous secrets to Fallon.

'He knows the precise whereabouts of the rest of your family, the condition of their health and the precise distance from their house to the gibbet. You have a daughter, don't you? I'm certain that you would not want to endanger her. Don't think your position keeps you safe. There is always someone else wanting the honour of being Fallon's Chief Spellstone Wielder. Do you understand?'

The Chief Spellstone Wielder nodded and, though he lost his colour so that his face became the grey of wood ash, he seemed to regain his composure. 'That is all very well, but I still don't know what you are talking about.'

'You are trembling.'

'You are an intimidating man, Haver-snatcher, and your years in the dungeon have not made you any the less so.'

It was perhaps true enough. Haver-snatcher grabbed the skinny spellstone wielder by the throat and slammed him hard against the nearest tree, a broad-trunked oak that was for some reason a vivid and unnatural scarlet. Haver-snatcher could not help but enjoy the feeling of power his strength gave him. He could feel the pulse of the man's thin neck, beating under his thumb, and knew he could squeeze out the life in him as easily as his ma wrung out her washing. He had always favoured throttling as a method of killing, it was so intimate somehow. Kalen's fear-filled eyes bulged and Haver-snatcher almost didn't stop, but then he heard the jingle of chain mail and the hiss of a sword being unsheathed and he let the man regain his feet.

'Just a friendly chat,' Haver-snatcher said to the guardsman. 'You know how it is? You've not seen a man to talk to for years and your feelings get the better of you.' The young guardsman swallowed noticeably. Haver-snatcher could see the concern in his eyes – was Haver-snatcher the Protector's dearest friend or his most dangerous enemy? Did he dare arrest a man who might be working for Fallon? Haver-snatcher turned on his smile. His looks were not what they were, but his smile could still promise friendship and warmth, could still disarm a man or a woman faster than his quick right arm. He patted Kalen's shoulder as if he were a friend from way back, and for some reason Kalen played along, merely clearing his throat and coughing fit to croak, but not instructing the guardsman to take action. He waved the guard away and managed some kind of grimace that made his thin face crease in a hundred unlikely places.

'All is well – it is as he said!' The guardsman sheathed his sword and stepped back out of earshot, if not out of bow shot.

'You can frighten me all you want, Haver-snatcher, but I am loyal to Fallon. I kept Gildea under guard and supervised his imprisonment. I witnessed his torture and his decline, and I never saw him use thaumaturgy. There is no plan of which I am a part, and if I knew of one Fallon would be told.' He sounded hoarse but convincing and Haversnatcher considered him critically. Would such a man risk his skinny neck when he had power and influence under Fallon?

He thought it unlikely. He had no evidence against Sibeal either, so their forgotten marriage was no proof of sedition. It had been worth a try and a little bit of intimidation made him feel much more his old self. He needed to spend a little more time out in the world, tracking down the apprentice, working out who had the potential to overthrow Fallon. He would start with finding the girl, Akenna, the one who'd been with Sibeal. The birds had defended her. Something was going on, he was sure, and he wanted to be part of it, to subvert it to his own ends.

CHAPTER TWENTY–EIGHT

Tommo walked the cold Macalley road in his borrowed shoes until his feet bled, then he rode it on the bony-backed mule until dawn broke. He knew it wasn't far to Broadford, but it seemed a long way to him. He had no idea what to expect and no idea what to do, but Grena had been very sure that Akenna was in trouble, or at least he thought she had been. He wished now that he'd asked her what she'd meant by her warning instead of meekly doing as he was told.

He didn't really know what he was doing, blundering his way to Broadford in the hope of rescuing Akenna from some unknown danger – as if he could help! He wished he'd been able to persuade her that they were better staying together, but he hadn't and now there was nothing else for him to do but to try to find her. He was out of the borough at last, so there was less risk of being hanged as an outlaw and more risk of being stoned to death; in a borough that banned the works of spellstones his skin alone was a provocation. He could not weigh up which was worse and so tried not to think about either.

He passed several low stone houses.

It was barely light, but the home fires were all kindled and wood smoke and cooking smells drifted in the air. They were up and about their business early in Broadford. As he passed one of the cottages an old woman hailed him enthusiastically and tried to sell him some bits of needle-work, while her yet more elderly neighbour tried to flog him some old bits of sheep's wool, the kind of bits and pieces that caught on thistles and thorns in sheep country. When he stopped to explain that he had no havers, he had a sudden debilitating bout of trembling and dizziness which had the wool seller ushering him indoors.

'Urtha's arms, legs and heart of warmth, come inside and you're welcome to a drop of cornmeal porridge which I've on the go. Nobody can trudge the Macalley road on a hollow stomach and you're pale enough to pass away altogether. Leave the beast there. My neighbour will keep an eye on him. There's water in the pail.' She fed him a generous half of the meagre contents of her porridge pot and waved away his thanks when he left. 'Put it down to Urtha's account, grandfather, and when you make it to her door, put a good word in her listening ear for fat Bertho from Broadford.'

Kindness was like rain in a dry spell, after so many years of brutality: it made him smile in spite of everything. Tommo felt more optimistic leaving Bertho's cottage than he had for a while.

Although the house was dim and the woman was not

overly intelligent, she had not noticed his skin or his other peculiarities and that gave him a measure of confidence to overcome his next obstacle – getting through Broadford.

Even so, he checked that his oilskin cloak wrapped round him tightly and did his best to keep his head down and his face partially covered by hair. He found a fallen branch of just the right height and thickness for a staff, and leaning on that thought he gave a fair impression of an old man bent by age, leading his mule behind him. He kept his steps small and careful, which was easy because he feared at any moment a severe attack of the quivers that would make his pretence of weakness no pretence at all. Perhaps he might not be caught, perhaps he might be able to help Akenna – if only he could find her.

He could smell the distinctive dank, almost metallic, tang of weed and slow water, the pungent stench of silty river mud, so guessed he was nearing the ford of the river. He did not know if it was a good sign that he could see no birds flying above the water, and hoped that it wasn't because the bird-catcher had caught them all.

It was market day and as the day brightened the road thronged with people cheerfully hailing each other and driving pack-laden mules. It was clear that Broadford was a thriving town and he must have seen twenty or thirty people coming his way, each offering him a polite 'Hoya!' in the peculiar accent of the region. He nodded his reply in what he thought was an appropriately elderly fashion.

Cottages bordered both sides of the road and beyond

them he could spot the fishers' bothies. The smells became more intense. At least five of the cottages bore the sigil of a clenched fist, which marked them as brewers and snugs, and the air there was tainted with stale hops and spiced ale. Further on it was all fish guts and the tang of the smoking boxes where the fish were smoked for sale. To his right there was a gap in the cottages so that the way was open to the riverbank and a path of large stones laid across the mud and shingle continued across the breadth of the shallow river. The cottages near this part of the road needed no sign to indicate their trade; the smell of fish was powerful and drying nets and fishing paraphernalia spilled out into the street.

On the other side of the street, the road itself formed one side of a cobbled square. It was busy enough to be confusing. To his guilty eyes the square was dominated by the wooden gibbet, mounted on a platform in the centre. A thick rope hung from it and swung a little in the light wind. He swallowed hard, blessed Urtha keep him from that fate. As was traditional, one half of the square was stained a dark red – to mark Unga's end of the market dedicated to the works of the flesh: to butchered meat and fish, to the gutters and the animal slaughterers and to the forge, the farrier, the chandler and the body burner, the teeth pullers and the muck sellers, even in some places the mattress-girls of Unga's watch. On the other half of the square, washed white by lime, lay the old Thaumaturgical Chapel, the local physicker and the Sheriff's manse. When

Tommo was a child there would have been a school at the Chapel dedicated to the study of thaumaturgical gifts, but these days it would be a fortunate town which even had a place to learn reading, runes and reckoning.

It was disconcerting to be in such a bustling crowd. Tommo had forgotten that noisy hymn to life in the spellgrinder's cellar. Everyone was shouting, shooing away stray dogs, singing out the day's prices, gossiping.

He spotted a bird-catcher by a stall stacked with wicker cages and he went cold. Surely he hadn't caught any of the human-faced birds? He felt sick at the thought. There was a rough trestle table with a couple of dozen bird carcasses laid out in a gruesome display. He had to force himself to walk up to the man's stall and peer at his bloody wares, but he had to know. The birds' wings were splayed out on the table in a mockery of soaring flight, their beaks were all turned to one side. They all had beaks. None of them had faces. Tommo let out a shaky sigh. The bird-catcher was an old man in a dark cloak, his one eye took in Tommo's shabbiness at a glance, and he didn't pause in his animated conversation with a peddler, some old-time quack selling third-night charms.

'Yep, the fortress wants the lot.' He spat. 'Protector's got to have what he's got to have. That's sure enough. He wants them for a fourth-night feast. It's nothing to me what he wants them for, so long as they pay me.'

'I heard you had spellstone birds,' the peddler said, with just the right degree of disapproval to get the bird-catcher started on what was clearly a preferred topic of conversation. 'I did. Some acolyte of one of Unga's demons from the depths let them free. I'm not saying such creatures should ever have been made, but once made I don't see why I shouldn't gain from them, and but for that lad I would have done too. I've lost some havers over them I can tell you, may White Urtha bless us and keep us all.' He added this last with mock piety.

Tommo pretended a sudden interest in his mule's ear in case eavesdropping was frowned on in this part of the Spine. He wanted to ask what became of Unga's demon's acolyte – a fair enough description of Akenna as he'd heard. He was as certain as he could be that seeing any of their birds in cages she'd have tried to set them free. In the end it was not necessary for him to ask the bird-catcher anything, as one of his customers, a hard-faced woman buying a brace of song birds, answered him.

'But I heard you handed the brat over, so the day didn't go all Unga's way.'

'Well, no, the Sheriff took him for what he'd done to me – freeing my birds, wrecking my living. But what's gone is gone.' The bird-catcher sounded angry still and his face was flushed with temper and with ale – a dangerous combination, particularly so early in the day – but the woman was one of Urtha's own, the argumentative kind not given to letting an untruth go unremarked.

'Well, you know what we hereabouts think of that. Losing demons of vile sorcery will do you no harm. I don't mind telling you straight, for all that I'm fond of braised-lark pie, I wouldn't be buying these birds off a hawker dealing in thaumaturgy. We've hanged men for less in Broadford.' Tommo did not wait to hear the bird-catcher's response to that. He now knew what kind of trouble Akenna was in. All he had to do was to find the Sheriff's gaol and release her.

CHAPTER TWENTY-NINE

Kalen let out a long sigh when Haver-snatcher left. He was shaking as though he'd spent the day spellstone wielding and had to steady himself on the red oak. Long ago when he'd trained in thaumaturgy they had done breathing exercises to focus the will and steady the nerves. He had little enough will left, but his nerves needed all the help they could get. He closed his eyes to banish his vision of Haver-snatcher's violet eyes boring into him. The physical pain worried him less than the memory of his fear. He was braver than he looked, as any spellstone wielder had to be. It hurt to use the stones, and the greater the user's thaumaturgic gifts the greater the pain. The spellstones made his bones ache and shake, and his body was covered in burns from misdirected power and the undeniable malice of the stones. Neither Fallon nor Haver-snatcher understood what a spellstone wielder battled with and it was well they did not or perhaps they might respect him more: the respect of the likes of Fallon and Haver-snatcher was something to be avoided.

Kalen was so busy trying to find the heart of Urtha's

inner calm inside his own tumultuous heart that he failed to notice Vevena's arrival in the garden. She was suddenly there like a spirit or an image of White Urtha herself.

As she came to stand beside him he could not help but notice that her face was wet with tears and Kalen found himself wiping them away with his fingers, a degree of intimacy he surely ought to have avoided with the Protector's wife and Haver-snatcher's daughter, whose violet eyes resembled her father's all too closely.

'There, there,' he said to her as though to a child.

'He is dead, isn't he?' she said at last, in a faraway sing-song voice. Perhaps the curse was making her mad. It would have destroyed a lesser woman long ago, of that Kalen was sure. How much reality seeped through the sorcery? He remembered the diamond ring and shuddered: at least one man had died because she could still remember how to trick.

'Who, heart's ease?' he said lightly, though he feared he already knew the answer. He let his hand fall from her face, which was soft as rose petals and similarly fragranced.

'The toffee man, in the blue like larkspur,' Vevena said. He knew that she meant Gildea and felt suddenly cold.

'Yes, beauty, he is dead and we are all doomed if his plan has failed, as I fear it must have done. There will be no victory – only Fallon, your dearly beloved, imprisoning people and having them killed, and pursuing his whims and keeping us from contact with anywhere else until – oh, until he dies, I expect.' He had not meant to speak so frankly or to let quite so much bitterness creep into his voice. Fallon's spies were everywhere and it was not impossible that they could be overheard or that somehow Vevena might remember that Kalen had threatened Fallon. He swallowed hard.

Vevena's pale, slim hand sought his and squeezed it gently. He had forgotten gentleness. He did not know how to interpret the gesture, for she was still as ensorcelled as any woman had ever been.

They sat down by common but unspoken consent on the coiled tail of a silver dragon, twisted into the form of a seat. The air was cool and damp as though rain might fall at any time. The damp made Vevena's long hair curl in tiny ringlets around her face and the cold gave her pale face a rosy glow of health. Vevena did not look at him, but traced the outline of the roses embroidered on her overdress with her nail, a slight frown of concentration puckering the smooth perfection of her face. Kalen did not know why he chose to tell what he had never told another soul, perhaps because she too was a soul trapped, the one person who could not betray him since her silence was part of Gildea's plan. Somehow he felt he owed it to her to explain.

He was not entirely a fool however and he drew out of his inner robe a small yellow-hued spellstone shaped like a giant arrow head. Vevena recoiled and he felt it buzz and hum with sufficient power to hide them both from view, to lose them and their voices in a mist of obscurity. It was one of the secret powers of spellstones he had been careful to keep from Fallon and from his own acolytes.

Vevena's eyes looked a little wild as though she was aware of the sudden expenditure of power that made his hands shake and beaded his forehead in a cold sweat. It would pass soon enough. He slipped the spellstone back into his inner robe pocket, and wiped his hands on his grubby outer robe. It made no difference: the strangeness of the stone's touch could not be wiped away.

'Oh, Gildea,' he sighed. 'He was my mentor, Gildea – your toffee man – High Priest of the Inward Power, philosopher, thaumaturgist and so much else.' He found that there were tears in his eyes as he spoke, tears he'd never shed and maybe never could. 'He never rested. He always wanted to understand what for most of us simply was. Long before he was imprisoned, when Sibeal and I were still together, he had been experimenting with what he called the "fragmentation of the soul", a way of transferring the Urthene essence of himself into other Ungine bodies.'

'Rosemary and lavender, cowslips and cabbage flowers,' Vevena sang softly, still tracing the pattern on her lovely dress with her lovelier finger.

'After Fallon had him captured at Tipplehead, he was so badly beaten, I was afraid he would not live. He was old and ill, even before the attack, and in need of a stronger, younger body. I tried to help. I took risks, honestly I did. I tried to find him a new Ungine body. I tried all manner of corpses.' Kalen suppressed a shudder. Finding corpses had been easy enough in Fallon's fortress, but their condition had made him sick with fear for what Fallon might do to him if he were discovered. He got temporarily lost in unpleasant reminiscences, but Vevena nudged him slightly by accident as she played with the flowers on her dress. 'Where was I? Oh yes, I tried to make those bodies fit for Gildea, with all the spellstone magic we could muster, with prayers and sacrifices to Unga-under-all-flesh, all done in secret here in the fortress, but it never worked. They rotted without Unga's animating spirit and Gildea could not enter them.' He glanced at Vevena to see if she understood a word of what he said, but he was safe: her expression remained unchanged, perplexed by the complexity of the embroidery before her. He carried on: 'Somehow, alone in that cage, Gildea learnt how to divide his Urthene essence into smaller portions and house it in other creatures, so that its own Urthene essence was not wholly usurped and Unga still made the creature live. Gildea entrusted fragments of his Urthene essence to many of the birds of the Protectorate so that little by little he escaped his spellstone cage. He saved the key to his true Urthene self until last. When that left his body, his Ungine flesh died. The golden eagle holds the key – I saw it fly to his cage and take what was left of the man I thought had the answer to everything. I think I was a fool.

'If Fallon's bird-catchers have caught that bird, there is no hope.' Vevena looked at him and smiled without apparent understanding. He smiled back. 'Thanks to Fallon and the zeal of the bird-catchers the eagle might be gone, all the birds might be dead and all the wisdom of Gildea gone for ever.

'I never wanted him to do it that way. I wanted a proper plan, but Gildea came to believe that his own fate was tied up with the eternal battle for dominance between Urtha and Unga, the realm of the soul and the realm of the material. He scattered his soul to the winds in the hope that Urtha and Unga would, between them, determine his fate. He refused to make any arrangements, refused to let me make other arrangements. He ensorcelled you so that you could not interfere – he saw something strong in you that would not leave his fate to the will of Urtha and Unga and the flight of a few hundred birds.' The tears he thought would never fall were running down his cheek unchecked. 'I am so sorry, Vevena, for what was done to you. It was done with my help and I am ashamed now, but I truly believed that Gildea knew what was best for all of us. Now I do not know what to think and I am in despair.'

Vevena's fingers wiped his cheeks, as he had wiped hers a few moments before. She met his eyes, for a moment intelligence gleamed and then she spoke.

'Spring flowers are never quite what you expect,' she said and shrugged. 'They come and the world is different. Spring flowers in the garden would be pretty,' she added, 'and they look so well with white silk.'

Kalen patted her hand, grateful that she could not understand him and sorrowful that such a strong soul should be brought to such idiocy.

CHAPTER THIRTY

Tommo crossed the market square to the only building large enough to be the Sheriff's manse. A woman in a widow's pale yellow scarf was in loud conversation with a companion about her neighbour's provoking ways. It was clear that she had some kind of complaint to register. Tommo allowed her to step into the Sheriff's chamber first and then followed, trying to keep her substantial frame between himself and the Sheriff.

He felt very uncomfortable to be back in such a place. The room followed the traditional layout for a Sheriff's chamber with lime-washed walls, a wooden law-lectern and a gaol – a small cell accessed by a single, solid wooden door. It was exactly like the manse in Tipplehead where he had sought sanctuary. The cell door reminded him of the dark door to his own cellar and he felt a familiar lurch of fear in his innards. He felt so diminished, so worthless and insignificant, he was barely surprised to be ignored by the woman in yellow and the Sheriff, to whom she was talking in very loud and self-righteous tones. He held on to his old man's stick for no better reason than the vague sense of

security it gave him and took a closer look at the cell door –
it was of strong, thick wood and it would take more than his
own insubstantial bulk to batter it down, even if he could
find a way to get rid of the Sheriff while he did it. He risked
a glance at the Sheriff who was dressed in his working robes
of dark green, embroidered with the interlocked symbols of
Red Unga and White Urtha which represented the perfect
balance between flesh and spirit. The Sheriff was listening
intently to the widow's noisy grievances with an air of
professional patience. He did not seem to have noticed
Tommo. The keys to the cell door dangled from a nail on
the wall behind his law-lectern. Tommo moved casually in
their direction, while pretending that he was merely waiting
his turn for an informal hearing and unhooked the keys as
silently as he could manage. It was not quite silently enough
because the Sheriff glanced in the direction of the sound,
but said nothing. Tommo decided that he should have tried
posing as an old man earlier: it seemed to make him
invisible.

With the keys in his hand he moved insouciantly towards
the cell door and unlocked it. He had only moments to act.
He opened the door just wide enough to slide himself
inside.

He kept his body in the doorway, blocking the interior of
the gaol from view, and kept one hand on the stick so that
he could defend himself if need be – even the thought was
ridiculous. Akenna was not alone in the cell, but he saw her
at once. She was sleeping with her head against the cell wall,

just where the high, barred window spilled most of its light. Two other prisoners – dark, indistinct shapes – were also sleeping in oddly sprawled positions on the floor. The air stank of ale and vomit and he guessed that Akenna's shadowy companions were sleeping off the last night's excesses. He did not dare shout, but leant forward into the cell and shook her gently, then slipped his hand over her mouth. She was instantly awake and biting his palm until she realised who it was. She got stiffly to her feet as though she had been beaten again and was by his side in a stride. She didn't say a word but her smile was broad. Tommo squeezed himself out of the doorway, and Akenna followed, like a wraith, an instant later. Tommo closed the door silently and glanced at the Sheriff who was now making notes into the Ledger of Malfeasance, which was housed in every manse. Akenna was about to bolt, but Tommo restrained her. Hiding her from view with his cloak, he held her arm and hobbled slowly out of the chamber. He unhitched the mule from the post where he'd tethered it and with fingers that trembled more with nerves than with the quivers whispered, 'Don't run – everyone will know there's something wrong. Oh, Unga's feet! If you're seen, someone will report you to the Sheriff. Here, cover yourself in my cloak.'

She shook her head. 'No, you're still glowing – they'll know you're a spellgrinder and probably lynch you on the spot. Why don't you beg for alms? That way everyone will avoid us.'

Much to Tommo's surprise they got away from the square without being challenged, as if two strangers were no longer worthy of attention. No one called out 'Hoya!' and no one gave them any alms. A few duck-girls selling eggs gave a puzzled look in his direction when he called out for alms, but their eyes seemed to slip over him without seeing him. He could almost believe that he had made both of them invisible.

'Thank you,' Akenna said, when they had walked a decent distance from the town and found a traveller's halt with a stone statue in the image of Blessed Urtha by a small stream. Tommo was delighted to see some of their birds flying high overhead again. He wondered what had happened to the rest of them. Akenna didn't look at him, but patted his arm in a casual way that he knew was anything but casual.

He didn't answer, because he could not think of a response that didn't sound embarrassing so instead he changed the subject. 'What happened?'

'I did some gutting and smoking work but then, when the gaffer sent me to get him a pot of ale, I saw the birds – our birds – in the catcher's nets. He'd got maybe twenty of them. I waited until he had them all in cages. I thought he might kill them, then I realised he was going to hang onto them because they had human faces.' She stopped to take a drink at the spring and Tommo could see that in spite of her ordeal she looked better than he had ever seen her, somehow her face looked fuller and less angular, even her hair seemed thicker and less limp. The bruises and abrasions to her face were quite gone.

'You look . . . different,' Tommo said.

'I feel different, I think it's the Inward Power.' The smile she gave him was quite dazzling and most un-Akenna-like – she had been snaggle-toothed but now her teeth were all straight and even. He found that disturbing.

'What do you mean?'

'I'll explain. After I let the birds go, someone called for the Sheriff. There was a big fuss because the human-faced birds were in the borough at all, as they were the work of thaumaturgy. The Sheriff took me to the cell. That wasn't too bad, but after a while the door opened and he threw in two more people.' Akenna's voice tailed off and she looked uncomfortable.

'So?' Tommo prompted.

'Well, one of them was Da and the other Old Garth. As soon as he saw me Da was on me. Old Garth tried to hold him back, but Da's fists were ready. I didn't have time to think and then suddenly he was on the floor just lying there and Old Garth was trying to wake him up.'

'What did you do?'

'I don't know. It must have been thaumaturgy. I thought about how I wanted to hit him harder than he'd ever hit me and then he fell as if I had hit him, but, by Unga-under-all, I never touched him. I didn't move. I was frozen scared when I saw what I'd done, I thought I'd killed him. I was sick where I stood with the shock of it. But Garth said he was still breathing and I'd just knocked him out. Garth was quaking, I could tell by his voice, and he doesn't scare easily. He said he'd rather be hanged for spellstone smuggling than face thaumaturgy. He pulled Da as far away from me as he could and kind of cowered there.' She paused for a moment before continuing. 'Then I knew that I did have power, maybe I'd always had it. It was like discovering that I had an extra hand that had been tied behind my back all these years. I thought I'd better practise using it on something – something useful. I didn't want to break down the door or anything because I didn't want the Sheriff to do me for having thaumaturgy, and I didn't want Old Garth and Da to get out, so I tried to cure myself.'

'But you're not sick,' Tommo said, in surprise.

'I was bruised and not so well grown. Da knocked a couple of teeth out when I was younger, but they've grown back.' She sounded triumphant and Tommo did not know what to say. He was pleased for her, he supposed, but he was still shaking and dying, which made it hard to make a fuss about a couple of knocked out teeth. Besides, Akenna with more power than was to be found in her gutting knife was a frightening idea.

'Maybe I can cure you properly now,' she said.

'Maybe,' he agreed, though he didn't believe it. He was not going to be duped into hoping again.

'What do we do now?' he asked.

Akenna glanced at him. 'You look done in. We could go back to Footsore Farm?' She paused. 'I've been thinking about what Sibeal said. I can't stop thinking about it. We do both have power – so maybe we are supposed to look after the birds like she said. The birds fought for me you know. I am certain we should take them to the Fortress of Winter. They've helped us both. I don't think they should be trapped. There are bird-catchers all over the Protectorate – what if more of the human-faced birds have been caught? I think we should release them all. I owe them a debt. I don't like owing what I can't pay back.'

Tommo opened his mouth to say that he thought she'd lost her wits, but he didn't want to argue with her. What did it matter where he went or what he did – the outcome was going to be the same soon enough? He was all done in, as Akenna put it, and he hadn't the strength to argue. Akenna seemed to hum with energy and vigour and Tommo felt weaker than ever. The triumph of his rescue of her seemed to pale into nothing beside her discovery of her tooth-regenerating power. He nodded wearily and started walking.

CHAPTER THIRTY-ONE

Vevena wandered around the garden thinking only of flowers. She knew that was a bad sign and struggled to remember the source of her fascination with horticulture. She had seen Kalen – that she remembered. He had been sad. There had been tears on his lined face as though someone had died. Someone *had* died. She remembered that too. The man in the cage, the toffee man with the white beard, he had died and some hope that she couldn't quite grasp had died with him.

Her head was immediately filled with irrelevant thoughts about gowns and colour schemes so that she knew that her thinking was on track. A small, undamaged part of herself was able to wait until the fog of sartorial obsession cleared, some part of her was able to float a fragile thread of thought above the tumult of irrelevancy and to hang on to the one word, 'Gildea'.

Perhaps that was why she knew the face when she saw it again, perched incongruously on the body of an eagle with a damaged wing. Blood darkened its plumage and its human face was ashen with pain.

'Gildea,' she said softly, when she saw it. 'You are important, though I don't remember why, but you are beautiful too and I know where I can keep you, safe from everyone, until I do remember. I see you in blue of larkspur, in spellstone glory, bright against the storm clouds in the sky.'

Vevena was not a large woman, but she was wiry and determined, and even the limitations of her thaumaturgical curse could not keep her from this task, though the reason for doing it at all escaped her for much of the time. She hummed a little as she worked, songs that would take the ensorcelled part of her mind away, busy business that would allow a small part of her to do what was needful, against all the odds. She constructed a kind of a stretcher – two longish branches to which she tied her cloak of dark red velvet.

'You must let me lie you on this,' she told the bird, which groaned a little with a human voice at the pain. The poor thing was as incapable of thought as she was and tried to elude her, hopping away and beating its one whole wing as if to ward her away. Its talons were sharp but its lack of a beak was a grave disadvantage and eventually she managed to chase it so it stood on her velvet cloak. There were some unseasonal spellstone berries on the silver-boughed trees of Kalen's creation and she gathered a few and laid them on her cloak so that the poor bird struggled and strained to eat them with its human mouth.

That day Vevena had worn a thick veil of gossamer-fine silk, as was her custom when she got tired of the endless bold-eyed stares at the Unga-cursed peculiarity of form that men called beauty. While the bird was distracted she unfurled the veil so that the light made it ripple like a stream and then she cast it like a net on the water to catch not a fish but a bird. Somehow she contrived, after several vain attempts, to wrap the bird in it and lay it on the cloak so that its wings were pinioned. She was sure it could still breathe as she could breathe when wrapped in its silken folds.

Although she was ensorcelled, she wasn't stupid and once she had completed her task it was clear to her that she would be quite unable to get the bundle past the guards, even were she to flash her eyes and flick her hair from now until the Feast of Urtha. She found herself at a loss. She sat on the hard ground and plucked away at the fabric of her dress, the pattern of which reminded her of something Kalen had said. His words had got tangled in the thorns of the embroidered roses, but she was sure if she tried hard enough she might be able to untangle them.

It was then that Dolina arrived. She was agitated and probably in trouble with Fallon. Anyone with that look of anguish and panic in their eyes had usually found themselves at the receiving end of the Protector's harsh tongue and malevolent stare.

'My lady, the Protector has need of you. Why, what are you doing without cloak or veil? You will surely catch a chill, sitting on the damp ground. Come, come! We must get you inside! Urtha's sweet breasts, what a mess you are in!'

Vevena took the opportunity to appear even more fey and deranged than was the case.

'The beauty, I want it in with the roses and the bright colours of my room,' she said vacantly, pointing at the veiled eagle.

The maidservant gave her a look of barely disguised contempt and turned to the guards who flanked her.

'The Lady Vevena wants you to bring that statue she's wrapped in her veil. Good Urtha alone knows what it is or why she wants it, but it is not for the likes of us to question our betters and may the Blessed Urtha reward us when we knock at her door, for the Protector will not, if we do not get her back to him sharpish and in a more seemly state.'

The guards were staring at Vevena with undisguised astonishment and admiration and Vevena chose that moment to smile. The effect was all too predictable: within moments they had gathered up the eagle and her strange stretcher contraption, and if the trapped eagle fluttered and bated, frightening them under its shroud of pale silk, they were wise enough to say nothing and to carry their burden silently into her chamber.

She did not quite forget about it while she permitted Dolina to robe her in the latest elaborate confection of her dressmaker's overstimulated imagination. Throughout her audience with Fallon her injured mind fluttered around other concerns so that it was not until the evening when she had retired, that she was reminded again of the eagle's existence by the strange noises that came from under her silk veil. The handmaid had drunk too much. She said Vevena drove her to it, to which Vevena said nothing but merely topped up her glass, adding just a little mother's comfort she had found in her husband's chamber and which was such a pretty colour that she thought it would look well in her own room and in Dolina's glass. Had Vevena been able to think, she would have thought that fear of Fallon would have kept the woman more virtuous, but fear seemed to make her worse and as the maidservant snored Vevena remembered and the name Gildea echoed through her memory.

It was a difficult thing devising a plan and keeping it hidden from the part of herself that wanted to think of flowers. It was like riding a one-legged pony blindfolded through snow, but it was not quite impossible. So while the maidservant snored and the eagle muttered, Vevena did her very best to overcome the flowery manacles round her mind and take the eagle to safety. She found a girdle plaited with wool, horsehair and silk, which was strong, as well as being of a colour that accorded well with the eagle's plumage.

When she loosed the eagle from the veil, she clamped her hand over its wet human mouth and cooed to it as if it were a lovebird. Its sea-coloured eyes, caught in the eerie light of a moonbeam, seemed to understand and when she took her hand away it did not make a sound, though tears dampened its wrinkled cheeks and she could feel it shivering with fear. She tied the girdle loosely round its leg as she had seen falconers do, and padding her shoulder with all the quilted fabrics she could find, she lifted it onto her shoulder. The moment the bird's claws bit into her she grasped the flaw in her plan. The bird was heavy, its feathers tickled her ear and its claws were sharp as pincers and would draw blood very quickly, even with the padding.

'Stay still, sweet beauty, please,' she whispered. The bird settled a little, as if it understood. She hoped she had the strength for the necessary and lengthy walk. She tried to lean her head away from the eagle, but it was too awkward and uncomfortable. With her every step the nervous bird gripped Vevena's shoulder more tightly and more painfully until Vevena had to discipline herself not to whimper. The padding was very little use and her flesh felt flayed raw. To keep its balance the eagle kept partially opening its wings only to find itself impeded by the rather necessary presence of Vevena's head. Strangely pain cleared Vevena's mind a little and she was able to elude the guards without resorting to complicated games to persuade herself that she was doing nothing of which her husband would disapprove. For the whole time she fought against the pain, she thought of neither flowers nor gowns, she gave no thought to Fallon or to the curse, but only focused on enduring the pain and getting the eagle to the tower and Gildea's cage where he would be safe, for a time at least.

As Vevena had assumed, neither the stairway nor the tower room was guarded and it was the work of moments to lead the bird into the open cage and close the door. There was food still there and water, which was a mistake on the part of the guards, but a relief to Vevena as she knew it was beyond the limited freedom of her thoughts to arrange anything so long-term as a raid on the kitchens. She arranged the food and water within the eagle's reach. By the morning she would perhaps have forgotten everything. 'May Urtha help me to remember,' she muttered, and she was sure that in the blue light of the spellstone cage she saw the eagle smile.

CHAPTER THIRTY-TWO

As Tommo walked on the quivers began to take a hold again. The shaking wasn't too bad. He was getting used to that but his mind seemed to drift away and he found it hard to concentrate on the simple business of walking.

'Let me try to heal you,' Akenna said, full of her new confidence in her Inward Power.

'Sit down!'

Even that wasn't so easy, as his knees didn't bend properly any more, and he more or less collapsed in a semi-seated position. Akenna grabbed his hand in hers, which was rough and worn with hard labour.

'Close your eyes and let me try to concentrate.'

He would have argued, but it took too much energy. He knew somehow that it would not work and he was determined not to be made a fool of by hoping for a second time. Akenna gripped his hand as tightly as the vice on a grinding wheel and scowled. Wild flowers burst suddenly into unseasonal bud, bloomed yellow and blue, then withered and died all round them. Akenna's face grew thin again and pale, but Tommo knew that he still had the quivers. In the end Akenna was shaking almost as much as he was.

'It's no good, Akenna, forget it. Thanks for trying, but I don't know that anyone has ever been cured of the quivers. I am strong enough to carry on a bit longer.' He sounded a good deal less brave than he might have wished and nowhere near as grateful as he ought to have been for her efforts. Akenna looked ill, her skin had something of the pinched look he remembered from their first encounter.

'I won't let you die,' she said angrily, almost petulantly, as if his dying was a personal affront to her newly gained power.

Tommo shrugged. 'Everything dies, Akenna. It's the living that counts. It's not so bad, at least I've seen the sea and a dolphin and . . .' He would have liked to say that he had met Akenna and that had meant something too, but he couldn't find the words, so he let the unfinished sentence tail away. He wished they could return to Footsore Farm and rest but once he'd explained to Akenna about Grena's cryptic warning she had reluctantly agreed that the farm was to be avoided.

It was a surprise then to see the sturdy figure of Grena standing on the Macalley road, hands on hips, a good long way down the road from the snug.

'He found you then,' she said to Akenna by way of greeting. Akenna looked startled.

'And what is that supposed to mean?'

'I have some secret sight so let's not waste words. Your da

is a friend of mine. There's danger for you back at the snug and I don't want you on my conscience when I stand at White Urtha's gate.'

Akenna seemed to take this at face value. 'They caught Da. He's in the manse cell.'

'I'd heard,' Grena said. 'Don't come to the farm – there's a man named Haver-snatcher, nasty piece. He's looking for you. The word is he's on the way to Footsore.' Akenna nodded tightly. The cloud of birds above their heads started to sing loudly of danger. Grena glanced upwards and smiled.

'The catcher didn't get them then?'

Akenna shook her head.

'He did. I set them free but I think more were caught.' Akenna paused and then added, 'Grena, I know about the Hand of the Island.'

'Oh yes. And what's your da been telling you about that? That's no business for young ears.'

Akenna's look made it clear what she thought of that and it was Grena who broke the suddenly chilly silence. 'What of it?'

'I've heard that the birds are a problem for Fallon, that if they were free they might do him harm.'

'You shouldn't believe tales for babes – there's nothing much that can do Fallon harm.' She sounded bitter, angry.

'What if they could though? Could you get the word out to the men and women of the Hand to release all the captured birds throughout the Protectorate? I think it's important.'

Grena appeared to consider that for a moment. 'I could do that,' she said at last, 'but why would I? What proof have you got that they could harm him in his fortress?'

Akenna opened her mouth but Tommo did not hear her reply because suddenly the world turned hot and black and blank.

Tommo woke up in bed in a bedchamber. He hadn't been in a bedchamber since he was a child and his mother had taken to hers for her confinement with the baby that killed her. His vision was blurred and it was dark as midnight until his eyes cleared a little and he could see Grena as a dark shape silhouetted against the red glow of the fire.

'Well lad, you certainly know how to sleep, I'll say that for you. You've lost a day to your bed. Are you awake now?' she said.

He did not seem able to nod and his 'Yes' came out like a groan, but that seemed to satisfy her.

'Akenna had a plan. I've given my word that the Hand will release the birds. We're not up to much, but we're up to that, and in return she's agreed that I'll give you to Haver-snatcher. He's an enemy all right, but he'll take you to the Fortress of Winter.' Grena let her great bulk settle on the thick straw mattress. 'Akenna's headed that way herself. Now that's the deal and she had to make it. She said to say she'll see you at the fortress and you're not to give up and die on her in the meantime.'

That did indeed seem so much like the kind of thing Akenna would say that Tommo believed her. The quivers were getting bad again, but he managed to nod his head, though he was beginning to feel as he had at Sibeal's cottage – as if his every moment was numbered. At Grena's instruction he rolled out of the raised bed on to the floor and crawled towards the narrow stairs.

Grena made no effort to help him and he virtually fell into the room below which was full of men. There was a pause in the conversation when he landed in a sprawl at the foot of the stairs.

'This is the apprentice.' Grena's voice rang harshly through the low murmuring of the men. 'I've given the Sheriff Naal and Old Garth. Now I give you him. If that isn't proof of loyalty to the Protector, I don't know what is. Now get out of my snug and leave me to my business.'

A man's face loomed in front of him, a well-made, even handsome, face with eyes the colour of violets.

'So you're the apprentice Fallon's so afraid of?' The man laughed a great shoulder-shaking belly laugh without any mirth in it. It was as if he thought the Protector a fool. Tommo did not know that Fallon was even aware of his existence, but the significance of that extraordinary piece of information was lost in his sudden desire for the kind of power to wipe such laughter away. The violet-eyed man reminded him of every bullyboy who'd tried his luck in the cellar. The man hauled him roughly to his feet and then lifted him up in one easy motion and threw him carelessly over his shoulder, as if he were as light as the carcass of a hare. All of Tommo's blood rushed to his head and he feared that he would surely be sick. The sawdust-covered floor bobbed and heaved like the base of Akenna's curragh just before it sank.

'Thanks for your hospitality, Grena, but don't think I'm done here yet. I have a nose for trouble and this place stinks of it. You can't guess how many people whispered to me about this place when I told them I hated the Protector. Remember the name of Haver-snatcher my friends, you'll hear it again.'

There was a groundswell of angry muttering from the men, but something about Tommo's captor kept them from acting. It was probably the look in his eye, the look of a man capable of anything and not overly worried about Urtha's reckoning.

Tommo did not know if Grena had betrayed him or not. He did not know if Akenna was safe or if the men Grena claimed she trusted were men of Haver-snatcher's ilk. He didn't know anything and he was finding it hard to care.

Haver-snatcher was not much interested in Tommo at all. He didn't even bother speaking to him once they were outside the snug. Grena's boy had readied a small horse and cart – not so different from Akenna's father's rig – and Haver-snatcher dumped him unceremoniously in the back of that.

'Don't die until I can get you to Fallon, lad,' he said and threw the horse blanket over the top of him. Tommo's shuddering had got to the point where obedience to Haver-snatcher's command looked improbable. His teeth had begun to clatter together again and his head kept banging on the base of the cart. After a time the noise of his head hitting the boards must have irritated Haver-snatcher because he stopped the cart and wedged some sacking under his head. Tommo could not express his gratitude. No part of him was under his control any more. His eyes could barely focus on the stars above which trembled and swam like things seen under water. He thought he saw the dark shapes of birds flying far above and heard the high, distant strains of their complex harmony. He could not make out the words and if they formed some symbol for him to read, that too was beyond him. He shut his eyes – he felt less sick that way – and let his mind drift. And still his life did not pass before his eyes.

CHAPTER THIRTY-THREE

Tommo knew nothing of the journey that took him to the Fortress of Winter. Haver-snatcher stopped at least once and gave him a drink of water, but beyond that he was aware only of intermittent fragments of sky, seen through bleary eyes, and the birds.

The birds sang to him in his dreams, they sang of longing and of hope and other things for which his experience provided no names. His dreams were haunted most by the vision of a huge eagle wearing an old man's face with its sea-coloured eyes imploring him.

Even in his dreams he was angry because the quivers were so bad he could barely move. How dare some creature of sickness-inducing spellstones demand anything more of him? How could he give it? He wished to be left to die in peace.

Haver-snatcher had no such intention. After an unknown passage of hours that might have been days for all that Tommo knew, they arrived at what was clearly their destination. He heard voices; a horse whickered and another snorted. He struggled to open his eyes and saw that it was dark and above him the stars shone almost as brightly as his skin. He sensed rather than saw the bustle of people, heard laughter and footsteps.

Someone – probably several people – approached Haver-snatcher and shone some kind of spellstone light in his direction. Tommo could feel the pulse of the spellstone, and felt immediate and overwhelming nausea.

'Gift of Urtha! What is that thing?' Haver-snatcher asked crossly. 'I'm sure the Protector will be interested to hear how you terrified my precious cargo and startled his oldest friend witless. It's Haver-snatcher you buffoon – let me through!'

Tommo could smell the ale on the guard, even from the back of the cart. Tommo heard the guard mumbling and caught only the word 'Protector' and Haver-snatcher's reply, 'There is no need, no need at all to trouble yourself, particularly as we have arrived on the Third Night of Unga.'

No wonder the guard was drunk – it was the night dedicated to the joys of the flesh and there wouldn't be a sober man in the whole of the Island of the Gifted. He had heard that the Protector had brought back a lot of the older customs from before the Convocation, to curry favour with the people. From what Tommo had seen it didn't appear to have worked.

This guard seemed to have sobered up quite rapidly, however, and loud male voices hailed each other in the dark as though commands were given and received. Tommo heard the sounds of armed men flanking them in a sudden regular clatter of military order. Haver-snatcher must be important then, and it seemed that Tommo was about to meet the feared Protector. It was probably a good thing that his hours were numbered because death at the hands of the Protector was rumoured to be exceptionally unpleasant.

They stopped again at what was clearly a stables and two big armed men lifted Tommo bodily from the cart and held him between them. The sudden change from horizontal to vertical set up a new bout of violent shaking in him. The men smelled strongly of meat and ale, horses and spell-stones. The combination was too much for him and the guards were less than pleased when he was immediately sick.

'The Protector won't like this,' one of them said with the careful diction of the inebriated.

'Send word to the Lady Vevena. She will have her maidservant clean him up. We do not want to offend the Protector's sensibility.'

'The Lady Vevena, but she's –'

'What, lad?' Haver-snatcher's voice threatened extreme violence and the guard, armed as Haver-snatcher was not, swallowed hard. The hand that held Tommo's arm was sweaty with fear. If Tommo hadn't felt so wretched, he might have found it more interesting.

Tommo wasn't sure what happened next, only that there was a great deal of activity, various important drunken people were called and Haver-snatcher repeated his demand and, though he never raised a finger, somehow everyone was cowed by him and did his will. Only Akenna, in Tommo's limited experience, was as effective at getting her own way.

A dark swooping form flying high above the tallest tower landed on the battlements and drew his attention to the silent gathering of many birds on the ramparts and rooftops. They looked dark and sinister against the night sky, with their strange beakless shapes giving them a bat-like look. It was a wonder no one else noticed them, but he supposed they were all busy trying to do whatever Haversnatcher demanded of them. He said goodbye to the birds in his head. He didn't know why they had been made or why they had followed him, but they had been companions of his last days and better company than most of the poor Unga-benighted apprentices. He was grateful to them and he did not expect to see them again.

Two new guards took him, lifting him bodily and carrying him upright through an apparently endless series of huge and oddly decorated rooms. Had he not found focusing so difficult, Tommo would have been interested in their strange, multicoloured wall hangings, the sculptures and the extraordinary furniture of spellstone manufacture.

The motion of the guards made him feel ill and his eyes were functioning so badly that it was less disorienting to keep them closed. After a good while, which alone gave him an indication of the vastness of the fortress, he was carefully lowered to the ground.

Someone with some authority was talking to Haver-snatcher, a woman who was clearly more afraid of her master, the Protector, than of Haver-snatcher.

'I know you are her father, my lord, but I have strict instructions that no man may enter my lady's bedchamber or my head is forfeit. I am uncommonly fond of my head, Lord, um, Haver-snatcher. I will allow this creature here does not qualify as a man, as you pointed out, and as my lady, by Urtha's grace, is kindness itself, we will take it upon ourselves to ready him for the Protector's audience. But, you, sire, must leave.'

Much to Tommo's surprise, Haver-snatcher did not argue, but only asked to be permitted to see Lady Vevena for himself. A woman entered the room then. Tommo got the impression of almost unearthly beauty, but she stank so badly of spellstone magic, and he could feel the pulse of it so strongly, that Tommo immediately and messily vomited again and he did not see what passed between Haver-snatcher and his daughter. When he had recovered himself Haver-snatcher had gone. The handmaid was wiping his face with a cloth and insisting he bathed before being permitted to enter the presence of Lord Fallon, the Protector. The spellstone woman entered the chamber as the handmaid left it and Tommo struggled to control himself.

'What ails you, child?' the Lady said quite gently.

Tommo's mouth worked for a moment without his being able to produce a sound and then he managed to stammer. 'You pulse with spellstone magic.' The woman looked quite startled, insofar as he could tell through the blurring distortion of his erratically focusing eyes.

'I love flowers,' she said. 'I am fond of roses.' Then with some difficulty she managed to mutter, 'I'm under a thaumaturgical curse.'

He could see it then: she was like a tiny ember of fire floating in water that almost, but never quite, extinguished it; she was a small struggling creature caught in a trap and paralysed by thousands of silken ropes, intertwined with flowers. She was someone powerful, rendered impotent by the spellstones which he hated above all else – a powerful, well-cut spellstone channelled a powerful malice.

'Take off all your jewels!' Tommo said in the rasping voice that was all he could produce. Why the woman did as he told her, he did not know, though he supposed her will was all but destroyed by the evil of the ensorcellment, but the next thing he knew the woman was throwing her gems on to the floor before him: ruby rings, diamond collars, bracelets and earrings of extraordinary beauty, marriage chains of such weight that it was a wonder she could stand erect when wearing them. The last thing she discarded was a ring, her fingers hovered above it but she could not bring herself to remove it.

'The ring . . .' he said. She thrust her hand in front of his face, clearly indicating that she wanted him to remove it, while she started talking loudly about gowns and fabrics and other things which made no sense at all. It was a strange mix of pity and anger that somehow allowed Tommo to gain enough control of his own hands to be able, tremblingly and haltingly it is true, to remove the ring. The stone was a small one, but cleverly cut and so pale a yellow it was almost white. When he got it from her, Tommo threw it with all his strength and, by some extraordinary good fortune or manifestation of Inward Power, it found the narrow arrow slit of window and disappeared, presumably into the moat.

'I am still not free,' she said, rubbing the place on her finger where the spellstone gem had made its mark. He had not the energy to explain that until the stone was gone no one could help her so instead he grabbed her hand clumsily with his.

He did not know how he knew he could help her, but he knew that he could. Perhaps because he was so near death he was aware of his power as he had not been before. He closed his eyes and, with his mind, carefully unpicked the silken threads that bound her. Sweat drenched him and his shaking made him worry that his brain might rattle out of his skull, but he did not give up until the last skein was untied. When he opened his eyes, Vevena was looking at him, her beautiful face wet with tears and her violet eyes brighter than her discarded jewels.

'Oh, by Gracious Urtha, I am free. You have freed me!'

CHAPTER THIRTY-FOUR

Vevena's mind was released suddenly from the shadows as if the silver boy had opened the curtains on a darkened room. Her first response was joy and surprise, her second concern for the poor boy, who must be the apprentice she had heard discussed.

He looked like he was having a fit, his whole body shaking like a puppet in the hands of some sadistic puppeteer.

'What can I do?' she asked him, helplessly. He couldn't speak so she did the only thing she could think of. She held him in her arms very tightly, as she might have held a child.

He was quite obviously not a child, though he was very slight and thin; his long hair, white as a gull's wing, gave him a prematurely aged look. 'Shush,' she said, 'you have saved me – tell me how I can save you.' The boy seemed to shake his head and then Dolina entered the room.

'Lady it is unseemly to touch that one. He's filthy and sick, and look what you have done to your dress.'

Vevena found herself responding very badly even to the sound of her handmaid and gaoler's voice, but she did not want to alert Dolina to her sudden liberation. It took enormous self-control to pretend meekness and do as she was told. She lowered her eyes because she could not control the expression in them, and got swiftly to her feet.

'Well, come on, my lady, help me to get him in the bath. I'm not a workhorse, whatever you and your husband might think.'

Vevena clenched her jaw tightly to prevent the sharp answer that had immediately come to mind from leaking out of her mouth. Between them, the two women lifted Tommo bodily and put him in the tub. It was of spellstone glass, like the bed, and within it exotic flowers bloomed. Tommo started to whimper almost as soon as they got him inside it, though the water was neither too hot nor too cold and the cleaning oils the handmaid had added to it were not too astringent. The strange lights under his skin glittered more brightly in the bath and could be clearly seen. It was as if stars lived within him.

'Get him out, quick!' Dolina said. 'I can't put up with that noise, I'll send for the footman to clothe him. It's not decent for us to do it.'

Vevena was so moved by pity for Tommo she did not know what to do for the best. She could not see that dressing him would do him any harm so she didn't argue when her gaoler bustled off to send for one of the footmen.

Vevena herself sat down heavily on her bed and tried to make sense of the sudden flood of images that overwhelmed her: Fallon desperately trying to gain her approval to the extent that he released her father from prison, a mistake for sure if Fallon wanted to hang on to his position; Haver-snatcher filthy and worn down by his years of incarceration; Gildea in his cage of spellstones; Kalen with all his talk of Urthene essences; and the eagle with Gildea's face, the eagle she had hidden in the tower.

She sat for a while putting her thoughts in order, thinking about what had to be done to overthrow the Protector, perhaps to kill him. She wondered that she felt so calm; the hate that had burnt in her before her ensorcellment had burnt away. She could bide her time. She did not have to kill Fallon yet. She remembered all the longing looks he had cast in her direction. She examined her chaotically organised memory of the last several years but could find nothing to incriminate him; in his relations with her, his behaviour had been exemplary.

When Dolina returned, Vevena did not have to feign confusion. Fallon's behaviour had not been as she would have anticipated and that was disturbing. She submitted to being dressed in some ghastly, over-heavy gown laden with bits and pieces of quite unnecessary decoration, and was amused to remember that it had been one of her favourite gowns in her strange ensorcelled state. The pattern was so elaborate that following it with her finger had been one way of sustaining and memorising her thoughts.

'I won't wear any jewellery today,' she said, fearful that some other gem might be of spellstone origin, and that she might find her thoughts locked again in the terrible oppression of magical control. She tried to make her voice fey and faraway as if she were still lost. Dolina gave her a sharp look.

'But the Protector likes to see you wear his gifts.'

'They are heavy and are giving me a headache,' Vevena answered, perhaps more forcefully than was wise.

'You are feisty today, my lady. Has that nasty apprentice upset you?'

Vevena struggled to come up with an answer. 'I'm tired,' she said petulantly, 'and hungry. Is it not time for the feast?' The woman seemed comfortable with petulance and merely brushed and arranged Vevena's hair, though she had to be reproached for attempting to fix it with a large emerald.

'No jewels,' Vevena said in a sing-song voice she re-membered occasionally using to amuse herself, and the handmaid seemed to accept that.

To her surprise Haver-snatcher came to escort both her and the apprentice to the feast. There were guards every-where, of course, but still she had not expected that he would be allowed such discretion. Fallon must have grown foolish to trust his former friend so far.

Haver-snatcher looked weary, thinner than she could ever remember, but she knew the moment she saw him that his ambition was undiminished.

'Father,' she said softly, with lowered eyes so that he would not see that she was restored. She had not yet decided how she wished to deal with him. She was no longer sure that they could work together. Haver-snatcher had ever been a powerful man who would want her to do

his will and not her own. She needed to understand what game he was playing before she revealed her own hand.

He must have been distracted to fail to notice the slight changes in her demeanour that gave her away. She tried to walk without purpose but it was difficult when she felt herself afire with new energy, exultant to be free.

Two guards had to carry Tommo, who was still shuddering as if he were some injured animal in its death throes. There had to be something she could do to help him, but she had no idea what that might be.

They were taken to the great hall, which had been furnished for the feast. Fallon was seated at the head of a vast table in his magnificent carved oak chair, painted and gilded to resemble a bower of pink and golden roses. He was elaborately dressed in silks and velvets, and yet he still looked like a toad, though an unusual toad with yellowed and misshapen teeth, and ill-matched eyes, one blue, one brown, that gave his stare a curious intensity. His face changed when he saw Haver-snatcher and the apprentice.

'Is he the one?' he demanded.

Haver-snatcher shrugged. 'If you want my opinion, his spirit will be in Urtha's arms within hours, but yes, he is the apprentice known as Tommo.'

Vevena was watching Tommo intently, willing him to keep breathing, when she saw Kalen's face out of the corner of her eye. The Chief Spellstone Wielder's face had turned white and he was gripping the table in front of him as if it were the only thing keeping him upright.

'I will question him myself. Have him taken to the dungeon!' Fallon said.

Vevena was acutely aware of the horrified expression on Kalen's face and she struggled to keep her own face blank. Tommo made no sign of having understood. His eyes were closed and his whole body was ripped by such violent eruptions of shaking that it was difficult to watch him.

'Kalen, go with him and use what skill you have to keep him alive.' Had Fallon noticed Kalen's face? Did he know that his Chief Spellstone Wielder would act against him if he could?

Vevena did not know and could not guess from her husband's inexpressive face.

'Please, old friend, join me. You have done well to find the boy. I would be glad of your company at the feast.'

Fallon had drunk little, but the same could not be said of the guests who had clearly been imbibing steadily for some hours. That was no bad thing from Vevena's perspective as she would stand a greater chance of passing herself off as still ensorcelled among the blunted wits of drunkards.

'I am glad of your news, Haver-snatcher, that you have found the boy, that is . . .' He beamed with most un-Fallon-like satisfaction. 'And now that Gildea is dead, I can at last concentrate on all the other things that need doing. It is good to see you, Haver-snatcher. Did you find anything further about a plot against me?' He dropped his voice to speak to Haver-snatcher in an undertone.

Vevena could barely believe her ears. Had Fallon forgotten who her father was?

Why would Fallon expect him to cooperate? She realised suddenly that she was herself the reason. Haver-snatcher believed that her own survival depended on his cooperation. That was a shock, but of course she had been quite incapable of taking care of herself all these long years. She had been utterly at the mercy of Fallon, of Dolina and of anyone else who cared to take advantage of her.

What would Haver-snatcher do, if he realised she were free? She was not entirely sure that she wanted to find out.

CHAPTER THIRTY-FIVE

Sibeal was dozing when they brought in the boy. He was as near dead as almost made no difference. She had never seen anyone in such a state. Had she had her knife with her she would have been tempted to finish him off, to save him from his suffering. Had she had her knife, of course, she would have finished herself off some days ago. They had tried to get from her anything she might know about a plot against Fallon. She had told them about the birds. She'd had no choice, but she was not even sure that the interrogator had reported that back to Fallon. He had after all killed all the birds. She felt desolate. There was no hope left.

The boy – her husband's boy, she was sure of it – lay twitching on the floor and she could not help herself. She scooped him into her arms and cradled him as if he were her own child. She stroked the white hair and rocked him back and forth. She thought he smiled a little and he let out a low moan. Encouraged, she started to sing to him in a voice cracked and hoarse from screaming. She found within herself some fragment of a melody from when she was young and hopeful, from the days when Inward Power was a gift not a crime.

When Kalen came she was still singing and Tommo was miraculously still breathing.

'You were right,' he said in a choked voice. 'He is my Tommo, he is the image of Eavan. Why did no one tell me? I am the Chief Spellstone Wielder of the Protectorate, I could have kept my son from the terrible grinding cellars. Oh, why did I never confirm for myself that he was dead?'

'I didn't want you to. I know I discouraged you,' Sibeal said, still rocking the boy and stroking his hair. Giving him comfort gave her some hope back, misplaced though that was. 'I think I was glad there was nothing left of her, of your beautiful Eavan. I was wrong. I'm sorry.'

Kalen gently touched her hand and leant over the shivering form of Tommo, his son, who was not long dead as he'd always believed but was, instead, just about to die. Was that the worst moment for reconciliation or the best?

'Let me take him,' he said and they sat down together sharing his meagre weight between them.

'I assume there is nothing you can do?' Sibeal shook her head without speaking as she sang some old nursery song. When the song ended she said, 'He is far beyond my help, even if these spellstones did not make any thaumaturgy a near impossibility. I've managed to keep the rats away and that's about all. Are you here as captive or captor?'

Kalen pulled a face, 'I think I am still Chief Spellstone Wielder. Fallon sent me to help Tommo. If he knows I am

Tommo's father, he will probably have me torture him myself. I am sorry, Sibeal, I have not been able to help you. Has it been very bad?'

'Well, you know. I've used what power I have to block out the pain, but I told them about the birds.'

'They already knew that the birds meant something to Gildea. You shouldn't worry about that.'

Sibeal nodded. 'I know and I don't think I explained the theory very well.' In the end she had wanted to tell everything she knew but agony did not help clarity of thought. She didn't think the interrogator had made any sense of any of it. That was something with which to content herself.

'I wish I knew how to use the spellstones to heal, but in all my experiments I have never managed to make them do anything so useful.'

'Only the Inward Power can heal, Kalen, and neither of us have enough of it for this. I have heard it said the spellstone dust acts as a kind of poison, killing the body of Unga and leaving only Urtha's part.' They were both silent for a moment, looking at the boy who lay over them.

Tommo's shaking seemed to have subsided a little. Sibeal did not know if that meant he was slipping away. She held him more tightly as if that were going to help.

Kalen was weeping huge great, silent tears that ran down his nose and dripped off his chin. Sibeal who had disliked him for so long found her heart softening. He had never loved her as much as she would have wanted, but then maybe she had not been very loveable. She did not approve of him becoming Chief Spellstone Wielder and Gildea's gaoler, but who else but a devoted acolyte could have done a better job? She had not changed her mind about spell-stones; if they were not malevolent things how could they have so harmed a spellgrinder? She found that her bitterness towards Kalen had evaporated: pain and pity had left her cleansed. All their disputes seemed very trivial somehow as they huddled together in Fallon's dungeon, trying to ease the passing of Kalen's son. She carefully slipped one arm out from under poor Tommo's body and put it round Kalen's bony shoulders. She was shocked at how thin he'd become. It was as if the spellstones had eaten him up, as the dust had destroyed his son. There was nothing left of Kalen but wiry tendon, bone – and grief, of course, she could not discount that. 'You could not save him. You didn't know he was alive, Kalen. It is not your fault.'

He did not move away from her, but he did not seem much comforted either. He still held himself stiffly, holding his son with taut muscles and a rigid back.

'Is it over, Kalen? Has Fallon won?' she asked.

'It is too early to say,' Kalen said softly, never taking his eyes off Tommo's face. 'We don't know what happened to the birds.'

'Don't we?' Sibeal said. 'Fallon's bird-catchers killed them. I doubt that anything like enough remain to house a quarter of Gildea's spirit. We needed all of him. Poor Tommo has more power than anyone in the Protectorate and look at him – he isn't going to save anyone. How could

Gildea enter this body even if enough of his Urthene essence remains?'

Kalen shook his head. 'There is still the other one – the one with the beads. Perhaps she –'

He had no time to finish his sentence before the door of the dungeon opened again and the guard pushed a young woman into the room with them. She was covered in blood and filth. She moaned a little as she landed hard on the impacted dirt floor, but then her eyes fixed on the burden Sibeal and Kalen shared.

'Tommo?' she said. She picked herself up and did not even pause to dust herself down before hurling herself at the boy. 'What are you doing to him? Leave him! He's my friend.'

It took Sibeal a moment to recognise her; she had filled out since she had seen her last, but the face was unmistakably that of Akenna, their last hope.

CHAPTER THIRTY-SIX

Akenna appeared quite distraught. 'But Grena said he'd be safe – she promised me. Tommo! Tommo! Don't die on me. Not now. I brought the birds, Tommo. We got nearly all of them, Tommo!'

'Hush, child. Get a hold of yourself,' Sibeal said sternly as Akenna's reaction looked suspiciously like hysteria. 'Tommo is not dead, at least not yet.'

'Then can you heal him?' Sibeal shook her head. 'He has gone far beyond my powers. Can't you?'

Akenna looked a little taken aback. 'Well, I might have stood a chance, if someone had taught me when they could have done,' she said tartly.

'It was a difficult time, and if Fallon had known a child of your gifts existed he'd have had you killed with the pox or something.'

'So you say. But how close to dying do you think I came with Da? At least if I'd known how to use thaumaturgy I might have had a chance.'

Sibeal shook her head. 'It didn't work like that –'

Akenna cut her short. 'Tell me how I can help him? Take your hands off him.'

Sibeal reluctantly pulled back from Tommo's prostrate form, though he still lay partially on her lap.

'Who's he?' Akenna asked indicating Kalen with a half-nod of her head.

'That is the Chief Spellstone Wielder.'

'Oh, so it's his fault Tommo was stuck in a cellar grinding spellstones and getting sick is it?'

Akenna looked likely to go for Kalen with her fists so Sibeal added quickly, 'He is also Tommo's father.'

'Unga's arse – and he let him use up his life in a cellar?'

'I didn't know,' Kalen said quietly. He looked as though it would have been a relief to him if Akenna had actually hit him, he looked wretched. Akenna sat down abruptly as Tommo's twitching continued: he neither spoke nor opened his eyes in response to her noisy presence.

'Has he not spoken at all?'

'Not since they brought him in.'

'Oh, by Urtha, tell me what I can do.'

'I don't know,' Sibeal said. 'You could hold his hand and try to will him well, but I have no experience with the quivers and I've never heard of anyone surviving them.'

Akenna grabbed Tommo's hand almost violently and clenched her eyes shut, concentrating furiously on making him well. Tears oozed out from under her lids, but Tommo's condition did not improve in any way that Sibeal could observe. At length Akenna's shoulders sagged in defeat. 'I can't feel anything happening. I can't find him to make him well.'

'There are spellstones all round us,' Sibeal said. 'They dampen down the Inward Power.'

'I'll try again, when I've caught my breath,' Akenna said and Sibeal noticed how ill the girl looked suddenly. She had a deep cut on her upper arm which was still seeping blood.

'What happened to you?' Sibeal asked.

'I suppose you know my father was in the Hand of the Island?'

Sibeal nodded silently. She had done a good deal of work for them herself, not that Akenna would know that.

'Well, when I realised that the bird-catchers were taking our birds, I asked . . .' she paused perhaps not willing to trust Sibeal with a name, 'a friend to get the word out to the Hand's members.'

'Grena, I suppose, of Footsore Farm?' Sibeal asked thoughtfully. 'She has some gift for thaumaturgy, you know, but she doesn't always use it wisely.'

Akenna hesitated. 'Well, she said she'd take care of Tommo, but I didn't think she meant like this.'

She touched him hesitantly on his brow. His spasms of twitching were less pronounced as if he'd used up all his energy.

'Go on,' Sibeal prompted.

'Oh,' Akenna had been lost in contemplation of her friend for a moment, 'I thought the Hand was something strong and noble, not just a few old men and women drinking in snugs. It was a hard job getting anyone to actually do anything.' She paused and then continued more calmly, 'Well Grena sent out word to those members who hadn't died since they last saw action and somehow they managed to get the birds released. I went out with one lot and when we were over Kimrick way the Sheriff caught up with us. Fallon had given a command that anyone interfering with the birds was to be brought to the Fortress of Winter. The men I was with bought the Sheriff off – I think they might have used Da's spellstones, but I didn't have enough havers. Anyway, one of the Hand members heard I'd turned on Da – though I don't know how. He told the Sheriff I was a witch and then I got beaten up and brought here.'

'Did you not use your power?'

'I couldn't – I didn't know how. I managed to hurt Da with it, but then I hated him. It'll be all right, I can fix myself. I can't help Tommo, though.' Akenna wiped her face with her hands.

'Did you use spellstones to keep my thaumaturgy hidden?' she asked suddenly, to Sibeal's surprise.

'I had some beads made of dead spellstones – I noticed when I wore them I couldn't do thaumaturgy. It was a spur of the moment decision. When I felt how strong your power was, I had to protect you. I –'

'What about the birds?' Kalen asked, interrupting Sibeal before she could get under way with her self-justification again.

'The birds all followed me. They stayed out of sight but they're all here. I brought them to the fortress like Sibeal asked me – much good it's done me and Tommo.'

'What about the eagle? Was the eagle with them?' Kalen asked urgently.

'How in Unga's name should I know?' Akenna snapped back. 'I don't know one bird from another unless they happen to be seabirds.'

'It's very important. It would have been a very big bird – probably the biggest of them all – and it would maybe have looked different, more knowing perhaps than the others.'

A brief candle of hope was suddenly extinguished, as it was clear that Akenna did not know what Kalen was talking about.

'I never saw an eagle, but the birds flew way above my head most of the time. Why does it matter?' Akenna looked from one to the other in some confusion. 'Sibeal, I did what you asked.'

'Yes, you did, Akenna, and I'm grateful – such obedience is probably more than I deserved.'

'It wasn't for you,' Akenna said firmly. 'I thought it might help Tommo. The birds helped us and I thought that if we did something to save them they might reward us somehow, like this was some croon tale for children. It was stupid. Tommo was always going to die. He told me from the beginning, but I didn't believe it until now.'

Sibeal suddenly felt very sorry for her. Whatever was going to happen to Akenna, it was extremely unlikely to be very good. They may all come to envy Tommo before too long.

'It's as I feared – Fallon's bird-catchers must have got the eagle,' Kalen said. 'Without that bird Gildea cannot reassemble himself. The eagle is his organising principle, the key to his soul. If the key has not survived, we are quite without hope.'

So that was that, Sibeal thought. It is over, after all.

CHAPTER THIRTY-SEVEN

Vevena tried to concentrate on the feast. It was the third night of Unga and a time to indulge the body in worldly delights, but the food tasted over-rich to her jaded palate and the rumbustious music irritated her. Most of the guests were already very drunk, which was at least part of the point of the feast, but Vevena was still coldly sober and looking with some distaste at the aristocratic Names and high-ups making fools of themselves and getting ready for the traditional wild man parade. It was more difficult to deal with fortress life now that she was fully herself. She was also very worried about Tommo, the boy who had saved her. There must be something she could do – somewhere she could hide him safe from the ministrations of her husband and his interrogators.

She was certain that Fallon knew that something was not right, that something was different about her. She could feel it. It upset her stomach, turning it sour as third-day milk. He kept glancing up at her, an odd expression on his face. How could he know? She had neither done nor said anything to arouse suspicion. She had tried to keep her expression neutral – what had her expression been all the long years of her ensorcellment? Haver-snatcher did not look at her. Did it pain him to see her so ensorcelled or did he too guess that she was changed and wanted to avoid drawing attention to her? It was frustrating not knowing. She observed that her father was sitting close to Fallon, wearing borrowed finery that made him look far more regal than the Protector, which was a mistake: Fallon was sensitive about his ugliness. Her father, rather to her surprise, was sober too. The musicians struck up the opening chords of a well-known song and all the high-ups and court servants were up out of their seats and cavorting round like wild men possessed by Unga. There was much laughter and giggling and falling over. Vevena clapped her hands in pretend delight and left the table as if to join the dance. While all eyes were elsewhere she slipped out for a breath of air. She needed to escape.

The guards took little notice of her. These regulars saw her so often her beauty had become commonplace for them. Though they were on duty, they had obviously been celebrating the third night of Unga among themselves and barely managed a shambolic salute as she passed them. Fallon was growing soft if he permitted such behaviour: she would not. She only prevented herself giving the guardsmen a sharp look and a sharper reprimand just in time – she was still supposed to be Vevena the vague and ensorcelled.

The air in the courtyard was pleasantly cool. Here she could no longer hear the discordant music of the drone and drum; here she could hear something else. She stood and listened. She had never heard anything like it before. The sound was a strange one – a long, keening chord sung by many male voices, endlessly repeated, echoing around the courtyard. She could not see where it was coming from, but the battlements were dark with the forms of hundreds of birds of every shape and size. They looked wrong, somehow: their silhouettes were beakless and most unbirdlike. Suddenly she had a picture of the dress she wore that evening, the dress in the garden and her finger tracing its complex pattern, and remembered Kalen's voice:

'Gildea entrusted fragments of his Urthene essence to many of the birds of the Protectorate, saving the key to his true Urthene self, until the moment of death. I think a golden eagle holds the key to unifying the whole.'

She shivered. It was clear what she needed to do. She would take advantage of the guards' drunken state to rescue the apprentice – that was an issue of honour – and then she would free the eagle. If Gildea somehow reappeared – she had not understood that part of Kalen's confidence – he would know what to do. He might be able to help her find somewhere safe for the silver boy.

Having made up her mind, Vevena went in search of Lord Awnan, whom even she knew must harbour some resentment against her husband. She was not sure she could command in the dungeons of Fallon. They may not know her there and might send for Fallon to vouch for her. She returned to the hall which seemed crowded, loud and stuffy after the cool of the courtyard – so many red-faced courtiers, the smell of wine and spices. She was briefly overwhelmed. Then she saw Awnan. He was sitting alone at the other end of the table from where Fallon and her father were apparently in deep conversation. Awnan too was a little drunk.

'My Lord Awnan,' she began softly, 'there is something I would have you do.'

He looked very surprised. 'My lady.' He tried to get to his feet but Vevena laid a pale, restraining hand on his and smiled her most charming of smiles. It took her some time to persuade him that there was no risk at all to him personally, but that now she had returned to her senses there would be advantage in helping her. He was a very nervous man, fearful and weak, but that was, of course, why he had been selected for his post. Fallon was careful to employ only people too cowed to get into trouble unless they were led there, and Vevena firmly intended to do some leading.

She flattered Awnan remorselessly and he, poor lamb, was quite unused to the attentions of a beautiful woman, particularly one who promised her help in improving his position with Fallon. He was not stupid, not by a long way, but he was fertile soil for Vevena's particular brand of manipulation. Fallon was not going to know quite where to turn once she had a better grasp of fortress business.

The fortress was in chaos, there was not a guard who was sober or a servant who was at his post. Awnan explained rather apologetically that Fallon had given dispensation that the festival should be celebrated by all. Lord Awnan was a familiar and respected figure, if only because he brought orders from Fallon, so no one argued when he entered the dungeon and demanded that all the prisoners there be released, by Fallon's own decree, in celebration of the third night of Unga. If the gaolers found it strange that Fallon should have changed his mind about the prisoners so rapidly, no one commented. No one dared.

They gazed at Vevena in undisguised awe and if they wondered at her presence in the dungeons, they kept as silent as very drunken men could manage. The dungeon stank. The floor was uneven and sticky with something she was grateful not to be able to identify in the dim light. The low buzz of spellstones made the base of her skull ache, perhaps her long ensorcellment had rendered her sensitive to their effects.

When the guard opened the door of the main holding cell, Vevena was a little surprised to find Kalen with the white-haired apprentice in his arms. He looked a little uncomfortable; he ought not to be holding the prisoner as a mother might hold her sickly child. She was less surprised to see the two women prisoners, as Fallon's dungeon was always full and she remembered seeing Sibeal when her father had brought her in. If her faulty memory served, she was a worker of thaumaturgy.

'Get out of here! Fallon has decreed that you are to be freed as a third night of Unga favour,' Vevena said as the guard fumbled to open the cell door. Kalen gave her a questioning look, but kept silent.

'I'll give thanks to Red Unga for that!' the younger woman said in the broad accent of the western coast. She flashed Vevena an unreadable look and then helped Kalen carry the poor trembling body of Tommo out of the cell.

There was a strange awkward silence as they shuffled slowly out of the dungeon. Sibeal cringed away from the guards as she passed them, her face averted. The guards ignored the prisoners but followed Vevena's every movement with their eyes so that she felt obliged to speak. 'Thank you,' she said, for no good reason. 'Unga's blessings on you.'

Lord Awnan said nothing, and looked uncomfortable, but then as far as she could remember he always did.

No one spoke as they made their way up the narrow stairs out of the dungeons. Vevena helped Kalen and the girl manoeuvre the unconscious body of Tommo up the narrow, twisting stairwell while Sibeal staggered after them. If Fallon had ordered her torture, it was a miracle of White Urtha that she could walk at all.

It was only when they left the stench of the dungeon below them that Kalen broke the silence. 'Lady Vevena, you are changed,' he said in a low voice as if it were some kind of a secret.

'So are you,' Vevena replied.

Kalen had never been much concerned with his appearance, but he was now filthy and bloodstained, though much of the blood seemed to belong to the young woman prisoner. Kalen also looked desperate. Vevena could not account for the change in him, nor his curious interest in the boy. There was no time to ask; she had to find a place to hide the prisoners before news of their removal from the dungeon reached Fallon's ears. She ought to have thought more about what she was to do with them. She had not been so impulsive before the days of her ensorcelled madness. She almost panicked, but then Kalen's worn, pleading voice brought her back to her senses. Pray to Urtha that her mind was not permanently damaged by the curse.

'Lady Vevena, the birds we spoke of – perhaps you do not remember – are they outside?'

'Please, for the love of Unga-under-all, take us to the birds.' The girl's voice was harsh and insistent.

'Hush, Akenna, you cannot speak to the Protector's wife like that,' Sibeal scolded breathlessly as she leant against the wall for support.

Akenna, for that was clearly the young woman's name, gave Vevena a look of such concentrated venom that she was momentarily quite discomforted. She had almost forgotten the power of her face to inspire slavish devotion and hatred in roughly equal proportions.

'I will take you to the courtyard. Lord Awnan, you should also return to Fallon, but remember it would be disadvantageous for you to mention the liberation of the prisoners for the moment. I will tell Fallon when the time is right.'

Lord Awnan looked worried, a characteristic expression, and, bowing, left them. Vevena was not sure how Fallon would react when he heard what had happened. She remembered his desire for her with a shiver of discomfort. How much could she bend Fallon to her will? He was proud, cruel and ruthless with regard to everyone but herself and now, inexplicably, Haver-snatcher. She wished she better understood how things lay between those old enemies and older friends. She allowed herself to consider how far she was prepared to go to protect Tommo from Fallon – the boy was clearly dying.

Vevena led a limping Sibeal and the more or less unconscious apprentice, supported by Akenna and Kalen, into the courtyard. Sibeal gasped when she saw the birds and gripped Vevena's arm. The skyline was distorted by their strange, black silhouettes.

'There are enough, Kalen, surely! More have survived than we could have hoped. You did well, Akenna.'

There wasn't much light in the courtyard, just a few storm lanterns marking the sentry posts, but even so Vevena could tell that Akenna was not much impressed by such praise.

'What about Tommo?' she said and to that question no one had a reply, least of all Vevena.

CHAPTER THIRTY-EIGHT

Akenna hesitated for only a moment at the entrance to the courtyard before shouldering Tommo's entire weight herself and half dragging him into the centre of the paved area.

Kalen looked on, somehow rendered even more useless than usual.

The courtyard had by and large escaped Fallon's spellstone improvements and remained unchanged from earlier days when villagers had set up encampments within the castle ramparts in times of trouble. The moment Akenna and Tommo came into view, the birds all launched themselves into the air at once until the sky above the fortress was dark with birds all singing together. It was so loud that Vevena covered her ears with her hands.

'They can't do anything without the eagle,' Kalen said despairingly. 'Listen, they are all singing different things. The eagle is needed for Gildea to make himself whole. I can't see it – it's not here is it?' He sounded old and desperate and despairing. None of which was very helpful. He was a man of power for White Urtha's sake, not some snivelling old man.

'It is in the spellstone cage,' Vevena said shortly. 'I took it there while I was still under the curse. It's hurt . . .' It might be dead for all that Vevena knew. She had forgotten about it until Tommo restored her. When had she taken it there? How many days had it been there alone and injured? She kept fear from her voice with some effort. She was not going to join Kalen in his hopelessness.

'I was hoping you might be able to use thaumaturgy to free it. Eagles have sharp talons – I have no desire to try to carry it again.'

'You took it to the tower cell while you were under the curse?' Kalen said incredulous, unbelieving. What had he expected of her? That she would do nothing to fight against the curse, give in to it and let Fallon win? Vevena found herself increasingly irritated by his strange, indecisive powerlessness. He was the Chief Spellstone Wielder. Why had he not fought Fallon?

She did not think it wise to let her feelings show, however. He appeared to be an ally of sorts and she did not know how many of those she might find within the fortress. She therefore merely nodded in response to his question. 'The curse has been weakening ever since Fallon released my father. I think my father was one of the things I wasn't supposed to think about, but I couldn't avoid it when he kept appearing. Father brought Tommo to me. I don't know if he thought he could help me with his Inward Power. It seems unlikely – the boy couldn't walk – but somehow he freed me. Not that it did him any good at all. Look at him! If I can help him, tell me what I should do.'

'We should release the eagle. I have not the power to open the spellstone cage,' Kalen said, apologetically. 'If I had that kind of strength Fallon would never have let me live.'

'Akenna might be able to do it – if you could show her how,' Sibeal said, shouting to be heard above the sudden cacophonous singing. The sound raised the hairs on Sibeal's neck; the voices were too beautiful to be human and yet horribly discordant.

Vevena had to force herself to walk with Kalen and Sibeal into the dark storm cloud of birds circling Tommo and Akenna, wailing their plaintive, pitiful song. There were so many birds all flying low and so close together they looked like tea leaves swirling in a diviner's cup or a whirlpool of treacherous water. She was irritated with herself for being so fanciful and so afraid. She had not been so foolish before the curse.

Akenna had laid Tommo on the ground, no longer able to support his weight, and was shooing the birds away from him, like a demented scarecrow.

'If you can't help him, go away! By Unga-under-all and all her demons, don't you hurt him or I'll sheathe my knife in your hearts.' She was crying hysterically and wasn't making a great deal of sense. Once more it seemed to Vevena that if she did not take control no one would. She was, like it or not, Fallon's wife and Haver-snatcher's daughter.

'Akenna, listen to me, if you are to help Tommo, you must release the golden eagle from its cage of spellstones. It's injured, but it might still be able to fly. Can you see it?

It's just over there – hidden behind the tower – you can just see the blue glow.'

'And why by Unga's arse should I do what you tell me? I don't trust you. What do you know? You're married to the Protector. I'm not taking orders from a woman in a flowery dress,' Akenna snarled. Vevena kept her temper with difficulty, she would have liked to have slapped this unruly girl, only the fact that she was apparently gifted in the power of thaumaturgy stayed her hand.

'Kalen agrees,' Vevena answered briskly.

'Kalen brought Tommo to this state – if it were not for the spellstones he would be as fit as anyone else.'

'Perhaps,' Vevena agreed as soothingly as she could manage. Urtha's heart but she wanted to shake her, this was so obviously not the time for recriminations. 'Sibeal thinks you can do it and also that you should do it.'

'And why should I trust her? She lied to me and trapped my power. The only person I can trust is Tommo and he's –'

'He isn't dead, is he?' Vevena asked in sudden fear. She still owed him and she was someone who paid her debts.

'As good as. What do you care anyway?' Akenna's plain face was a mess of tears and dirt and fury. Vevena could understand fury and suddenly found some small grain of sympathy for the scarecrow of a girl.

'He saved me. I was ensorcelled and he saved me. I want to pay him back.' She paused for a moment trying to think of something persuasive to say, then decided honesty was the best course: 'Listen. I don't know what will happen if you release the eagle, but I do know that nothing will happen unless you do. Gildea was the most powerful thaumaturgist this land had ever known, maybe . . .' She did not finish her sentence. Frankly she had no idea what might happen if the eagle and the birds somehow came together, but it could hardly make things any worse.

Akenna in turn looked as if she understood about debts. She wiped her running nose on the back of her hand and turned to face the tower. The blue spellstone glow was just perceptible – it made a kind of corona round the top of the tower.

Vevena couldn't say exactly what happened next only that there was a sudden stillness.

The birds ceased their dizzying circuit and flew back to the roofs and perched there silently, ominously. No one breathed. The wind dropped, but the candles in the storm lanterns went out. All that was visible was the moon, the tower, Tommo and his glowing skin and Akenna. Vevena had the impression that all the passion, the energy, the fury of that young woman was suddenly focused, sharp and deadly as a knife point on the eagle's cage. Akenna's face was damp with sweat and every muscle in her slight body seemed to be straining with effort. She grimaced and suddenly in the darkness there came a long, high cry and the form of the eagle was outlined against the bright moon. The blue spellstone glow went out as abruptly as the candles had guttered and died. The eagle was free.

CHAPTER THIRTY-NINE

Perhaps Lord Awnan was not the kind of man Vevena would wish at her side in a crisis, but she had not expected him to reveal her whereabouts to her husband quite so quickly. Just as the eagle soared into view, Awnan arrived, accompanied by Haver-snatcher, Fallon and a contingent of rapidly sobering guards.

'What is the meaning of this?' Fallon bellowed, striding into the courtyard. He looked shaken when he saw the birds. 'What is going on?' he blustered.

'Watch and you'll know as much as anyone else,' Vevena answered tartly. Fallon looked at her, startled as if she had hit him. Haver-snatcher seemed scarcely less surprised, but she could not waste her attention on them. The birds were circling round and round the eagle. As she listened their song, which had been so dissonant, began to blend and harmonise so that it became almost unbearably beautiful: a song of longing and terrible hope.

Fallon appeared unmoved and tried to impose his own order on the scene:

'Take those prisoners back to the dungeon! Who has

defied me by releasing them? They will join them at once and I will punish them myself!' He signalled to the guards to arrest Akenna, who was shielding Tommo's prostrate form from the avian maelstrom.

Vevena turned away from the mesmerising sight of the vast flock of human-faced birds flying in tight formation round and round the Gildea-faced eagle. She had to stop Fallon harming Akenna and Tommo. The guards slunk forward, heads low, their swords at the ready. They were for some reason led by Lord Awnan who looked ridiculously out of place in his festive court clothes. All of them looked as fearful as Vevena herself felt. She was about to beg Fallon for Akenna and Tommo's lives when Akenna raised her thin right arm and glared at the approaching troops. The guards hit an unseen wall, falling or stumbling back in confusion, dazed as though they had encountered a physical barrier. Awnan looked to Fallon for orders.

'Who is she?' Fallon stormed.

Vevena might have answered, but the birds' voices became suddenly comprehensible and compelling.

'Be still! Listen and learn!' the birds sang in their strangely inhuman human voices.

Even Fallon was duly silenced. The whole of the court-yard was bathed in a pale light that was not moonlight but had something of its ethereal quality. It was not clear to Vevena what the source of it was, it might have been Akenna or Tommo or the birds themselves, but it was as eerie and as disturbing as the birds and their song. For a pause of several heartbeats there was complete silence, as if the whole courtyard had been muffled by a blanket of invisible snow, as if silence had fallen like snowflakes and buried all noise, and then a new sound began that was even stranger than any that had preceded it.

At first Vevena had assumed that all the birds had different faces, but in the uncanny light she could see that many of them had the same face, some that of a baby, others of a golden-haired child, some of a youth, others a middle-aged man, while many more had the face of an old man with a white beard. The eagle was not the only bird to bear the face of Gildea as she had known him. All the faces had the same strange blue-green eyes that had so distinguished the old man. She began to understand. All of these birds were in some way Gildea; they all bore a fragment of his soul. That thought chilled her more than their music. Kalen had tried to explain, she remembered, but until that moment it had made little sense. As she watched and listened she could better interpret the sound. It began softly with a musical babbling, incoherent but melodic, and Vevena saw all the baby-faced birds singing together in wordless unison, then the high, pure treble voices of the boy Gildea soared above their childish babble. Little by little, the other birds joined in, so trebles were joined by tenors and countertenors, by baritones and basses, until they all sang together in the perfect, unearthly harmony that was beyond her power to describe.

'It is time to choose,' they chorused. 'Who offers an Ungine body for the Urthene spirit of Gildea?'

In the silver light that seemed to grow ever brighter Vevena could see the face of Gildea at all the stages of his life repeated endlessly through the vast flock of birds; ranks of babies and children and young men, all with the same face planted on an array of bird bodies and all encircling the eagle, which had come to rest a little way from Tommo and Akenna. The eagle hopped awkwardly towards Tommo and gave him a hard look. Akenna had her arms wrapped protectively round him.

'This one! This one!' the birds sang.

'No, you can't have him,' Akenna yelled savagely.

'This one, this one!' the birds sang.

'I thought you were our friends! No! Leave us alone!' she shouted, grabbing the gutting knife from somewhere about her person and waving it wildly in their direction.

Vevena was about to rush forward to protect the dying boy herself when the eagle turned its sharp sea-coloured eyes on Akenna and the birds sang, 'The girl, the girl!'

To Vevena's surprise Tommo contrived to move jerkily in Akenna's arms and made a sound that might have been 'No!' It happened so swiftly she could not be sure it was not her imagination.

Sibeal shouted, 'No, leave her!' in a voice that was almost as fierce as Akenna's. Vevena was impressed that Sibeal still possessed such spirit. Now the bird hopped towards Kalen, who was ashen with fear, and Akenna shouted, 'No, that's Tommo's da.'

Sibeal muttered, 'No! No! He hasn't got as much Inward

Power as the girl. Why would the birds want him?' She seemed totally unprepared when the eagle hopped towards her and the birds once more sang, 'This one! Take her!' She shook her head bemused, uncomprehending, like someone waking from a bad dream to discover it was no dream at all.

This time it was Kalen who shouted in a clear voice, 'No, she is my wife!'

Vevena sensed rather than saw the sudden retreat of the guards and Lord Awnan so that none of them remained within range of the eagle's strange hopping. Those who were sober enough had run away. The remainder were held in thrall, as Vevena was herself, by the voices of the birds' and the eagle's choice. When the eagle paused by Vevena, as she knew it must, she faced it squarely as she had faced everything else. She looked into the eagle's eyes and wondered if she saw a glimmer of recognition. What would happen if it took her? She had no Inward Power at all. To her surprise it was her father, Haver-snatcher, who cried out, 'No!', quickly followed by Fallon who let out an incoherent but anguished cry.

When the eagle moved on, she found she was trembling all over as if she, like Tommo, were dying. Haver-snatcher put his large hand on her shoulder and she could feel that he was trembling too. She should not have been surprised when the great bird also paused in front of Haver-snatcher, but it still shocked her. Once more she tried to stare down the eagle.

'No! He is my father!' she shouted, louder than she had intended.

The pressure on her shoulder increased and her father's voice whispered, 'My girl. I am so glad to see you whole again.'

She found her eyes filling with tears, but she dared not turn to look at Haver-snatcher for fear of missing the bird's next move. The only person now left in the tight circle centred on Tommo and Akenna was Fallon. The huge bird fixed Fallon with its human face and for the first time, Vevena heard it sing, 'This one!'

It sang in a resonant voice deeper and stronger than any voice she had ever heard. The sound made her guts churn. She thought of standing up for Fallon, the man who had not taken advantage of her ensorcellment, who had tried so hard to make her love him. But she could not make the words come out of her mouth: she had hated him for too long.

'No!' It was Sibeal who spoke out, stepping forward and addressing the eagle directly. 'This is an evil man. Do not give him the only power he lacks – the power of thaumaturgy. Please if you must have an Ungine body take mine!' She stumbled and fell prostrate in front of the bird.

'I see you were right about saving me,' Fallon said, his voice no longer the steady tone of command Vevena had grown used to. His face too seemed changed, distorted by an odd mixture of fear, astonishment and hunger.

'I don't want your sacrifice,' he said. 'I'll take the power, Sibeal, and finally I will have nothing to fear from the likes of you and Kalen and all the other little thaumaturgists.'

'But it was supposed to pick someone with Inward

Power!' Sibeal's voice broke and Kalen stepped forward to grab her hand. He held it tightly as she wept, murmuring his agreement.

'No, no. This was not the plan. This wasn't supposed to happen.'

'What do you think you are doing, Fallon?' Haver-snatcher began.

'Fallon . . .' Vevena started, but Fallon waved them both silent.

'This is what I want,' Fallon said and smiled, a smile part-nervous and part-triumphant. With admirable self-posses-sion he nodded at the eagle as though the creature were just another servant at the castle. The eagle's face remained impassive, but its eyes glittered in the strange light and Vevena was suddenly very afraid not for Fallon but of Fallon. What would Fallon become with Gildea's Inward Power as an adjunct to his temporal power? She would have liked to prevent the eagle from hopping towards Fallon, but her body would not obey her.

The eagle spread its wings around Fallon as, somehow, it had grown so that it all but concealed him from view. The assembled birds all took to the air at once in a great surging flapping of wings and a ringing refrain. 'At last, he is chosen! He is chosen,' they sang.

Then, from every corner of the sky the birds dived towards Fallon and the eagle so that he disappeared, lost among multi-shaded feathers. There was no singing now, just the sound of flapping wings and Sibeal's terrible, choking sobs. Vevena found her father's hand and held it tightly. It gave her some comfort as they watched the extraordinary scene.

As each human-faced bird flew down it kissed the just visible crown of the Protector's head with its soft, human mouth, then flew away, bird-faced again with a flutter of wings to disappear into the night. It took a long time. Vevena could not say how long. She grew cold, but none of them seemed able to do more than stand and watch with wonder and fear.

No one spoke until the eagle itself had planted a kiss on the vacant, bemused face of Fallon. Vevena saw it turn its eagle eyes just once on Tommo and Akenna before taking off, high into the dark sky. With the eagle's kiss, Fallon lost his bemused look. He cleared his throat. No one moved or spoke and once more it seemed to Vevena that it was up to her to break the strange spell that seemed to hold them all transfixed.

'Are you all right, my lord?' Vevena asked, stepping forward to where her husband stood alone among a circle of feathers. The strange light was gone and they were peering at each other through the ordinary gloom of the night. The storm lanterns, magically reignited, shone on Fallon's mismatched eyes and Vevena had to use all her self-control not to run.

'I – I don't know,' Fallon said, distractedly. 'I'm not sure. Why are we outside?' His voice was still Fallon's voice, though without its imperious quality.

'But where is Gildea?' Kalen cried. 'You should be Gildea now.' He was holding on to Sibeal like a drowning man and she clung to him as desperately.

Fallon paused for a moment, as though listening to some voice that no one else could hear. His voice was hushed with awe when he replied, 'Gildea is here.'

'Where?' Sibeal screamed. 'He was this island's last hope! This was not supposed to happen. Gildea was supposed to save us from you – not become you!'

Vevena had to admire Sibeal's courage. Fallon had ordered her torture for no crime at all, who knew what he would do to her now?

'Gildea is with me,' Fallon answered softly, which was somehow more terrifying than his usual bluster. 'I know what he knew and what he felt, but I am not Gildea.'

'Prove it – let him speak to us.' Sibeal demanded, her voice hoarse and quavering out of control.

'I cannot let him speak except through me. Gildea is with me, but he's not separate. For Unga's sake I do not know how to put this. I am not Fallon any more, not like I was and he isn't Gildea – we are both something else, something new.'

'Oh, Urtha, no! I knew it. It didn't work,' Kalen said. 'We failed.'

Fallon opened his mouth but his response was cut short by an anguished shriek that set Vevena's heart pounding still faster.

'Tommo, Tommo!' Akenna screamed, shaking the limp

body in her arms almost as violently as the quivers had convulsed him. 'He's stopped breathing! Oh, by Urtha's mercy, he's dead!' Akenna shrieked.

'No!' Kalen was at Tommo's side in a stride and picked him up in his arms. 'He's still breathing just – Fallon, Gildea, whoever you are, help him!'

Fallon snapped his fingers and Tommo was bathed in pale silvery light. Vevena felt sick at such casual thaumaturgy. Fallon's attention was wholly upon Tommo.

'His body is all but destroyed by the quivers. He should have died days ago but for thaumaturgy. He has been sustained by a strong gift of Inward Power – yours, girl, and his own.'

'I don't suppose you care – you imprisoned him and were about to torture him. Sorry you won't get the pleasure.' She really was a reckless girl, but amazingly brave.

Fallon ignored her. He walked towards Tommo a little unsteadily, as if finding his balance, and gently put his head against Tommo's head. The lights under Tommo's skin winked out one by one.

'What are you doing to him?' Akenna was about to throw herself at Fallon to drive him away as she had tried to drive away the birds. She might have been successful if Kalen had not got to her first and held her tightly so she could cause no harm. Fortunately she did not think to use her Inward Power or who knows who could have stopped her. 'He is your son,' she howled. 'Stop that monster of Unga! Don't die, Tommo, don't die! You are all I've got!'

'Hush,' Kalen said. 'Can you not feel it? Whoever and whatever he is, he *is* healing Tommo. Stop crying. Be still.'

Vevena had not a thaumaturgic bone in her lovely body, but even she could feel the power that flooded into Tommo from Fallon. Tommo just soaked it up as parched ground swallowed rain.

'Fallon has no Inward Power,' Haver-snatcher said as though repeating a strongly held tenet of belief.

'He is not Fallon any more,' Sibeal said shortly. She seemed to have recovered a little and was watching Fallon intently. 'It is perhaps what Gildea always had in mind. I can see how this might be his idea – the reconciliation of opposites, Unga and Urtha, brute force and peaceful contemplation, enemies united. By Unga, Gildea might have taken that much of a risk. Pray that he was right or we are all under the protection of a Protector with political and thaumaturgical power, a tyrant to end all tyrants.'

'But the usurper has not been usurped!' Haver-snatcher cried out. 'He will not have everything and, drawing his sword, he charged at Fallon who was kneeling, with his eyes closed, by Tommo's side. Vevena screamed as Haver-snatcher struck. Fallon never saw the blow coming, but then neither did Haver-snatcher.

As Haver-snatcher raised his sword to deliver his death blow, Akenna's gutting knife was out and in his guts. Haver-snatcher collapsed, clutching at his spilling innards. He fell with a groan over Tommo and Tommo opened his eyes.

Vevena ran to Haver-snatcher, 'Father!' She sounded hysterical. 'Father,' she repeated more calmly.

'Vevena – I am so glad to see you again as yourself before I go. The silver boy freed you? I didn't dare hope. I am proud . . .'

'Don't talk, Da. You saved me – you brought me the boy. Hush! Save your strength.'

It looked like a fatal wound to her – the kind that killed you slowly. By Unga's udders, that child Akenna should have been strangled at birth: she was trouble for all that she had courage and power. She could not help hot tears spilling from her eyes. She whom Fallon called his ice queen. There was nothing else to do but turn to him, beg if necessary.

'My lord, Fallon? If you ever loved me . . .' It pained her more than she could say to ask her husband to do anything, but some things were more important than pride.

Fallon was already turning his attention on her father, proof enough that he was not the old Fallon, who would have milked that moment for all that it was worth. Fallon looked at her just once, full in the face, and he looked as if he saw straight through her to the unlovely person she truly was, so that she felt briefly ashamed. The man with Fallon's toad-like face and mismatched eyes gazed at her dispassionately.

'Fallon did love you, Vevena. I think you know that. You were the love of his life. There is no need for you to worry. I will help Fallon's old enemy and friend all I can, and, if

Unga and Urtha will it, save him.' His tone was gentle, unassuming. He turned away to care for Haver-snatcher and she felt the power of his healing will reverberate through her own bones. It was then that she knew for certain that it was true: Fallon was no longer Fallon.

The Protector she had hated with such energy, even through the depths of her ensorcellment, was no more and she did not know whether to rejoice or not.

CHAPTER FORTY

The first thing Tommo saw when he opened his eyes was Akenna and her blood-stained gutting knife. The second thing he saw was a man with a face that resembled a toad's trying to staunch blood oozing from the stomach of Haver-snatcher. He was not at first sure that he was not dreaming. There was a strange light around him, which had no obvious source, and there was a smell of power in the air. He did not know where he was, only that he was cold and he had stopped shaking.

Akenna was looking at the bleeding man, her stained gutting knife in her hand, her face an unreadable mix of emotion.

Although her arm was round his neck, she did not seem aware that he was awake.

'Akenna?' he said.

'Tommo? You are alive!' She dropped the blood-stained knife and hugged him.

She was shaking and her filthy face was wet with tears. She smelled of power.

'What has happened?' he asked when he could breathe

again. He could not believe that the quivers were gone and that he was alive.

'The birds were all bits of Gildea, the old High Priest – or his Urthene spirit anyway. One of the birds – one we never saw – got to choose which of our Ungine bodies he would take and he chose Fallon's.'

'What? But Fallon captured Gildea – I thought they were enemies.'

Akenna shrugged. 'I know. Don't look at me like that. It had nothing to do with me. Except I wouldn't let them take you.' She looked embarrassed and pulled away from him so that her arms were no longer round his neck.

'Thank you, Akenna,' he said. He still could not quite believe that he was still alive. The last thing he remembered was lifting the curse from Vevena, after that everything was a haze. 'I'm sorry I wasn't much help.' He thought for a moment. 'I thought bringing the birds here was supposed to help get rid of the Protector – but Fallon is still Protector?'

'Yes. Oh, Unga's arse, I don't know Tommo. All I know is that you're not dead.'

The 'not yet' hovered unspoken between them.

Tommo looked at the plain-faced man he guessed was the Protector healing Haver-snatcher with an incredible outpouring of raw power and felt very afraid.

What would such a man do to him, a renegade apprentice, and Akenna who had apparently tried to murder Haver-snatcher?

Vevena was the only person who seemed able to move.

Everyone else looked dazed and confused and very cold. The light was fading in the courtyard and the wind began to blow, tugging at his hair; his hair which was no longer white but black as it had been when he was very young, before he first entered the cellar.

'Akenna . . .' he began, but Vevena was speaking, giving orders to terrified-looking guardsmen, demanding that all the participants, in what must have been a very odd drama indeed, were escorted indoors to the hall. Reinforcements were called for and suddenly Tommo was being wrapped in blankets and led into the warmth of the hall.

Vevena ordered the remnants of the feast and the tables to be cleared, fresh food to be found and all the drunken revellers lying comatose around the hall to be escorted away to their lodgings in the fortress. Servants sobered up rapidly when she spoke. Furs were found for Haver-snatcher and hot food for himself, Akenna, Sibeal and the tall, thin man who sat with them.

'Well?' Akenna said sharply to the thin, tired-looking man. 'Are you going to tell him? Tommo, this is Kalen, the Chief Spellstone Wielder.'

'Are you Tommo, son of Eavan of Tipplehead?' Kalen asked.

'Well, yes, I am,' Tommo answered slightly bemused. There was something familiar about the man's voice – they must have met when he was not quite unconscious.

The man made a kind of strangled cry and said, 'You were supposed to be dead!'

'Yes, I've got that impression myself,' Tommo answered. 'But somehow I've managed to stay alive. I'm not sure how.'

'Oh, merciful Urtha, I do not know how to ask you for forgiveness. They told me you'd died with your mother, Tommo, and I never doubted it.'

'What do you mean?'

'Tommo, I'm your father and I'm sorry. If I had known you were still alive, but . . .'

Kalen's voice tailed away and Tommo said nothing. He remembered his father – just: a shadowy figure who played with him in the sunlit garden of his memory. It came to him then that this man could have saved him from the cellar, and the quivers and his wild fight for sanctuary. He could have saved him from all of it and he hadn't. Tommo couldn't speak.

'Your mother and I fell out for a time and I didn't see you – I was away studying the properties of spellstones. I was away for more than a year and when I got back the house was shut up and I was told that Eavan and her child were dead. I had no reason to question it, especially as there were more rumours of the blue pox at that time. Lots of children died in infancy,' Kalen said talking too quickly. There was so much pain in his voice that Tommo might have been moved if there had not been so much more pain in his own life.

'I don't know what to say,' Tommo said. 'You bought the stones I nearly died to grind. You have served the Protector.'

Kalen looked down, avoiding Tommo's eyes. 'Yes. But I

fought him in my heart. I knew about Gildea's plan to escape the spellstone prison and to be whole again.'

'Why didn't you help him get free while he had his own body?' Tommo asked. 'I don't understand why this – this nonsense with the birds?'

'It is the way Gildea wanted it. It is better this way.'

'What, with Fallon having all of Gildea's Inward Power as well as command of the army and Unga knows what?'

'I have a daughter, Tommo, and she would have been tortured if I had not done what Fallon wanted. It was the best way.'

'You had a son too,' Tommo answered, 'but you did not save him.' Any further discussion was halted by Fallon himself.

He stood up, his hands still covered in Haver-snatcher's blood. Tommo doubted that Haver-snatcher's was the only blood on his hands.

'Enemies of the Protectorate,' he began and Tommo felt a tightening in his guts that was probably fear. He glanced at Akenna who had grown pale.

'I am hereby renouncing my position as Protector of the Island of the Gifted. I am disbanding the Guild of Spell-stone Wielders. It is my intention to find and remove all spellstones from the island and to return them to their natural home in the living fire of the mountain from which they came. As Gildea I had long suspected that they are alive and have been punishing us for our abuse of them by corrupting all they have touched.

I Gildea—Fallon, once High Priest of the Inward Power, once Protector of the Island of the Gifted, will leave the island and do not plan to return. I take with me Haver-snatcher who in punishment for his attempt on my life will serve me in my vocation. I will take others who have kept children in cellars, smuggled spellstones or traded in them so that they too can atone for their wrongs. I leave the care of the island in the capable hands of Vevena until such time as she can rebuild the Convocation and restore the land to good order. Our three-heir dynastic marriage, which was performed under duress, is annulled. May blessed Urtha and Unga both smile on you.' He smiled too then in a most un-Fallon-like way and then both he and Haver-snatcher disappeared. They disappeared with no preliminaries, no sound, just a sudden absence.

Sibeal screamed and Vevena swayed as if she were about to faint, but steadied herself on the table and all that could be heard in the stunned silence was Akenna's voice saying very loudly, 'Well, by Unga's arse, I didn't expect that.'

Tommo was unconvinced by the disappearing trick. He had after all performed it himself even if it was by accident. So he was surprised, but not shocked, to hear Fallon's voice in his ear whispering, 'Forgiveness is a gift of Urtha. You would do well to remember it. Kalen did what he could. He has more courage than you might believe. What was meant to happen did happen so do not blame him for failures he could not help.' Tommo opened his mouth to answer, but before he could reply he sensed that Gildea—Fallon had gone.

EPILOGUE

'Did you foresee any of it, Sibeal?' her stepson asked, years later. It was a good question and one it was hard to answer honestly. Her stepson, a tall man with thick dark hair, waited patiently for her answer. He had grown into a gentle servant of Urtha, with a strength of Inward Power that far exceeded his father's. Sibeal struggled to see any trace of the quiver-afflicted silver boy he had once been in his smiling face.

'I don't know, Tommo, I had no hope then. I saw little with my secret sight. I think I was afraid to use it too much.' She shrugged. 'Gildea saw more than I ever could and for that perhaps we should all be grateful.' Tommo did not press her but left her to join his bride. Sibeal was glad. She no longer entirely trusted her inner vision. She had seen so many futures then, and in only one had Tommo lived out his boyhood. Strangely, that one hopeful vision bore no relation to this joyful present, this marriage to Akenna. She had never foreseen this and she did not know what that meant.

She watched Kalen in his full regalia as High Priest of the Inward Power. In time he would retire and Akenna or Tommo would take over the role for no one in the island matched them in thaumaturgic talent. It amused her to see how Kalen had gained weight and gravitas with the years. She smiled as she watched him smile at the Lady Protector, Vevena, as she added her blessing on the union to his. Vevena had served the Protectorate well these last seven years. She was strong enough to rule, but wise enough to temper her natural ruthlessness with justice. She looked lovelier than ever despite the simplicity of her dress. Since the day of Fallon–Gildea's departure, she had worn no jewels or other adornment to complement the plain dark robes she favoured. Of course, unlike most other women, she needed none.

The ceremony was almost over and Sibeal rose to congratulate the bride and groom. It was as hard to see the skinny fisher's brat in the grown Akenna as it had been to see the spellgrinder's apprentice in Tommo. Akenna's gaunt pinched face had filled out so that, though she would never be pretty, her face had a strength and grace about it that lent her a kind of beauty. It did not take any special power for Sibeal to know that despite the outward changes there was a part of them that would always be fisher's brat and apprentice – their shared memories bound them tighter than golden marriage chains ever could. She saw little of what lay before them, but knew that whatever came their way Akenna would be at Tommo's side and at his throat, his most ardent critic and his staunchest friend. That was, perhaps, the greatest blessing anyone could bestow.